"It's your land." Aubrey s ⸱⸱⸱ ⸱ked. "You can come and go as you wish."

"What if it wasn't my land? I mean, what if I let you…" Cort expected he would regret his next words. "What if I just worked a piece of it until I leave? What if you registered the land in your name?"

Miss Huxley narrowed her eyes. "What are you saying, Mr. Stanton?"

"One hundred and sixty acres is big enough for both of us, is all. What if you let me lease the land from you?"

Miss Huxley's lips parted. She blinked several times before whispering, "You'd give it to me?"

"Sure. Doesn't seem right that I keep it all to myself when I might—" Cort cleared his throat. "I'll be away more than I'd be working it." *And sooner rather than later if that surveyor recognizes me.*

"I—I don't know what to say." She clamped her mouth shut. Her lips grew thin as she frowned. "What's in it for you, Mr. Stanton?"

Angie Dicken credits her love of story to reading British literature during life as a military kid in Cambridgeshire, England. Now living in the American heartland, she blogs about author life along with her fellow Alley Cats on *The Writer's Alley* blog. Besides writing, she is a busy mom of four and works in adult ministry. Angie enjoys eclectic new restaurants, authentic conversation with friends and date nights with her Texas-native husband. Connect with her online at www.angiedicken.com.

Books by Angie Dicken

Love Inspired Historical

The Outlaw's Second Chance

Visit the Author Profile page at Harlequin.com.

ANGIE DICKEN

The Outlaw's
Second Chance

HARLEQUIN® LOVE INSPIRED® HISTORICAL

Recycling programs for this product may not exist in your area.

LOVE INSPIRED BOOKS

ISBN-13: 978-0-373-42541-9

The Outlaw's Second Chance

www.Harlequin.com

Printed in U.S.A.

For we are His workmanship, created in Christ Jesus for good works, which God prepared beforehand so that we would walk in them.
—*Ephesians* 2:10

To my dad, who raised me to dream big,
and to my husband, whose support is unwavering.

Chapter One

The Cherokee Strip
September 15, 1893

Aubrey Huxley rushed over when her father shoved his bony finger against the customer's shoulder.

"You're crossing a line there, boomer," he threatened. Aubrey cringed as she approached the tense business negotiation. Of course, her brother was nowhere to be found. It was up to her to deal with Pa. Ed Huxley would try to sell a jar of the red Oklahoma dirt and label it "Gunpowder," if it meant an easy profit. Just the same, the skinny horses with matted manes did nothing to live up to the sign tacked on the fence post: "Fastest in the West." Yet he'd talked himself blue trying to convince any challenger that afternoon.

After all, it was the day before the land run. Thousands of settlers bustled around the sprawling camp, preparing for the next day's race for free land. Each one had a flag, waiting to stake their claim at the precious markers dotted about the prairie. Leave it to her father to take advantage of the poor land-hungry boomers who'd need a horse to claim their own quarter section tomorrow.

She sucked in her dignity with a swallow of air. "Excuse me, sir."

The disgruntled customer turned toward Aubrey, and her breath caught. Beneath his cowboy hat, green eyes squinted with cynicism—a handsome, stirring cynicism that made doubt look like a cool drink on a hot Oklahoma day. Aubrey doubted she'd change his opinion at all.

"Ma'am, this isn't any concern of yours." He smiled cordially then tipped his dusty hat. Her temptation to melt slid away with his smoldering look. She was not a pretty little fixture to be brushed off. This stubborn man, adorned with a shadow of stubble along his jaw and dark hair curling against a sunburned neck, had no idea he was dismissing the wrong girl.

Aubrey cleared her throat when he tried to turn his attention back to her father. "This is as much of my concern as it is my father's." But their reasons were as polarized as the sun to the moon. Her jaw ached from clamping her mouth shut day in and day out during this shady operation. Her mother would have never agreed to any of this. She was probably stomping around in Heaven knowing her beautiful horses had been sold to double Pa's inventory with these pathetic creatures.

"Oh?" A grin hooked one corner of the man's mouth. "Is it?" He leaned an elbow on the corral fence, which creaked beneath his weight.

"Yes, *boomer*." She lifted her chin and ignored the flutter in her chest. Must he stare at her that way? She shoved her hand out for a shake. "I am Aubrey Huxley.

If you have any questions, please direct them to me." She spoke those last words through her teeth, trying to sift through the desperation in her voice. The last thing she wanted was to arouse Pa's anger. Not when she was this close to completing her plan.

"Good day, Miss Huxley. I am Cort Stanton." The cowboy's grip was firm.

Aubrey tried to mimic his strength in her own grip instead of allowing it to distract her. Swooning at the first handsome man who crossed her path on the prairie would not add any courage to what she intended to accomplish.

"Mr. Stanton, please address your concerns with our horses—" she raised her voice over the yells of men pouring into the next-door tent set up as a temporary saloon "—to me."

Mr. Stanton whistled a minty breath more pleasant than the mangy odor of her merchandise. "I've never been much of a businessman. But I know horses. And if you'd like to call *that* a horse…" He arched an eyebrow and wagged his head. "Then those pretty brown eyes of yours might need checking."

Anger coursed through Aubrey's veins, red-hot like the setting sun bleeding on the horizon beyond the myriad of tents. "I know horses just fine, thank you. You don't know me, or the specimens we've sold before this." Well, they were at least decent, anyway. Why was she fighting him? This would be her last day as an accomplice to her father's schemes.

"Believe me, any specimen is finer than that one." He threw another glance at the tawny mare and kicked his boot on the fence post.

Her father puffed out his chest, looking like he was ready for a duel, but then a holler from the saloon stole his attention. "Aubrey, take care of him." He flung open the gate. "Got some business to take care of yonder."

A heavy weight settled in her stomach as Pa abandoned their only customer in hours. He slipped into the pulsing tent. Exactly why she was leaving him. Just like Mama couldn't trust him when she was alive, Aubrey couldn't trust him to follow through, either. As much as she'd tried to revive her affection for the broken man, the ache of all he'd inflicted was too much to bear.

She'd had enough.

"So, Mr. Stanton, are you interested or not?" Aubrey folded her arms across her torso, the steam of the challenge changing its course with the wind of surrender. Her efforts to help Pa this one last time deflated, because he'd just walked out on her once more. Even if this cowboy, with his rich voice and gorgeous eyes, encouraged her to snap back, she just didn't have it in her to continue this charade.

"Sorry, ma'am." He shrugged his shoulders. "I'll have to look elsewhere." His face softened with true regret as if he felt he owed her more. Her heart sped up at the small glimpse of compassion from the rugged man. It'd been a long time since someone showed concern for her feelings.

"Fine, then." Why did his split-second glance of tenderness inflict such a fury of emotions deep within her? She brushed a strand of hair from her face and tucked it into her braid. "If you don't mind, I've got to clean up before nightfall." *And get ready, myself.*

Her nerves frenzied at the urgency of all she had to do.

First, she needed a horse. That was her only way to have a fighting chance tomorrow. The only fools who ran by foot in the last race ran the night before, even with the risk of getting shot for running early. Every time she spied the scouts guarding the line, she nearly buckled in fear.

"Are you running tomorrow?" Mr. Stanton seemed perfectly content to stay and chat awhile, even leaning up against the fence with one worn-out cowboy boot crossed over the other.

Aubrey tilted her head and studied his face for any sort of malice. While there were many good-hearted folk around, she'd met her share of scoundrels in these three long weeks. This cowboy had nothing but a kind smile.

She lifted her shoulders, arching her eyebrow.

"Just wondering." He held his hands up like she'd threatened him. Perhaps she had. Aubrey didn't have the restraint to control her emotions like she used to.

Mr. Stanton took out a handkerchief and wiped the back of his neck. "Just some friendly advice from one of the thousands of men running tomorrow." He squinted into the crimson light beyond the camp then pushed away from the fence. "I think you'd do better running the race on foot." He glanced at the horse, shook his head and then walked onto the crowded path. "Good evening, Miss Huxley."

Aubrey rolled her eyes. *Arrogant boomer.*

Temptation to race the cowboy to a better horse deal pulled her toward the fence. She could cut through the tents, but she had to wait on a customer until seven. If Aubrey was any bit of her father, she'd do what was best for herself and forget the appointment. Yet she couldn't follow Pa's selfish way, could she?

Besides, she'd do nothing to hinder this chance to start over—to fill a dream at last, her mama's dream. Provoking Pa to anger by shirking her duties was the last thing she wanted to do. If she did him wrong by leaving now, he'd make sure she'd pay for it. No matter how much money she'd leave behind.

Hiding among a hundred thousand men on wild horses would be her only chance to escape, whether on foot or on horseback. Either way, she would leave Pa in his misery and find land of her very own.

Cort inhaled the aroma of a mesquite campfire and tried to ignore the tug in his heart. If he'd allow his footsteps to follow his heartbeats, he'd turn himself around and insist Miss Huxley give him a chance to redeem himself. How could he treat a woman that way? Mock her mangy horses? Or worse, socializing as if he had any hint of a future to offer a woman? Her brief look of hurt after her father abandoned her had Cort almost consider a purchase of one of those miserable beasts. Perhaps then he'd see her smile. But that could be torture in itself. And between the unknown of when he'd get caught again, and the known of all that had happened, he had enough torment to contend with. His future was as bleak as the Texas Panhandle where trouble found him. No use daydreaming about a pretty smile. A woman would only complicate things.

Two boys scaled chests and furniture securely fastened to a wagon. Their creeping shadows crawled across Cort's path. He watched the boys as they played a game of keep-away just like he'd seen his nephew do a hundred times. There was nobody more important than Trevor right now—because he was the first of a generation that could change the Stanton ways. To become noble and right. Kind. Pure. Everything the Good Book preached about that had only begun settling in Cort's heart this past year. His brother, Charles, had promised to change, too, when Cort was arrested for that murder Charles had committed. Charles had said he'd raise his son right, and Cort had agreed to take the blame because of his nephew. A boy needed a father. The Stanton brothers knew that the hard way.

He flicked a glance over his shoulder before heading to make an offer on the stallion down by the land office. Miss Huxley busied about the corral, the burned orange light kissing her midnight hair. Cort sighed. He'd never met a woman with such a fighting spirit, yet brimming with softness beneath.

A man approached Aubrey from the many tents crowding around the makeshift corral, stalling Cort's attempt to dismiss the lure of temptation. Perhaps Miss Huxley was taken, anyway? That'd help ease his gnawing interest.

Miss Huxley placed her hands on her hips and both she and the man focused on the mare. But before she turned toward the man, Cort saw it. The scouring look of a dangerous man.

The stranger inched closer to her, his teeth resting on his bottom lip. Words seemed to slip from his mouth, and Miss Huxley spun around. Her neck flushed crimson, and she spoke words no doubt sharpened with the same bite that Cort had witnessed earlier. The man snatched her waist, provoking a quick slap across his face.

Cort tunneled through the crammed tents and wagons. His heart pounded against his chest, and an angry heat crawled up his spine, invading his neck and ears with fire. The man, unable to keep his hands to himself, pathetically assaulted her, giving Cort the chance to redeem his own rude behavior to Miss Huxley.

"Hey now." Cort grasped the man's shoulder and yanked him around. The man's surprised expression turned to one of vehemence.

"Are you her husband?" the culprit growled.

"No. But I know when a man has overstayed his welcome." Cort returned the hateful stare, slowly moving his hand to his holster, just in case. "Leave the lady alone."

A quick glance at Cort's hand dimmed the spark in the man's eyes, and he backed off. "She ain't worth it," he muttered and stumbled away.

Aubrey smoothed down her skirt and kept her eyes lowered.

Cort's throat was tight. He shoved through the corral gate. The woman was a whole head shorter than him. Her ivory brow was framed by silky ebony hair gathered in a loose braid across her petite shoulder. A strand skimmed her lowered nose. Cort clenched his teeth. The desire to gather that rebellious hair between his fingers and tuck it behind her ear rattled his senses. He tried to take a step back, but her dainty aroma of lavender soap tempted him to stay close. He breathed deeply. His hand lifted regardless of the battle within him, and he reached out to tilt her chin up. Was she crying? Or, perhaps, humiliated by that man's forwardness? Aubrey lifted her eyes and met his gaze.

He jerked his hand back to his cowboy hat and tipped it. "Are you okay?"

Her chocolate eyes were perfectly dry, and her mouth was set in a curt rosy smile. There was nothing unsure about this woman. She even held her shoulders in a soldier-straight line, her chin perfectly angled in confidence. Only a slight ripple across that ivory brow softened her cool demeanor. Cort swallowed hard. This woman intimidated him, no matter that he was nearly twice her size and towering over her.

"Thank you, Mr. Stanton. I do believe I could have handled him, though." With a large grin, she patted her skirt pocket and eyed his holster.

Torture. The smile brought torture just as he'd expected.

He nearly shoved his hands in his pockets. "Good to know you're not a woman to be messed with." The horse behind her whinnied and stomped its knobby leg. "I'd better let you get back to your business, Miss Huxley." He stepped back. Yes, that was the wise thing to do. Walk away.

He didn't need any prospective distraction. If he gave himself an inch, the implications would be a mile long and would hurt more than the torturous smile that now burned in his memory. But as much as he tried to focus on the busyness of settlers around him, he couldn't escape from the Aubrey-induced fog in his mind.

Could a woman clothed in such God-given beauty be so utterly content in her own skin, even in the face of strange men on the wild prairie? Perhaps Cort had been around too many women who used their looks only to gain advantage or a marriage proposal. But it didn't seem that Miss Huxley depended on her outward beauty in any way, exuding only a strength he could hardly reckon with in his baffled state.

"Wait!" She rushed up to him and put a hand on his arm. "Are you on your way to buy a horse?"

Cort dared a look in her bright eyes. "I am heading over to the dealer by the land office."

"Mind if I join you?" She glanced away and scrunched her nose. Her petite frame lifted with a deep sigh. "I mean, I'd like to see the competition." The words came out as more of a question than a statement.

"You think you'll have much more business out here?" He looked beyond her shoulder at the deep pink clouds painted with the setting sun. "I mean, the race is at noon tomorrow."

"You haven't found your horse yet, Mr. Stanton." She crossed her arms, cocking her head to one side. "Who's to say that there aren't a few more negotiations left tonight?"

"You have quite an eye for business, don't you, Miss Huxley?"

She looked over her shoulder. "One day I hope to use it for my own ranch." When she looked up at him, there was a flush in her cheeks and her eyes brimmed with moisture. "May I join you, Mr. Stanton? Please. I…I just need to get away." Her soft admission allowed him a glimpse of her vulnerability in that moment. Cort's fierce desire to protect her was stronger than it had been just moments ago in the face of that rascally man. But now, he had no idea what he would protect her from. Just that there was something threatening her strength.

He held out his elbow and she placed her small hand in the crook of his arm.

"Thank you," she said as they strolled forward.

When they arrived at her competitor's corral, the owner rode up on a slightly older male horse. Cort worried that his own advice to Miss Huxley about it being too late to buy a horse was his own fate.

"Sir, didn't you have a stallion earlier?"

Miss Huxley left his side and went up to the horse as the owner dismounted.

"Yes, sir. He's out back. Got this one for sale, too. Just purchased him from a poor guy who's been struck by the heat and won't be racing tomorrow. Paid a pretty penny."

"You have two horses for sale?" Miss Huxley's voice cracked, and her face lit up like she'd stumbled across gold. When her gaze crossed Cort's, she cleared her throat and brushed her fingers through the horse's fine black mane.

"Yes, ma'am. He's back behind the tent. Those boys over yonder were getting him all stirred up." He began to jaunt across the dusty dirt. "Let me bring him 'round."

Miss Huxley stayed by the horse, stroking his nose. A loud whinny from behind turned Cort's attention to the stallion being led by its owner.

After negotiating a price, they both paid for the horses. Aubrey was content with the older male, while Cort paid a little more for the stallion.

"You will do wonderful in the race with that horse,"

she said over her shoulder as she led her own horse out of the gate. "Wish I could see him run."

"Maybe you can come see me off." Cort chuckled. A pain reached across his chest—something he'd much rather focus on than the dangerous trail of thought leading his senses astray. The good Lord may have softened this ranch hand, but his edges were still rough. Cort was certain if he let anyone get too close, they'd feel the sting. And he promised himself no more regret. He had enough already. It was too much to bear most days.

She stopped her horse and spun around. A mischievous grin appeared. "Don't think I'll be around to see you off. But I do wish you the best, Mr. Stanton." She walked up to him and offered an awkward handshake. "I think I'll cut through between the tents and head behind the corral. Don't forget us if anyone needs a horse."

"That one is sure to be gone soon," he said.

She raised an eyebrow, and he did the same. What was she thinking? Or plotting? "We also have goods for sale like saddle soap." She clutched her skirt, avoiding a puddle near a water trough, then briskly led her horse out of view. Not a trace of lavender left in his dim surroundings.

Good. Only good would come from widening the distance between himself and Miss Huxley. He tried wrapping his mind around the relief of avoiding heartache since his days of freedom might be limited. If she knew he was an outlaw, she wouldn't stick around long anyway. They'd never see each other again, and that realization should be a salve for his wounded soul.

Then why did he feel like he was walking away from hope when Aubrey left him behind in the fading light of dusk?

Chapter Two

Aubrey couldn't sleep. Pa had returned to his own tent clear after nightfall and was snoring loud and long. How did her brother, Ben, put up with it? How could he put up with many of Pa's ways like he did? Ben was eighteen and a little puppet for their father.

She tried to breathe in rhythm with the snoring next door, but could only grimace with her effort. Her eyes caught the outline of her flag sticking out of her bag. She tried focusing on the waiting land and on staking her claim, but Cort Stanton crept into her mind. Even if she was offended by the cowboy at first, Cort had redeemed himself when he came to her rescue. She'd never let on what it meant to her.

But it meant something. It had been a long time since someone looked out for Aubrey Huxley. After Mama passed away, she'd never felt cared for. Not until this afternoon when that handsome cowboy threatened that horrible man at the corral did Aubrey realize how much she longed for such honorable attention.

The sound of nearing footsteps interrupted her thoughts.

Who was about at this time of night? Maybe sooners? In past land races, they'd been known to steal into the night looking for land—would they take a horse also? As she dressed, she slipped her pistol into her pocket, ready to fight for her new horse.

The warm night air was coated in fire smoke and murmurs of folk preparing for tomorrow.

"Hey there, sis." Ben startled her before she could look for a prowler. He held open the flap to his and Pa's tent.

"Were you walking around just now?" She peeked about the corral, then quickly glanced behind her tent. Her horse was still tied to the hitch. She blew out her tension. "I thought you were asleep."

"I was trying to convince that neighbor to take our last mare." Her eighteen-year-old brother was taller and broader than their father, but he wasn't much different than Pa. Always ready to help his father take advantage of a customer. "Wouldn't budge. Ah, well. Guess Pa will have to sell her back in Kansas."

"Or you can. Maybe get that money for your wedding. Liza's already got the dress," she said, recalling the details she'd sewn on the gown.

"Yeah, true." He scratched his head as he peered at his boots. He leaned forward, whispering low, "You sure you're going to run tomorrow?"

Her throat thickened. "Course I am. And you promised to keep Pa from looking for me. I left the money I earned for sewing in the bread box. If only I'd found Mama's savings for the ranch. Can't stand knowing that if he finds it, he'll squander it."

Ben shrugged. "You don't have to leave at all if you don't want to." His forehead crinkled.

She wrapped her arms around his neck. "I'll write. Just as soon as I'm settled." He returned the hug then stepped back and opened the tent, releasing Pa's heavy snores as he disappeared inside.

Aubrey'd never fall asleep now. She meandered toward the campfire lighting up the clearing just beyond their fence. In the flickering light she could make out a few men crouched down in a huddle, no doubt planning their route tomorrow. Two of the women she'd grown acquainted with this past week rocked their babies on one side of the fire. They'd brought their children over to pet the horses and make small talk.

Aubrey took careful steps as she neared them, wanting to say goodbye but not wanting to disturb their sleeping infants. Someone else caught her attention, though. All by his lonesome, Cort Stanton sat on a barrel, reading a book. What was it about Mr. Stanton, besides those emerald eyes and compassionate grin? Tiny flutters filled her stomach.

He caught her staring at him across the fire. "Evening, Miss Huxley."

She stepped around the steady flames, lowering her face as humiliation washed her from head to toe. Gathering breath in her lungs and willing her heartbeat to calm down, she gave him a curt smile upon her approach. "Good evening, Mr. Stanton." He stood up and tipped his hat. "What are you reading there?"

Good. He'd think her blatant attention toward him was out of curiosity for his book choice.

He held it out beneath a sincere smile. "The Good Book. Nothing better." He winked.

Aubrey swallowed. "I see. And I must agree." Her shoulders relaxed. He offered her his seat, pulling up a wooden crate for himself. "Shouldn't you be resting for tomorrow?"

"Couldn't sleep." He gave a slight wince as he stared off into the fire. "There's a lot at stake tomorrow."

"Yes, there is." What if she didn't get to the land she'd need to fill Mama's dream? "What kind of land are you looking for, Mr. Stanton?"

"Just land. I want to work and live. That's all." He looked down at his Bible.

"Yes, me, too." She bit her lip. "I mean, working and living are what I want also."

He narrowed his eyes her way. "You *are* racing, aren't you?"

She gave a quick nod. "If my father found out, he'd ruin my chances to run. Can't risk anyone knowing." Aubrey wagged her head and let out a sigh. "Guess you know now. You and my brother are the only ones."

"It's okay. I won't say a word. Believe me, I know how to keep a secret."

"You do?" She arched her eyebrow, feeling a connection with this near stranger. He didn't pry, just gave her assurance.

"It's the only reason I'm here, Miss Huxley. To keep a secret safe and sound." His face hid beneath the brim of his cowboy hat and he turned to the next page of his Bible. "And the funny thing is, my brother's the only one that knows about it, too." His jaw clenched, and he shook his head.

"Seems we have much in common, Mr. Stanton." She didn't look at him, just stared into the flame.

"Miss Huxley." He said her name in a rich, deep tone. Aubrey met his gaze. Fire danced in his intent, lively eyes. He opened his mouth as if he'd speak, then shut it again. His face grew dim with a sorrowful smile. "Be careful tomorrow."

"I will," she said. "You, too, Mr. Stanton." What was it about this man that made her feel safe? "Good night." As she walked back toward her tent, she wondered why he hesitated. What was he going to say? Would he have shared his secret just like she shared hers? Whatever it was, she'd be careful to stay clear of that cowboy on the start line tomorrow. Her finely crafted defense from years of dealing with Pa's shenanigans quivered next to this man.

As she neared her tent, a whinny came from her horse. She held her breath, hoping it wouldn't wake up Pa and give away its hiding spot. Thankfully, the snoring continued.

Only a few more hours and Pa would find the note and the money. Her brother would keep him calm. Ben had promised he would after she made the wedding dress for his sweetheart without payment. Soon, the Huxley men would be back up in Kansas where they belonged, and Aubrey would have a piece of the Cherokee Strip.

She couldn't resist a smile as she ducked inside her tent.

Readying for tomorrow morning, she carefully placed her pistol in her bag. As she sat on her cot, she strained her ears. Did she hear whispers on the other side of her canvas wall? She stilled every breath and movement, hoping her imagination had got the best of her. Nothing but cargo and her horse were on the other side of the tent. It was a perfect hiding place from Pa and anyone else. Or so she'd thought. Another very loud, very real whinny startled her quieted body, and she sprang from her bed. Rummaging through her bag for her pistol, Aubrey burst into the darkness.

She kept her eyes lowered, careful to not trip over any tent stakes. When she came round to the back of the tent, her heart plummeted to her stomach.

Her horse was gone.

Rattled by anguish, she nearly lost her grip on her bag. Could all these months of planning slip away with a rotten thief? She thought about the years of marriage her mama had endured with a thief. Her anger grew. Her mama's dream was so close to coming true, she'd not let anyone get in her way.

Her legs had never moved so fast. The warm prairie air tunneled through the alley of tents. She barreled into the open at the edge of a lonely grove of post oaks. About twenty yards away, she spied a shadowy figure of a man climbing on top of her horse near the perimeter of the encampment.

"Hey! That's my horse," she whispered loudly, acutely aware that the camp behind her was asleep and the scouts ahead were no doubt awake. They most likely waited along that charcoal-gray horizon, ready to fire at sooners trying to run early.

The thief turned his head then leaned down close to the body of the horse. Surely he knew the danger ahead. But before she could reach him, he darted into the forbidden prairie. Her temples pulsed with fiery blood at the sheer obstinacy of the thief. She couldn't let him get away with this. There was no way another crooked man would take away her mama's dream to build a ranch so easily.

Lord, protect me.

She screwed her face up as if she were about to enter a tightly spun briar patch and ran into the black of night. Prayer sprouted from her heart as she ran, begging God that the scouts were sound asleep. She sliced through the warm night air, keeping her eye on the tiny figure ahead. Sweat slid down her hairline and across her jaw. She licked her lips, tasting the salt of her perspiration. Soon, her eyes blurred. Was it sweat or tears? She couldn't tell, but there was no doubt that her eyes wept at the effort. The fright of being out in the open hung in the back of her mind. She dared not look back to see how far she was from Camp Kiowa now.

Her legs couldn't push her through the tall grasses fast enough, and the thief grew smaller, disappearing for a moment. The distance between them seemed to stretch as wide and vast as the prairie, shrinking Aubrey's hope. He wouldn't get away with this, would he? She couldn't let him. No, she'd get her horse back—for Mama.

An explosive shot rang out. The silhouette of her horse lifted up on his hind legs, not as far away as she'd expected. A muted whinny met Aubrey's pulsing ears as she dropped to her stomach. Before tucking her head behind a stand of tall grass, she spied her horse, riderless, galloping across the horizon, running as fast as her dreams of racing tomorrow crumbled.

How could she even try to catch him? He was spooked

by the gunfire. Did the rider take a bullet? A flood of terror and uncertainty filled her heart. She just wanted her horse back. Now blood was spilled and her horse was frightened away.

She squinted, hoping to catch another glimpse of her horse's silhouette. Jagged sobs filled her throat as the weeds scratched her cheek. Her heart thumped hard against the packed soil. The earthy aroma filled her nostrils as she dragged herself toward the direction of her horse.

The ground beneath her began to rumble, and every inch of her stiffened again.

"I didn't find anything," a man called out.

"We'll find him in the morning. I know I got him. Probably wounded," another man said. "Let's go to the watering station and then return to our posts. It's going to be a long day tomorrow." Their horses' trotting faded as they rode away.

When she was certain only stillness filled her surroundings, she relaxed her clenched fists and stilled her grinding teeth. She continued crawling through the coarse grass. If she could just find her horse, she'd return to camp and run the race. The moon was bright now. While her eyes adjusted, her ears played tricks on her. She cocked her head. What she thought was a whinny ended up being a distant train whistle. The locomotive's rhythmic trudge across the land gave it away. She crawled forward but stopped at a nearby rustle ahead.

A wave of fear skittered across her heart.

Just a few feet in front of her, boot soles inched forward through the tall grass. A white flag was tucked in the back pocket of the culprit, bobbing in and out of view. Aubrey's nostrils flared and she bit her lip, scouring the contents of her shoulder bag. She'd packed her flag issued by the land office earlier at camp. Now it was gone. A wave of realization struck her like a twister hitting the ground. All her fright turned upside down.

She knew the thief all too well.

When she was close enough to grab his familiar boot, her courage bolstered, she lunged forward, hooking her arm around his neck.

"Ben Huxley. How dare you?" she seethed in his ear as he tried to wriggle away. Years of wrestling him gave her the advantage of surprise. He splayed flat, giving up immediately.

"Get off, Aubrey." He tried squirming, but she tightened her grip on his neck and dug her knee into his back.

"Why would you steal from me?" Her voice wobbled. Emotion was thick in her throat. "I am so disappointed." She let go with as much force as she'd tackled him, then snatched her flag out of his back pocket. The storm inside her drowned out the fear of being caught now. She sat up and draped her arms across her knees.

Ben sat up carefully, rubbing his neck. "I just got tempted. The thought of having land to sell…"

He was just like her father. Bending the rules, hurting those who might love him, all for his own gain.

"I thought I could trust you with my plan." She should have known better. There was not a man in the world she could trust.

He ran his fingers through his hair. "Got spared back there. Heard the bullet whiz by my ear." His hand was shaking as he rubbed the side of his stubbly face. "I give up. You can keep the flag."

"Oh, really?" She fiddled with the one-by-one post. "Of course I can keep it. It's mine! Now I need to figure out how to get my horse and get back to camp without being killed."

She looked across the horizon behind her. No horse in sight. The sky was silver with the onset of dawn. Sadness overwhelmed her.

"There's something I wanna show you, Aubrey," Ben whispered.

She wouldn't budge. Defeat bolted her to the warm ground.

"Come on, sis. It'll make up for all this, promise."

He began to crawl deeper into the prairie.

"Wait. Aren't you going the wrong way?" She tried to grab his ankle but he was too quick.

"I'm not going back and risk crossing those scouts' path," he said.

He was right. She felt trapped between her dream and the law. How did this happen? Because she was a Huxley. That was how.

Ben stopped and sat up again. "Look. Saw it as I rode. Just before the scouts shot at me." Ash-colored light peeled away the darkness of night more rapidly now. Aubrey followed his pointing finger. A flutter of movement hooked her gaze and quickened her heartbeat.

A marker, just like the land official had explained when she registered for the race, stood by its lonesome about half a mile away.

The marker waited for her like a treasure.

Ben poked his head above the prairie floor, swiveling as he spied all around them. "Come on, Aubrey. It's safe. Let's stake your claim." He stood up.

"Wait!" Aubrey tackled him to the ground. "You might have forced us into this situation, but I am not breaking any more rules. We'll wait until noon."

"You and your rules," he grumbled. She narrowed her eyes and waited for him to relent. He flicked his head, and she crawled past him.

Just beyond the marker, they came to the top of a steep bank. They slid down. Relief coursed through her now that they were no longer in the open. A shallow stream snaked through the narrow creek bed. They crept along some rocks and came to a bend where the bank had eroded and left a cave-like nook. A perfect hiding place. Aubrey crawled inside the nook first. Ben cozied up next to her, his head skimming the muddy ceiling while his body blocked most of the opening. Aubrey's eyes pricked with exhaustion.

"If we wait just past noon after the race begins, then I'll stake my claim fair and square. At the same time as everyone else." She brushed off dirt from her skirt and rubbed her tired knees.

"Don't you worry, sis. I'll make sure you do." Ben yawned.

If she could only believe that. Last night was proof that she needed to get away from the likes of Ed and Ben Huxley. Even yesterday, he was nowhere to be found when that customer had tried to take advantage of her just before Cort Stanton came to her rescue. The handsome cowboy's gallant gesture shone bright amid the dark memories of all the times her father had proved he couldn't care less. Mr. Stanton didn't know her at all, and yet he'd tried to help her in a time of need. If she had made it to the land race this morning, would she have been tempted to find him on the line?

Aubrey pushed her back into the packed dirt and closed her eyes, shoving away any more thoughts about the handsome distraction. Ben's breathing was slow and rhythmic, lulling her to a dreamy state. They hid out in this little nook that she'd soon own. Chills squirmed their way up her crouching spine. Miss Landowner. Mama would never believe it. Aubrey couldn't contain her smile. She spied the other side of the creek bed through the crowded opening. Untouched soil, wild grasses and freedom.

She was in the same sleepless predicament as she had been back at camp. How could she manage to rest at a time like this?

But when her eyes grew heavy and her smile faded, there was only one thing to do before sleep invaded her. She forced a little prayer:

Wake me up when it's time to stake my claim. Quarter past noon would be best.

He really shouldn't do it. The intense glare of sunshine promised the day would be agonizing enough. During the morning of the race the only thing Cort *should* be doing was preparing for his venture on the prairie—finding his spot among the other settlers, waiting for the start and then racing to land of his own. Why did he choose to go find Miss Huxley instead?

He *did* run out of saddle soap. That was a good excuse. A fine reason to visit that shoddy corral and its beautiful owner once more. But, as he went against the flow of settlers, away from the starting line, he knew his notorious Stanton bloodline would be the death of him. He was just drawn to making wayward decisions, it seemed.

The Huxleys' tents were all sealed up, but Mr. Huxley was outside, his feet propped up on a barrel as he snoozed in a rocking chair. Two old horses knocked around an empty pail with their dusty noses, and the gate of the corral swayed in the hot wind. Cort approached, closing the gate behind him. He pulled off his hat as he walked up to the old man.

"Excuse me, sir?" he said, but the man kept snoring. Cort spied the saddle soap on a table under a small canopy. He went up to the closed-off tent and cleared his throat. "Uh, Miss Huxley?"

He felt as ridiculous as a schoolboy trying to prove himself to be a man. He crammed his hat on his head. He could do without the saddle soap. As he turned, his boot crushed a piece of parchment.

It was crumpled up in the red Oklahoma dirt. He blew it off. It was a letter, not addressed to him, yet he couldn't help but read the elegant handwriting:

Dear Pa,
By the time you read this, I'll be riding in the race, praying that I have the chance to find some land of my own. Ever since Mama passed, I've wanted to honor her with a proper horse ranch of her dreams. I know you weren't able to give that to her, but as her daughter, I must try.
*   Please don't look for me. I am twenty-two*

*years old and need to find my own way apart
from you and Ben. I have left you the last of my
savings from sewing, which should help with your
expenses to get back home and even buy a couple decent horses for profit. That's the last I can
offer you, Father. I'll send word once I am established. Take care of Ben. He needs you, and
you need him. But right now, I just need to do
this on my own.
Your daughter,
Aubrey.*

Cort let out a long whistle. Mr. Huxley slept in his
rocker even though his daughter had just bidden him
farewell forever?

Cort and Aubrey had talked about their secrets last
night. Aubrey's was out in the open now. The hope Aubrey had kindled in him as they parted ways last night
flooded him now. He wondered what it might feel like
to have his secret out. Sure, it would clear his name.
Give him a chance at freedom, but at what cost? If he
told anyone the truth, he'd risk the chance of his brother
being taken away from his young family forever. Cort
would never forgive himself.

No. His innocence would never be found out. It would
jeopardize his brother's freedom and his nephew's future.

He lifted his gaze from the letter to the distant horizon already shimmering in the heat.

She was somewhere along the start line, ready to
build a ranch of her own. Now that Cort was a praying
man, he said a prayer for Aubrey's safety. And then,

against his own reasoning, he prayed that one day they'd meet again. He couldn't look for her today, but one day. And he hoped it would be a day he wasn't ruled by the fear of the law catching up with him. Perhaps when he was certain of his freedom, he might even share his life with a woman like Aubrey Huxley by his side.

He shook his head. Dreaming was no pastime for a cowboy who'd run out of chances. He may be free now, thanks to his dear friend Sheriff Conway, who'd allowed him to escape that prison fire and run away. But now that the sheriff had died of typhoid, he didn't stand a chance against the rest of the state of Texas. Cort Stanton could outrun his fellow land seekers, but he couldn't outrun his past. If anything, he should pray that God would keep him far away from Miss Huxley.

Before he left the corral, he crumpled up the paper again and threw it down where Mr. Huxley had tossed it. He would only focus on the race now.

The swarm of settlers fled the camp, yanking their whole lives in wagons, carts and packs. Cort was blessed in that way. He had nothing but what was in his small pack. Once he untied his horse and led him to the start line, he swung himself on top of his saddle. The anticipation around him frenzied like a kicked beehive. It was a day of all days. The day where he would cling to living and leave everything else behind. Live in the moment and do what he did best. Work the land.

"Whoa, boy." He tried to calm the horse as he kept his place in the bulging line. It was tough to expect much from the animal amid the chaos, but talking to him was at least calming Cort's own nerves.

Was he really this close to possessing his own piece

of land? His heart stuttered. Just two years ago he was content working someone else's land clear up in Wyoming. But now?

He loosened the bandanna around his neck. Either the heat was getting to him, or his conscience was starting early. Usually, he did well to not think about it until the quiet of nightfall. Perhaps the quieting mass as they neared noon gave him too much room to ponder. Ironic to think of this as a thought-provoking place. He was packed in between thousands of horses, hundreds of carts and sweating settlers hungry for what a fourteen-dollar registration fee bought them—a slim chance at acreage. A baby's cry pierced the aggravated silence. Regret niggled in Cort's core while he tightened the grip on his reins, leaning forward as most everyone did around him. He'd yet to have a family to provide for. Would he ever? His costly mistakes before now may have jeopardized any chance for that.

Aubrey Huxley slipped across his mind again. How could one woman have such an effect on him in such a short amount of time? One thing was certain: he could not endanger her happiness by linking his future with hers. No, he couldn't pull anyone else into his life now.

His horse slung his head back and snorted.

When an explosion coursed through the stifling heat and the line lurched forward, Cort kicked his horse to a roaring gallop. He left behind the billowing dust and toppling wagons, focusing only on one thing—staking his claim where God knew best.

Chapter Three

Aubrey woke up with a gasp. Ben was leaning most of his weight on her, blocking any view to the creek bed.

She shoved him. "Wake up." The air was hot and the light outside was a bold afternoon shine, not a weak morning glitter.

What time was it?

Ben stretched his arms, but Aubrey couldn't wait. She scrambled over him, elbows and knees battering her brother in the process.

"Ow!"

"We overslept. I know it." Her voice was as hoarse as the train whistle in the distance. She grabbed her sack and ran down the creek. "Come on, Ben. Look at the sun. Is it straight above?" She refused to consider that it was on more of a western crawl.

Please, let there be time.

She heaved the sack on the higher ground then pulled herself up. The clip-clop of hooves grew louder, louder still. Her heartbeat skipped ahead of the noisy gallop.

Upon the horizon, a man appeared, racing straight toward the marker.

"No!" She yanked out her stake from her sack and clambered to her feet. Her legs were weak from the marathon run last night. As she took her first stride, her knees buckled. The rocky ground met her splayed hands while the stake lay without purpose just beneath her.

"Are you okay?" Ben rested a hand on her shoulder.

Aubrey whipped her head around and screamed, "Go!"

Her hands burned like fire, yet she could only focus on one thing—the man leaping off his horse and racing her brother to the marker.

Ben was closer—she was sure of it. That was, until the man swiped the marker away and lifted his stake above his head. When he pierced the ground, Aubrey's dream came crashing down like pouring rain after the final crack of thunder.

Everything she had planned—to break free from her father, to revive her mama's dream, to make something of this life—slipped into a sour memory. Her stomach twisted. How could this happen?

A wild groan erupted from Ben. He flung himself at the man, wrapping his arms around the man's knees. They rolled away from the stake and Ben's fists pounded into his opponent. Aubrey knew Ben's effort was futile. The man had claimed the land. Nothing would change that. Yet a swell of awe struck her as her brother fought—for her. But when Aubrey spied the man's holster on his hip, panic puffed her with fear.

She must warn her brother. "Stop!"

Ben looked up from the brawl and the other man

hunched over, his shoulders heaving with big breaths. Ben's brows turned downward into a sharp V. She'd seen that look when he was planning a devious scheme. She began to take brisk strides toward him. He couldn't continue, especially with the rightful owner retreating. Before she could speak, Ben swiveled around and barreled toward the unaware stranger. His head lodged in the man's ribs. Grunting and groaning eclipsed Aubrey's screams. Ben wouldn't relent. Every time the man tried to escape, he'd clutch at him.

"Ben Huxley. You stop this instant," Aubrey yelled from the back of her throat. The man tried to push him off, and Ben's foot slipped from under him. He didn't let go. Suddenly, they fell in a heap, Ben trapped under his opponent. The thud shook the ground beneath Aubrey's feet.

She ran to them. "Ben, are you okay?" The man rolled off. Her brother lay there, moaning and reaching for his leg. "Ben, talk to me." His leg was bent in an awful shape and his eyes fluttered open then rolled back.

"Ben!"

Slapping his face did nothing. His head became a heavy boulder in her arms.

Silence hung in the air, thicker than the dust that refused to settle from the fight. It seemed everything floated in a trapped moment of time. Aubrey listened as Ben's heart began to slow from its quickened beat. The same rhythmic breathing from earlier this morning tickled her arm as she swiped away his hair to check for any open wounds. She tried to gently shake him awake.

His eyes fluttered open. Then he screwed his face up, reaching his hands down toward his legs. "It hurts, sis."

"Just don't move. We'll get you help."

A shadow blanketed her. Aware of her vulnerability now, Aubrey held her breath and skimmed her gaze upward. The man stood with a ray of sunshine around his silhouette. His body was indeed a shadow, dark and indistinguishable against the bright Oklahoma sky.

"Is this man with you?" His voice rolled away Aubrey's timidity. She knew that voice. Her mouth fell as she tried to make out his features.

She swallowed hard and said, "He's my brother."

"Miss Huxley, I didn't mean for it to go this far." Cort Stanton squatted in front of her, and his face came into focus. His chiseled cheeks and strong jaw were covered in a thick layer of black dust, no doubt from the stampede of horses at the race. His green eyes pierced hers eagerly. There was that compassion again. He swiped his hat from his head, hanging it on his knee. "I tried to step away. I—I…" A crease appeared between his eyebrows, and he placed a hand on her arm. "I am so sorry."

Aubrey stared at his strong, sun-stained hand—brown against her cotton sleeve—the hand of a hard worker but the soft touch of a dear friend. "He's in pain, Mr. Stanton." She searched his face once more for any sign of malice. If only she could find it then she wouldn't feel so bad that he was the one person who'd destroyed her chance to own land.

His face transformed with an apology, but it would never be enough to comfort her. After all she'd gone through, she'd not only lost her one hundred and sixty acres, but injured her brother in the effort. A tender look on a handsome face did nothing to soothe her broken heart or restore her shattered dream.

"I can't tell if you're devising a plan of revenge, or if stealing my breath away is revenge enough." Cort managed a smile that would've tempted many a woman to swoon and forget their current situation. But Aubrey was not just any woman. His charm only trivialized her loss.

"I do not intend to devise a plan." She cleared her throat. "My only plan is ruined." All her hope skittered away when he staked her claim.

Aubrey encouraged her brother to rest then carefully left his side. She brushed off her skirt, making sure her ankles were hidden away. Her world might be falling apart, but she needn't lose her dignity. Her boots crushed the grasses as she headed toward her belongings. Sensing Mr. Stanton following her, she stopped and spun around.

"Do not accuse me of stealing away your breath, or anything, for that matter." Aubrey leveled her gaze, her nose just barely aligned with Mr. Stanton's dimpled chin. " I am the one who's been robbed. My horse was taken before I even had a chance to run. And another thing has been stolen right beneath my nose. Thanks to you, Mr. Stanton. You, sir, have stolen my land."

Cort didn't understand how delusion could look so beautiful. Under no circumstance was this Aubrey Huxley's land. He glanced at his flag flapping in the hot breeze, looked about the land, then tilted his face toward her. "I am confused. How's this your land?"

Miss Huxley flared her nostrils and narrowed her

eyes. The prettiest little "hmph" came from behind her lips. She flicked her dark hair over her shoulder, freshening the air with the scent of spring flowers, then took brisk strides and snatched up her lifeless flag.

He eyed her brother's crooked leg.

Please, Lord, forgive me for hurting him. I tried not to—

Cort's horse grunted behind him. "Hey there. Decided to stick around?" Loyal after a day? What a creature. He hitched him to a tree. Cort had thrown himself off so fast when he'd seen the man running for the flag, he didn't even consider his horse's whereabouts. His only belongings were strapped to the back of the horse. And really, nothing was worth much in a change of clothes, cooking utensils and some blacksmith tools. But his pay from horseshoeing these last couple of months would get him started on building. His fingers itched to work land of his very own.

Miss Huxley tied a bonnet around her hair, the straight long locks fanned out upon her shoulders. If ever there was a beautiful mess, it was those dark strands catching the breeze.

Enough, Cort.

Where in the world had his reason gone?

Miss Huxley returned to her brother. Kneeling down, she held her hand high above his face, seemingly blocking out the sun. A whimper bleated from her lips, and her tiny figure began to tremble. She was crying. He steeled himself. He did not need to be a hero right now by rushing to her side to console her. Besides the fact that every fiber in his being told him to do just that and he couldn't trust himself, he was tired of what she did to him when she was close. To see those large brown eyes swimming with tears? Well, that would be the end of him.

"Miss Huxley, I'll get some water for him," he offered and didn't wait for her answer before heading toward the creek. When he returned, Miss Huxley approached him with her own canteen in hand. A crude tent made from a quilt draped over an upright shovel and her unused stake shaded the injured man.

"Here." He handed her his canteen.

"Thank you." She hesitated. "I'll go fill mine for good measure."

"Here, I'll do that. You stay with him."

Miss Huxley swiped her moistened forehead with the back of her hand. Tilting her head to one side, she examined his face. "That's kind of you." Lowering her focus to the canteen, she reluctantly gave it to him.

He hesitated, wondering how they'd ended up in this predicament. "Miss Huxley, did you run by foot? You said your horse was taken."

"Mmm-hmm."

"Your father didn't sell your horse, did he?" The thought of that sleeping man with the crumpled-up letter at his feet frayed Cort's nerves.

Aubrey cocked her head, her lips parted in a slight smile. "No, he did not. But I lost my horse to another thief." She glanced over at her brother. "Chased him through the night. The horse ran off before I got him."

"Wait—you ran early?" Cort asked.

"I didn't have much of a choice. Tried to get my horse back," she said. "Doesn't matter, though. Should've stayed put."

"That's a long run for coming up empty-handed," he muttered.

Her lip trembled. "This is not how I expected to end up, I promise you that."

His insensitive remark surely prodded her next sob. Cort didn't hesitate to gather her in his arms. Her shaking body was warm against his chest. She melded into him, prompting a powerful instinct to tighten his grip and assure her that he'd protect her. His cheek rested on her bonnet while she cried. Lavender mixed with the dry prairie air filled his nostrils. That strange storm of hope brewed again, filling him with a boost of life.

Oh, Lord, give me strength.

Miss Huxley began to quiet, and as she did, her body stiffened. She pulled away. "All I care about right now is that my brother heals. I didn't expect to take care of anyone but myself out here." Her eyes were red, just like her flushed cheeks. "But I was also planning on having land of my own." Her mouth turned downward.

Cort remembered the letter she'd written. This woman was trying to escape her past, just like he was. A twinge of sorrow plucked his heart. "You mean, you were going to run by yourself today?"

She folded her arms across her chest. "Well, having a horse would have been nice." She rolled her eyes then sighed. "I know plenty about working the land and caring for horses in a proper way. Not like my pa. This was my chance to get away from him once and for all."

Cort swallowed away his guilt. It was not his fault that he got there first. "You should've claimed it, then."

Her eyes flashed with frustration. "And I planned to, after the race had started. Fair and square." She pouted.

"If you don't mind, my brother and I will stay here until he recovers. Then we'll get off your land, Mr. Stanton." Her dress rippled behind her as she took brisk strides to her brother. She offered him a drink from the canteen.

Fine. Stubborn woman could throw a fit about not getting her way. He couldn't allow his heart to soften toward her anymore. What did she expect? For him to pull out his flag and give her one hundred and sixty acres out of sympathy?

When he returned with a second canteen, Miss Huxley was leaning against a lone tree, facing the sunny prairie just to the north. He set the canteen by her brother, who was asleep beneath the quilt.

A horse appeared upon the horizon to the north, barreling their way. Cort grabbed his holster. Would he have to ward off another person from his land?

"Miss Huxley, why don't you come beside your brother. I'll take care of this."

"You forget, Mr. Stanton, I can take care of myself." She walked over to her bag, pulled out a small pistol and shoved it in her pocket.

"Fine. You can help guard *my* land if you'd like." He smirked. She glared at him in response.

The rider slowed to a trot. When he was on the edge of the western tree line, he waved above his head.

Miss Huxley shaded her eyes with her hand. "It's a soldier."

Cort's stomach fell. The law. He tried to maintain his confidence. He couldn't help but consider the fact that anyone dressed in a uniform might be his doomsayer. A part of him knew he was being irrational. The man couldn't have known who he was—yet. Cort was different without his beard. And it was not as if he had his name written on his forehead.

But he couldn't hide forever. If anyone knew how small this part of the world was—no matter its million acres of prairie—it was Cort Stanton. He'd seen first-hand how quickly familiar faces popped up when you least expected them. Wasn't Aubrey Huxley proving this to be true right in the middle of the Cherokee Strip? He would take it as a warning to be more careful.

"Hello there." The soldier stilled his horse just a few yards away from them. His attention fell on Miss Huxley's brother. "Is that man okay there?"

She stepped forward. "His leg appears to be broken. Do you know if there's a doctor nearby?"

"I sure don't. But I'll keep my ears open for one. I'm riding around informing everyone that a land office is set up about two miles west of here, near the Alva depot. The quicker you get there the better."

Cort rubbed his hands on his trousers. Why was he sweating so badly? This wasn't Texas.

"I'll get there soon. Thank you, Officer." Cort pulled at his collar.

The scout tipped his flat-brimmed hat. "I'll be sure to send a doctor over if I come across one." He nodded at Aubrey. "As quick as everything's happening, there's bound to be one around here soon. They've already brought in a land surveyor from Amarillo. Y'all will have a town quicker than you can say 'Alva.'" He galloped away.

A land surveyor from Amarillo? This wasn't Texas, but it sounded like Texas was coming here. Cort would've never expected to see someone from his hometown in the Cherokee Strip. He began to head over to his horse, praying that his weak legs would carry him that far.

I just wanted more time.

If he risked showing up at the land office with an Amarillo man about, then his time may as well be up. He'd seen wanted posters with his name on them on his way out of the Panhandle. Even if he changed his name, the Amarillo man would recognize him, wouldn't he? This whole venture to hide seemed useless now.

"Mr. Stanton, I wonder if you could ask around for a doctor also? The faster we find one, the quicker we can leave." Miss Huxley's voice was as unstable as Cort's heartbeat. He could hear the hurt.

"You can stay as long as you like." His shoulders slumped.

"Believe me, it's better than what's waiting for me in Kansas. But I assure you, I don't need the reminder of all I've lost."

All she'd lost? Guilt began to swim around with his hopelessness. He'd taken the land from beneath her nose, and he might not even be able to keep it. What right did he, an outlaw, have to hoard land when this woman's whole future lay ahead of her?

He grabbed the horn of his saddle and pulled himself up. When he turned his horse around, he spied Miss Huxley squeezing her brother's hand. She bent her head and mumbled. Cort's throat tightened.

Lord, what should I do? I just want some time.

Maybe he could buy some time? He clicked his tongue and tugged the reins. The horse approached the two siblings. Miss Huxley stood as Cort dismounted. An awkward silence passed between them. She stroked his horse's mane while he tried to form words.

"You know, this is an awful big chunk of land for a man to live on by his lonesome." He gritted his teeth. "I'm not even going to stay long. It'd be vacant for most of the time." He swallowed hard.

How yellow can a man be to give all this up for a chance to hide?

"It's your land. You can come and go as you wish." The longing in her eyes ignited an ache in Cort's chest. She wanted to run horses. She wanted it badly.

"What if it wasn't my land? I mean, what if I let you…" Cort expected he would regret his next words. "What if I just worked a piece of it until I leave? What if you registered the land in your name?"

Miss Huxley narrowed her eyes. "What are you saying, Mr. Stanton?"

"One hundred and sixty acres is big enough for both of us, is all. What if you let me lease the land from you? Maybe one day, if I stay, I'll buy a parcel of it. But until then, all I'd want in return is a chance to work it. I am a pretty decent farrier once you're stocked with horses."

Miss Huxley's lips parted. She blinked several times before whispering, "You'd give it to me?"

"Sure. Doesn't seem right that I keep it all to myself when I might—" Cort cleared his throat. "I'll be away more than I'd be working it." *And sooner than later if that surveyor recognizes when I go to town.*

"I—I don't know what to say." She clamped her mouth shut. Her lips grew thin as she frowned. "What's in it for you, Mr. Stanton?"

* * *

Every hair on Aubrey's arms stood up on end. In the distance, a covered wagon blurred in and out of vision as she considered all that Mr. Stanton might be saying.

Giving up his land? And offering it to her?

He took a step closer. "I just want to work the land, Miss Huxley. Every decent man enjoys hard work. I might be long gone before winter, anyway." He gazed across the plains over her shoulder. "Have you ever wanted to run away and not be found, Miss Huxley?"

The cowboy searched her face with such intensity, she wondered if he could see into her heart and know that she didn't want to be found, either.

"That's why I'm here, Mr. Stanton," she half whispered. "But how can I trust you?" They'd spoken of their secrets last night. But he had never revealed his. What secret could be so big that a man would give up a piece of land?

"I promise you, all I want is honest work. I am a gentleman and a hard worker. You have my word." He took his hat off and placed it over his heart. A tousled mess of dark hair was slightly smashed on his head. Moist brown curls framed his suntanned forehead, and his emerald eyes sparkled.

Against every beat of her overactive heart, she wanted to believe this man. Why was that? Both dubious men in her life, her pa and Ben, forced her to believe that trust was an ideal more than a virtue. How could she be tempted to give it to this stranger? If his generous gift wasn't the exact thing Aubrey had placed her heart's desire on, then she would turn and run the other way.

But now this handsome cowboy waved his property flag in her face, even offering to help her get the ranch started. Agreeing to such an arrangement wasn't as much a matter of trust as a matter of business. Wasn't it? There wasn't a boomer in all of Oklahoma who wouldn't take such an offer as this. Maybe she could ignore the fact that he had secrets. This was her only chance to continue with her plan.

"It's a deal." She pushed her chin to her neck, smiling while tears slid down her cheeks. Mr. Stanton held out his hand. She shook it. "You might have something to hide, but whatever it is, it has made me a brand-new landowner today." She squeezed his hand. His face beamed even in his own loss.

"You can thank the horse for getting me here just in time." Mr. Stanton winked. "Guess it's a good thing you ran on foot after all."

Aubrey slipped her hand away. *No need holding on to him any longer.* She shouldn't entertain him any more than a rattlesnake on the toe of her shoe. Even if he was her first tenant and employee, exchanging as few words with him as possible would help keep him from becoming a distraction or a future regret.

Mr. Stanton offered his hand once more and helped her onto the horse. Her heart leaped at the thought of riding to the land office to officially register the land in her name. But she spotted Ben's collapsed body beneath her makeshift tent and gasped. She had nearly ridden off and left him with a practical stranger.

"Don't worry about him. I'll be sure to dodge any flying fists." Mr. Stanton winked again, an unnerving habit, to say the least.

A wave of nausea stopped Aubrey from acknowledging his jest. Could she really leave her brother with this man who hid something big enough to give up one hundred and sixty acres?

He closed his hand upon hers as she gripped the reins. "Miss Huxley, you have my word. And if that doesn't mean anything to you, you can rest assured that I won't do anything unworthy with such a window to the heavens as the Oklahoma sky." He cast his tender green gaze upward. A warm smile revealed a dimple beneath his stubble.

She might be leery of him, with his hidden motives for giving up his land, but he'd been a noble refuge twice yesterday—on the way to purchase horses, and last night, around the fire as he read his Bible and discussed their secrets. Perhaps his secret was the very thing that gave Aubrey this sweet providence?

"Very well, Mr. Stanton." She breathed in the hot prairie air. "I'll hold you to it." Patting the horse and clutching the reins, she squinted upward. "May that window above remain wide-open," Aubrey mumbled as they trotted along.

When she arrived at the land office, she stood among hundreds of people eager to register their land in the already thriving town of Alva. She couldn't believe the haggling that was already taking place among settlers who had just run the race of their lives. Tents were set up just like at the camp before the run—saloon tents, lawyers and even a doctor tending to many men and women who'd been injured in the shuffle. Aubrey was able to speak with him about Ben and he had said he'd follow her home after the town's first church service tomorrow morning. Although she was glad to leave behind the chaos in town, Aubrey was also thrilled to be counted among these settlers who were not lazy about making life here and making it quick.

Aubrey galloped most of the way back. She hadn't planned to spend so much time away, and her anxiety was heightened as she thought about Ben. When she approached the grove of trees on the western part of her property, though, she slowed to a trot. The peace of the prairie invited her back like she'd been living there for years. Every shadow, every blade of dry grass upon which they would now tread, was hers. Mr. Stanton walked over and offered his hand to help her off the horse. The excitement roaring through her veins made it difficult to refrain from wrapping him in a celebratory embrace. Instead, she crossed over to check on Ben. He was breathing just fine and had a wet handkerchief over his forehead. She twisted a bandanna in her hands and walked up to the cowboy poking at a fire near the ridge above the creek bed. "Thank you for caring for him."

"Glad to help. Don't think he knows who I am. Barely opened his eyes when I offered him a drink." He gave a warm smile and rubbed the back of his neck.

"I'm not sure what you're hiding from, Mr. Stanton, but it can't be too bad." Should she say what was on her mind? She'd thought about it all the way home. "You've been quite the gentleman today." And yesterday, for that matter. She fixed her eyes on the flame as she gave him praise for his chivalrous ways, hoping he'd stay accountable to those ways throughout the evening.

"That's kind of you, Miss Huxley." His scratchy voice

tempted her to look up at him. The dancing flames were trapped in his eyes. He grinned warmly.

She sat down and leaned back on her hands. "It's going to be a long day tomorrow. I'm planning on building my first sod house."

Mr. Stanton threw back his head and chuckled. "That's quite a feat, Miss Huxley. I told you I was here to help."

Her neck crawled with heat. She scooted back from the fire. "You're better off taking care of yourself, sir. I don't want to depend on anyone, especially a stranger."

"Aubrey—" He curled his lip in, then continued, "Do you mind if I call you that?"

She shook her head, trying to ignore the delight of hearing her name on his lips.

"I said I'd help you get the ranch going, and I will. I'll do my best to not disappoint you."

Aubrey stood to her feet and began to place her hands on her hips, but reconsidered and dropped them to her sides. "Mr. Stanton—"

"Cort."

She swallowed hard. A nervous stampede pelted its way across her stomach. How could such a rugged cowboy not only cast off his land, but swear by his word in such a way that every ounce of her spirit believed him? She refused to depend on him, though. No matter how much he offered his assistance. Leaning on him would wreck the independence she had finally found after escaping a man like Pa. Anything else would lead toward her demise, just like Mama found out after years with Pa.

"Cort. It's obvious that you try to be a man of your

word. You kept it while I was away, and for that, I thank you. But don't think that I am ever going to count on anything you say you're going to do, or anyone says, for that matter. I am only here for one person—my mother. If I get help along the way, then so be it. But I have my assumptions that your leaving might not be of your own accord. I can only take what you offer to do with a grain of salt."

If Cort's stare could, it would burn the very fire that blazed between them. His look barreled through her. Was he angry? Why in the world would she turn away the only able person who'd help her willingly? She must preserve her hope and expectations. It was the only way she could stay strong enough to do this.

"Okay, Aubrey." He leaned back on an elbow and crossed his feet on one side of the fire. "I've got my own sod house to build anyway. But of course, only if you say so, Miss Landowner."

Warding off a rush of uncertainty, Aubrey pulled her shoulders back and spun around on her heel. She'd better get some rest if she wanted to be the first to borrow that neighbor's steel plow she had her eye on.

"Good night, Mr. Stanton," she said.

"Cort," he retorted.

Goose bumps plucked her arms and she walked away.

Now to figure out where her house would go, and how many acres she should place between Cort Stanton and herself.

Chapter Four

The last of the embers died, snuffing out Cort's view of Aubrey's makeshift tent. He could just see the soles of her boots sticking out as she lay next to her brother.

Stubborn woman.

How could she expect to manage a plow and the task of building four walls of sod all by herself? Cort winced as he lay back and tucked his bag beneath his head. She would have had her brother's help if it weren't for him.

Wasn't that just typical of Cort Stanton? To fight for something that wasn't really his and hurt people in the process? He'd proved this back in Wyoming during the range war. He'd protected his boss's land but ended up fighting against his own brother. Charles had joined the unlawful gunslingers, forcing Cort to choose between standing up for good and his own flesh and blood.

How many ill deeds had Cort witnessed because of his loyalty to Charles?

Cort slung his arm across his face and tried to calm his mind and get some sleep. Before he could even consider blinking away the image of Aubrey's brown eyes from the backs of his eyelids, an unsettling groan drowned out a chorus of crickets.

"Ben, just stay still." Aubrey's voice rang out.

Another agonizing noise. Cort skittered to his feet and dug through his bag for his lantern and a match. By the time he made his way to Aubrey, she was frantically rummaging through her own belongings. Cort knelt down. The light shone bright upon Ben's face as he gasped, squeezing his eyes tight.

"Don't move, Ben." Aubrey laid her hand on his forehead then swiped it downward along his cheek.

"It's killin' me." Tears streamed down Ben's cheeks.

"I know, brother." She cast wide, questioning eyes in Cort's direction. As if he had answers. He wished he did. But the only sure answer was that her brother's hurt was all his fault.

"You spoke with a doctor?" Cort whispered.

She confirmed with a quick nod. "He's coming tomorrow."

"Good."

Aubrey's petite fingers clasped Cort's hand tightly. He shot a look of confusion at her. She grabbed Ben's hand and bowed her head.

"Heavenly Father, watch over Your child tonight. May Your healing hands lie upon Ben's body and begin to mend whatever might be broken. Give the doctor wisdom tomorrow, and let Ben rest well tonight. In Jesus's name. Amen."

As quickly as she'd held his hand, she let go and turned completely toward her brother. The hair on Cort's arms stood up on end. Her earnest prayer moved him.

Aubrey's hum trickled into the night air, blessing any

listener with its melody. The crickets' lullaby met its match. He tried to forget the warmth from her touch and the aftermath of her prayer on his heart. She was wise to not attach herself to Cort's promise to help. He wondered if he could follow through himself. A woman of such courage and tenderness would only be destroyed in the long run if he pursued her. He shouldn't wait for the authorities to come looking. He should leave now while he had her complete confidence in his unreliability.

Then again, she may not know it, but she was a woman in need of immediate assistance. No woman, or man, could care for a brother with a broken limb and build a dwelling in good time. In the heat of this drought, Aubrey and Ben Huxley would not find much relief beneath a rudimentary tent for more than another day.

The only way he knew how to begin to make up for Ben's circumstance was in a way that he'd always done well. He'd work.

Cort bade her good-night and headed back to his bag. He settled down again and managed to sleep on and off. Finally, at daybreak, he stretched his arms to the gray morning sky then headed to the creek.

After splashing his face with the lukewarm water, he clambered back up to higher ground. Aubrey was sleeping, curled up next to Ben. He fought the urge to peek in at her and, instead, explored the wide plains around them. In the near distance, their neighbors had already started on a soddie. While he'd stayed with Ben yesterday, it'd seemed that every time he glanced over that way, there was a growing stack of sod bricks.

A moan came from beneath the tent. Cort winced, remembering the gnawing pain of a broken bone. He was only eleven when he'd broken his wrist, but the undulating ache was seared in his memory. An urgency to ease Aubrey's burdens swelled up inside. Mostly because Ben's condition was his doing, and it was the only compensation he might offer. But there was something else, and no matter how much Cort tried to shove it away, it clung on like a cocoon in the shade of a broad leaf.

What were the chances that the very woman he'd prayed for back at camp would be the first woman he'd meet on this expanse of land?

Now they were tied to each other in a way. Their destinies were bound together because of a desperate bargain to work the land she longed to own. If only he could offer her a future based on more than a "maybe."

Settling by his pack, he read a couple of Psalms while eating leftover corn cakes he'd carried from camp in his bag. Once he inspected the steep embankment of the creek bed, he decided he would at least make a dugout home for the Huxleys until they'd purchased or borrowed the supplies for a proper home. If he had time, he'd get started on his own down the creek a ways. No reason to live right next door.

"Good morning, Cort." Aubrey startled him as he unstrapped his shovel from his pack. "Mind if I take your horse to the church service in Alva?"

He stood up and wiped his hands on his trousers. "Of course not."

Her face was pallid, a troublesome color compared to its usual creamy ivory. "Ben and I just ate. He's trying his best to keep his leg still. Told him you were nearby if he needed anything."

"I'll keep my ears open."

Weariness cloaked the woman. Her shoulders drooped, and her eyes were red. If he could gather her up in another embrace like yesterday, he'd beg her forgiveness for this mess. Forget any strength of his own. He clenched his teeth and pushed away his spiraling thoughts. He knew the woman beneath the worrisome shell. She was strong, adamant and not to be pitied. At least, that was what she would demand. It had only been a couple of days, and Cort was pretty sure his impression of Aubrey Huxley was correct.

So instead of an embrace, he helped her prepare his horse, saw her off, then got to work.

At first, the dry, packed earth resisted his shovel's blade. Cort leaned his whole body against the handle. It was nothing like the moist soil of northern Wyoming. He fought against the memory, but his mind had already stumbled backward. He may as well have been digging post holes for the south fence along John Buford's small cattle operation. John had been a good boss. One who had given Cort the chance to escape the Texas heat and the family name—or at least to live as a Stanton with no recognition by any townsmen in Buffalo, Wyoming.

Cort wiped away the sweat dripping down his nose with his sleeve and grunted at his next plunge into the earth.

John Buford had spoken on salvation many times as they worked his cattle. Cort had even attended church with the Buford family. But it seemed like family loyalty had caught up with him just as he surrendered to the Gospel as truth.

He'd seen much adversity growing up in Texas and had played along when his brother wormed his way out of trouble time and again. Could Cort truly see the goodness in this life without being pinned down by his cumbersome roots? How did a redeemed man truly find forgiveness on this side of Heaven?

A faint rumble came from above as Cort stepped back and examined the four-foot-wide hole he'd dug. A couple more feet were needed on each side. And then there was the problem of a good front wall. He'd start cutting sod with his spade tomorrow. Aubrey could string up her quilt until then.

He left his shovel and climbed up the embankment. Aubrey had ridden up with a man on a black horse following behind. They tied the horses to the only two trees that seemed secure enough.

"Dr. Mills, this is Mr. Stanton, my tenant," Aubrey said.

Cort tipped his hat then followed in step behind the doctor, praying that God would redeem this situation and at least take away this most recent guilt.

"You appear to have a fracture below the knee." Dr. Mills looked over his spectacles at Ben, then turned to Aubrey. "Might take a couple months to heal."

Her spirit dimmed. Shame swarmed her like fierce mosquitoes. She'd yelled for him to go fight for her land. She'd pushed him into it. Just like Pa dragged him into his schemes.

She was no better.

Aubrey fluttered her lashes to ward off tears. "Will he be able to walk normally again?" The thought knifed her. She knew what it meant to break a leg. Mama's best friend, Maureen, was never the same after falling off a horse.

Ben's eyes widened.

"I think he'll be able to, eventually. But it will take time to heal. I'm going to give him a splint for now. Hoping to get some plaster in the next shipment so I can make him a cast." Dr. Mills adjusted his hat and placed his spectacles in his front pocket. "The heat is unrelenting. I'm more worried about him dehydrating out here than dealing with a broken bone. It's crucial to get him to shelter before another day of this heat." He gave a quick glance to the pile of their recent shelter. They'd taken down the quilt for Ben's examination.

"Yes, sir," Aubrey mumbled, feeling as small as a mouse. There was no way she could build shelter that quickly. Cort gave her an assured nod. Even with his extra help, surely a shelter wouldn't be possible so quickly.

Cort came up beside her, gently cupping her elbow. "Don't you worry about shelter, Miss Huxley."

Before Aubrey could question him, Ben growled, "What's he still doing here?" He struggled to prop himself up on his elbows, his brown eyes lit with anger.

"Ben, you need to calm down—"

"That's the man who did this to me!" He curled his sweaty lip against white teeth and glared at Cort.

"Son, you must calm yourself." The doctor rushed over, placing a hand on his shoulder.

"Doc, wonder how my leg broke? That's the cowboy who did it." Ben's knuckles bulged as he held them in tight fists. His glare remained fixed on Cort.

"I tried to stop you… I didn't want any trouble."

Cort removed his hat, wiping his hands through dampened curls.

Aubrey placed a hand on Cort's arm. "Let's discuss this later." She glared at Ben, who just narrowed his eyes. The doctor didn't need to witness this dispute. Her skin crawled with the memory of every outburst she'd witnessed from the Huxley men over the years. Some men walked away from conflict and others, like the Huxley men, tended to barrel right into it without a thought. Just as Ben had taken Cort head-on the day of the race, he was now wanting to pick a fight even in his miserable state.

While Dr. Mills applied a splint, he advised, "You must keep your leg still. We'll try to get a nice flat board to move you tomorrow. There's supposed to be a railcar full of lumber delivered to Alva's square. A stretcher would be best, but that's one more day out here." He peered up at the baking sky and lifted his brow in uncertainty.

"We'll get to work on a better shelter right away." Aubrey pulled her shoulders back and offered a hand for a shake. "Thank you, Dr. Mills. We may not have come as prepared as most, but thankfully we have a creek nearby for plenty of water."

"Even the most prepared didn't have the chance to hunker down out here. You're blessed to have your quarter section and water. They're selling it by the bucket in Alva. Just be careful of sunstroke. I've already seen plenty die of it during my stay at the camp." He looked around the vast prairie sprawled out like a grassy cloth on earth's barren table. "I'll be back soon. Comfort him as best as you can. I gave him some laudanum. It will help ease the pain, but may make him sleepy. Be sure to drink plenty, son." Ben nodded weakly.

Aubrey saw him off, then remembered that Cort had disappeared shortly after Ben's accusation. His horse was grazing in the shade, so he hadn't gone too far. A tremor of defeat threatened to crush her. How could she manage to build a home, care for her brother and find work to afford the expenses of starting a horse ranch?

Lord, show me Your will in all of this.

If she thought of Mama—how she worked as a seamstress, her fingers bleeding, how she had stashed away her money in the jar at the back of the pantry, and she'd poured out every ounce of her energy for this dream— then the least Aubrey could do was make it come true. Even if the jar had been raided often by greedy paws, and the dream was dashed by her father's dishonest deeds. Aubrey's own pay from the dress shop was her assurance that Pa would leave her be. At least she didn't have to worry about that. She had come this far, and she must persevere regardless of what might stand in the way.

Dr. Mills disappeared beyond the mesquite trees. He had called Aubrey blessed for surviving the land run with something to show for it. She thanked God for the land and the creek. In town, pails and barrels of water were being sold for a price. Yesterday, she'd breathed in the black dust that hung over the newborn town of Alva, smelling the sweat of hundreds who had settled for a small plot in town instead of a homestead on the prairie. It was time Aubrey rekindled her determination.

No, she wouldn't give up. She had dealt with the challenges of living under the same roof as Ed Huxley all these years, hadn't she? Nursing a broken leg and building a ranch from scratch couldn't be any worse than that, could it?

"Aubrey, why's that man hanging around?" Ben called to her.

"I'll talk with you soon, brother," she said. He looked like he might get up and chase her down. "Don't you move." She didn't want to face his anger yet. First things first. Take the good doctor's advice and get some water.

Aubrey slid down the ridge to fill her canteen. A large mass of dirt was piled against the embankment to the east. The soft plodding of tossed soil alternated with labored breathing. She wormed her way around the pile that was close to damming up the very creek that she'd thanked God for. Cort's back was to her, his sleeves rolled up to his elbows while he shoveled soil in a constant rhythm. The muscles along his tanned fore-arm flexed with each movement and his shirt clung to his skin with perspiration.

Aubrey filled her lungs with a jagged breath and glanced away. "Mr. Stanton?"

He stopped midshovel. When she managed to look his way again, she saw that earth smeared his glistening face.

Aubrey's mouth went dry. Their eyes locked on each other. The freshly disturbed dirt scented the air just as it had done when she'd crawled through the night. Cort had crossed her mind more than once during that long venture. Now he was part of her new beginning. For how long, she didn't know.

She cleared her throat. "I do wonder why you are digging on *my* land?"

Cort cocked his head but kept her in his sights from the corner of his eye. Was he trying to gauge if she jested? She did not. It seemed he was building himself shelter without even consulting her on its placement. It was a fine hole, though. Big enough that he could probably lie in its width or its depth with room to spare.

"Well, I figured if you owned land, you would need a shelter better than a quilt strung over a shovel." He placed his finger on his upper lip as if trying to contain a smile.

Aubrey swallowed hard. "This is for me?"

"And Ben, I suppose. Dr. Mills seemed pretty adamant."

"But I told you, I was going to build a sod house…" Her voice was barely audible. His work had stolen her boldness.

"This is temporary but necessary in this heat. A soddie will take time to build." He released a broad, charming smile showcasing white teeth and his usual dimple.

"Oh." Aubrey diverted her eyes. How could she stop the flood within her? Her emotions were at war. Gratitude leaped higher than her reservation. This man was stubborn in keeping his word to help, wasn't he? A gentleman to a fault? How in the world could she protect herself from dependence when Cort Stanton kept on like this?

"That's mighty nice of you, Mr. Stanton—"

"Cort. Using my first name is fine by me."

"Okay, Cort. This is a fine shelter."

"Thank you. I just can't sit by and—"

"For you."

Cort's mouth hung open like he'd been snagged by her words.

"I'll build my own, though." She forced herself to appear unwavering, with a cool facade and a confident posture—even if her insides were melting by his gesture.

The cowboy's brow pulled over his eyes like an angry storm cloud above broken land. All joy dissolved from his face, unveiling an undeniable defeat. He gathered up his shovel and approached her in such a deliberate move that she took a step back.

"Fine. If you're so stuck on being self-sufficient, start digging." He pushed the shovel toward her, the handle inches from her nose. As soon as her fingers wrapped around it, Cort slid between her and the dirt pile and stomped down the creek bed.

She blinked away tears as she stared at the product of all his effort.

Of course the man was angry. He'd done all this for her. She'd allowed her stubborn walls to deflect his act of kindness.

How could she so easily reject the nicest gift that she had ever received?

Cort maintained his attention on the distant flame, his only sure proof that he was heading back in the right direction. He had spied Aubrey building a fire through the hazy dusk while he became acquainted with the neighbors. Frank and Mildred Hicks were kind enough, no doubt friendlier now that they'd exchanged the use of their plow for Cort's help in getting the rest of their house up. He would work with them until the noon hour then use the plow for himself and return it first thing each morning. The downside was that he'd work on his own soddie in the heat of the day. But that was the price he would pay for the use of a plow to cut sod.

His stomach was a tumbleweed of nerves after the way he'd left things with Aubrey. It was probably for the best, though. Now he was sure that he wouldn't grow any attachments. He'd be a good tenant and help only if she asked. Besides renting a small section of land from the woman, he really had no other reason to associate with her at all.

Except, of course, if he let her magnetic strength and wits have anything to do with it.

Lord, give me self-control.

He sure needed that fruit of the Spirit with a woman like Aubrey Huxley as his landlady.

By the time he trotted over to his horse's sleeping spot, the pinpricked quilt of the night sky twinkled above. Cort ignored the tug to look around for Aubrey.

Self control, remember?

He traipsed toward the ridge and tried to look forward to sleeping in the hole he'd supposedly dug for himself. It'd be nice to sleep on dry dirt and not the coarse grass of the prairie. It was cooler down in the creek bed, too. Cort talked himself into it, moving at a more certain pace until Aubrey came around from the small fire and stood in front of him.

"I just have one thing to say to you." She crossed her arms over her torso. Her face was dark except for an orange shaft of firelight cutting across her cheek and highlighting a deep carved line between her brows. He was captured by the medley of color in her eye. "We had agreed the only thing I owed you in this whole land exchange deal was a plot of land for you to work yourself. I know you offered help until you supposedly leave, but there's one thing about that." Her nostrils flared. "I need to know why." The wrinkle between her eyebrows smoothed.

"Why? I dug it for you because it was the right thing to do."

"No, not that." Aubrey dismissed his defense with a wave of her hand. She took a half step forward. "I mean, I understand. And I really do thank you for doing that." Relaxing her rigid posture, she stared downward as she fiddled with her fingers. "Why don't you know how long you will stay?"

Cort inhaled the spicy smell of burning wood. It comforted less than the question tormented him. What could he say? He couldn't lie. Lying would make him no better than the other Stantons. Every Stanton was a liar, a cheat and a—

He closed his eyes and prayed the verse, *Put on the new self, created to be like God in true righteousness and holiness.* He was stuck between the old and the new, hoping he could earn his new self from here on out, no matter the cost.

Aubrey's hands trembled while she stood there waiting for his answer. He wondered if she'd guessed it already. "What do you think?"

She clicked her tongue then frowned. "I—I can't say. It could be a million things."

"But you have a guess, don't you?"

Her hands fell to her sides, and he couldn't tell if the

right one still shook, or if it was the firelight dancing upon it. "I suppose."

"Then tell me. I'll tell you if you're right."

"Are you in trouble, Cort?"

Cort's insides began to quiver. He'd been in trouble for so long. But to hear someone else say it? Defeat rained down upon him and he was drenched with shame.

"Has it got something to do with the law?" Aubrey spoke this with more certainty. Did he just imagine her spreading her hand upon her dress pocket where she kept her pistol? The woman did not trust him in the least.

Why would she?

"I'd followed in the wrong crowd, Aubrey, until I gave myself to Jesus. But it wasn't long after that when I found myself in the wrong place at the wrong time." Cort stepped closer and Aubrey's hand slid up to the mouth of the pocket.

"Was it the law, Cort?" She spoke through her teeth.

"Yes." He clenched his fist, knowing she'd only see him as a criminal now. "I don't blame you for wondering or even for being scared. Trust me when I tell you that I would never bring you harm. I hope to never bring harm to anyone."

"What did you do?"

While she might eventually trust him, he couldn't tell her what had occurred. He had never spoken it to anyone, nor would he for fear of destroying his brother's family. He had given his word, and now he must stick to it for any kind of true redemption. Besides, claiming his innocence would make him appear more guilty.

Cort reached his hand out instinctively, hoping to clasp her arm with an assuring touch.

Aubrey twisted her body away from him and stumbled backward. "What did you do, Cort?" She spoke louder now.

"Please, Aubrey. Don't make me say it. It's in the past. I've been given a second chance."

"A second chance?" She narrowed her eyes.

He thought back on the prison fire. After he'd been given permission by Sheriff Conway, he had run faster than he'd ever run before. That was as good as freedom, right? Conway had always liked Cort and knew that he was nothing like his brother. The sheriff had tried getting the whole story out of Cort during his few weeks behind bars. The law was on his side in that respect. As Cort ran from the burning cell and his only friend, he'd sobbed and prayed.

Aubrey dug her fist into her hip, her elbow sharply bent. "A second chance by who?"

"By who?" Cort backed up a couple of steps. "By the good Lord, Aubrey. Only by His grace, and only by Him." He walked toward the ridge. There was nothing else he could say tonight.

Chapter Five

The whipping breeze was no less torrid than the curtains of sunshine that fell from the cloudless sky. Aubrey guided Cort's horse at a steady pace and waved to her new neighbors. The man gestured with his hat in his hand, and the woman just lifted her chin. Sunlight glinted off their plow, which sat amid piles of sod cut for building. Her stomach churned with anxiety. She had never used a plow before, and the thought of using a hand plow rather than a horse-drawn one seemed tedious and difficult. But a plow of some sort would be necessary for her home, even if she couldn't afford a plow or a horse. Borrowing from her neighbors might be the only option. Were they friendly? How long would their house take before she could start on hers? Aubrey couldn't make out their features. From the corner of her eye, someone else caught her attention.

Cort.

He covered the land with long brisk strides, heading away from the neighbors toward her land. He'd set out earlier while Aubrey was giving Ben his breakfast. Cort had said he was helping the neighbors after she'd asked to ride his horse to Alva. They had carefully avoided each other this morning, speaking only as needed. But why was he headed back so early? Hopefully he wouldn't get Ben all riled up.

Their conversation last night was not what she'd expected. Instead of upheaving his secret past, she'd unveiled his dependence on God's grace. And for some reason, that was enough. He was a faithful man. With that came respect and admiration. Faith had been hard to come by living under Ed Huxley's roof. Most days, her inability to forgive him only pushed her to a corner of guilt, not toward God at all.

Another reason why she needed to leave Kansas. She didn't like herself while living with him. Maybe Pa would be easier to forgive at a distance?

She looked back one more time. Her breath caught.

Cort began to hesitantly wave his arm in her direction. Before she could get her hand up to wave back, the horse let out a loud whinny and jerked to a stop. Aubrey gasped, tightening her grip and facing forward again.

A toppled-over wagon stood in their path a few yards ahead. It hadn't been there on her last ride to town. The ribs of the covered wagon lay crushed on one side while the canvas flapped in the breeze.

"Come on, boy." Aubrey gently stroked the horse, but he stuck his hooves into the ground and refused to budge. "Are you spooked?" A rustle from the wreckage sent a shiver down Aubrey's spine. It'd been a couple of days since the race. What if someone was trapped in the wagon? Or what if it was a ploy to get her off the horse and rob her? She'd lived her whole life with a thief, and this seemed to be an excellent opportunity for one.

Panicked, she whipped around to get Cort's attention. She frantically waved for him to come over. He waved back but didn't change his course. "Please, understand," she said under her breath, then used both arms. He began to run toward her.

She scrambled down and headed toward him, her feet crushing the dry grass that crunched as loudly as ripping parchment in a silent schoolroom.

"What is it?" He hunched over, planted his palms on his knees and gulped for air. "Are you hurt?"

Of course he'd ask her if she was hurt, because of her frantic motions, but she relished his concern.

"There's a toppled wagon, and the horse won't go closer. Something—" Aubrey nibbled her lip, giving a sideways glance toward the wreckage. "I mean, someone moved inside it. I heard it. I—I thought you could—"

"Help you?" He raised an eyebrow and straightened to his full-head-taller-than-her height.

She smirked. "Yes, I'd ask any nearby gentleman for help in this situation." She flicked her head toward the wagon, her bonnet slipping back. "And you have proved to be a gentleman, Cort." Admitting this frightened Aubrey. Only because she was tempted to attach herself to this man more than she should. The tragedy of her mother's attachment to her father was an ever-present warning in her mind.

Cort approached her, his eyes narrow beneath the brim of his cowboy hat. A flash of concern then cynicism then solace. "No, you were right to call me over. It's not safe for a lady to come up to a strange property."

Aubrey began to open her mouth in protest, but Cort leaned toward her and whispered as he walked past, "No matter what you carry in your pocket." He chuckled, heading toward the wagon.

She tried to grow angry, but instead released a sigh. Wasn't that why she had asked him to come over in the first place? Never in a million years would she admit it to him. But, for now, she'd bottle her emotions and follow the cowboy.

A property flag flapped nearby, and distant voices carried from the south—probably from the creek bed that ran through her own property. The wagon's wood was split where it came in contact with the ground. Aubrey prayed that nobody had been hurt. At her last utterance of prayer, a whimper traveled from beneath the wreckage.

"It sounds like a child." Cort's pace quickened. He dropped to his knees then crawled toward the entrance of the deflated canopy.

Aubrey's blood pumped hard in her ears. A second whimper smudged away her fear and only brought to mind one image—her helpless brother sprawled out on the dying grass. If there was someone in need, she was ashamed to think that fear had stopped her from helping right away.

While Cort half disappeared inside the wagon, Aubrey bent down to see as best as she could. The shade was too dark in the intense sunshine. The far-off chatter hadn't lessened or grown any, and the horse snorted a couple of times. The immediate silence surrounding them swelled louder. Cort had stopped moving. Only his boots stuck out in the daylight.

Another whimper. "Hello?" His muffled question tugged Aubrey closer and she dropped to her knees, trying to adjust her eyes to the darkness.

"Daddy?"

Cort was right. It was a child.

"No, but I'm here to help. Just grab on to my neck." He began to back out, tenderly so.

A small child, probably five years old, flailed about in Cort's arms as they hit the light of day. The girl wiggled about then leaped from him. Straightening her soiled dress, she then crossed her arms. "You ain't my parents." Her button nose was all scrunched up and her lips thrust out in a pout.

"No, but we can help you. Are you lost?"

"I ain't lost, but my dolly is stuck. Her pretty dress is caught. I know I wasn't s'pose to come back. Daddy told me so. But I knew my dolly was here. I just knew it." The little girl headed back toward the opening of the tipped wagon.

"Where is your daddy?" Aubrey asked. Why wasn't he looking for her? Pa wouldn't have looked for her, either. He hadn't, that time that she'd been lost.

Cort stood and brushed off his knees. "It's not safe for you to be out here by yourself. What with snakes and robbers and…" His warning trailed when the child's eyes grew the size of very large buttons. He obviously had little experience with children. Scaring her to death wouldn't do anyone any good right now.

"Cort, that's no way to talk to a child." Aubrey crouched

down to level with the fair-haired girl. "Where are your parents, child?"

"They went down to the crick to check on Jolene. She scraped her knee pretty bad when we tipped, and they're done carrying all our things to the place Daddy dug out for us yesterday." She dropped to her knees then sat back, cross-legged. "You think you could help me get my dolly? Mama just sewed her dress brand-new. It's made of silk."

Aubrey looked over her shoulder at Cort. "I am certain Mr. Stanton will happily rescue your doll. Won't you, Cort?"

His lips parted. He gave her the same look as when Pa had tried to sell him the pathetic creature back at camp.

"Contrary to your expression, I am very serious." She swiveled, chewing on her cheek to stop her smile from growing. Taking the girl's hand, she stepped aside for Cort.

He rummaged through the inside of the mess. The little girl hopped up and down in her scuffed boots, golden curls bouncing from beneath her bonnet.

"Aha." Cort backed out. He flipped over and sat beneath a crooked hat with a doll hanging from one hand and a cast-iron skillet clutched in the other.

A grin crept wide on Aubrey's face. She couldn't help it. This grown cowboy held a dolly in his massive grip. Well, it was sweet and ridiculous all at once.

"You ripped her dress!" The girl yanked the doll from his hand then ran toward the creek. Stunned, Aubrey's smile disappeared and her mouth dropped in near-perfect unison to Cort's.

"Ungrateful little girl," she grumbled. "Thank you anyway." Helping him up, she yanked a little too force-fully and he stumbled toward her. He grasped at her arm and she steadied him at his waist.

"Adelaide!" A holler carried across the plain.

Aubrey spun around. A woman struggled to run toward the little girl. Her hands held on to her very pregnant belly as if her precious bundle threatened to escape.

"You do not run off, you hear me? I had my heart in my throat lookin' for you!" She clutched Adelaide's arm. "Hello there." The mother walked toward them, shading her eyes. Both mother and daughter had round faces with bright blue eyes and golden hair. Although Adelaide's face was screwed up in a scowl while her mother's was bright with excitement. "It is so thrillin' to meet others who made it through that terrible start." She was breathless as she spoke. "Are you near here?"

"Looks like we're your neighbors to the east. I'm Aubrey Huxley." They shook hands.

"I'm Cort Stanton." He tipped his hat. "Is this your skillet, ma'am? I rescued it from the wreckage. Mighty fine piece there." He handed it to her.

"Thank you, Mr. Stanton. I thought we'd emptied most everything from the wagon. I'm Sarah Jessup."

"Back when I was a cookie, I'd have been hard-pressed to lose a skillet like that." He scratched his jaw. Aubrey just stared at him. He was a horseshoer, cattle rancher and a cook? She wondered if she would discover everything about this jack-of-all-trades.

Cort must have felt her stare. He nudged her with an elbow. "Didn't know that about me, huh? My best days were cooking for cowboys."

Mrs. Jessup piped in, "My pa used to cook, too." She tousled Adelaide's loose curls then admired her skillet. "Your grandpa. This was his."

"Now I'm working for Miss Huxley here to get a ranch going." Cort cleared his throat. "Her brother will help, too, once he recovers from an injury." Aubrey was certain he added that to secure a sense of propriety.

Even so, Mrs. Jessup's cheeks glowed red, her blue eyes glittering as she bounced her look from Aubrey to Cort. "Why, you all are a handsome pair, aren't you?" She winked. Aubrey gritted her teeth as she smiled back. And Cort? Well, she wouldn't dare look in his face.

"As you can see, our hardship met us right at the end of it all. Mr. Jessup had taken it to town for supplies one last time." Sarah nodded toward the wreckage. "One of our horses got spooked and flung that wagon around like a wild dog on a leash. But fortunately, we were mostly unloaded." She shook her head.

"I'm sorry for that. Is it just your husband and your daughter besides yourself?" Cort asked.

"Oh, no. I have three more daughters, Jolene, Caroline and Beatrice. My hands are full, but so's my heart." She giggled.

Three sisters for this little girl? Aubrey had always wanted a sister. Perhaps Mama's death would have been easier to handle with a sister nearby. She could tell that Sarah was a good mother already. Her joyful countenance reminded Aubrey of her own mother in a way.

"I look forward to meeting your family, Mrs. Jessup," Cort said. "If you need help getting your wagon upright, let me know. I better head back now, though." He gave a cordial nod. "I am working with the Hickses today, but forgot my canteen back at my dugout." Cort turned to Aubrey, his shadowy jawline clenched. "I'll see you this evening." His voice was scratchy and low. Almost a whisper. His lips parted as if he would say something else. But he seemed to think better of it and strode past her.

Aubrey sighed. "I'd love to meet your family, too, but I am on my way to find some work in town before dusk."

"Work?" Sarah blew a strand of hair from her face. "Isn't building a homestead enough?"

"You would think. I am going to have to work to... um, work." She flung a gaze over her shoulder, squinting in the brightening daylight. Cort was growing smaller in the distance.

"Your ranch hand seems mighty capable."

"Oh, he is. He's only around for the short term, but he...he has helped already." Aubrey fiddled with her lip, tasting a bit of the Oklahoma dust on her fingertip. Sarah was a good judge of character, it seemed.

"Oh, my. With an injured brother and only yourself out here, you certainly do need an extra hand." The mother laid her hand atop her belly. "If you need anything, you just holler. Mr. Jessup is always willing to help out a neighbor."

"That's kind of you." Aubrey looked down at Adelaide. "I'm sorry your dolly's dress ripped. Maybe you can come down my way, and I'll mend it for you. I love to sew and I have just the perfect button to add a nice touch."

Adelaide's cheeks perked with a smile and she hopped

up and down. "Will you? Oh, thank you, ma'am." Perhaps she wasn't so unmannerly after all.

"You sew?" Sarah asked.

A swarm of flutters filled Aubrey's stomach. The mention of sewing, first from her lips and then from Sarah's, stirred old memories of Mama, threads, fellowship and love. She could only nod. Her mouth seemed stitched closed by the emotional knot tangling in her throat.

"You might want to check in with the tailor. We were in there yesterday tryin' to find some quilt scraps to get ready for the baby. He seemed quite overwhelmed." She shrugged her shoulders. "A woman's touch might be all his operation needs," she said, taking Adelaide's hand then turning to leave. "Hope it all works out for you, Miss Huxley. And a pleasure meeting you."

Cort watched Aubrey mount his horse and continue on to Alva. This time, at a speed much quicker than before. A train whistled and chugged from across the plains where she was headed.

Ben was propped up on his elbows, the quilt blanketing his shoulder. "Why'd you give my sister the land?"

"Don't worry. I have no ill motives." Just cowardly ones.

"You seemed pretty intent on fighting for something you'd go give up at the next turn."

Cort let out a jagged laugh, trying to keep his tone even. "Well, friend, you were pretty persistent."

"A broken leg's not going to stop me from protecting my sister. If it weren't for me, she'd have never found this land."

"Oh, do you mean before or after you stole her horse?" Cort held his knit brow, seeing right through his threat. "Ben, you think you need vengeance because I hurt you. I am sorry for that. But I am here to work. There's nothing else I want."

"We'll see about that, Mr. Stanton. I've got a pretty good reason to sit here and watch, thanks to you. And trust me, you won't get away with whatever you're scheming."

"Scheming?" Cort hung his head, thinking to himself, *You've got the wrong Stanton.*

"There's something going on for you to fight so hard and give up so quickly. Aubrey's hard-pressed to get her ranch going, so she's let you be. But I won't be so easy to impress, cowboy." He glared, then rolled over on his side, blocking his face from Cort's view.

At least Aubrey had a brother who cared about her well-being. He'd give Ben that. But a thin spindle pricked Cort—one that had pierced him with fear at the mention of the land surveyor. What lengths would Ben go to to find out exactly why Cort had given Aubrey the land and why he planned to stay in this quiet corner of the world indefinitely?

He quickly grabbed his canteen and headed back, praying that he could convince Ben, along with his sister, that he was trustworthy.

When Cort returned to the Hickses, he was glad to guide the conversation to focus on the Jessups and away from the stormy current set in motion by Ben's scrutiny.

"Glad everything was okay." Mrs. Hicks handed Cort a tin mug of thick coffee.

"Yes, ma'am. Just a little girl in need of her doll."

He chuckled and took a sip. Bitter, but enough flavor to warrant a second gulp. "Now it's time to get to work."

"If you could bring over some of those bricks, Cort, I'll go ahead and start on the south wall." Mr. Hicks tugged at his suspenders and rolled up his sleeves. "Mrs. Hicks is mighty thankful that you are helping now."

"Why, yes, I am." She patted Cort's arm. "My back isn't what it used to be. You sure you don't want Mr. Hicks to head back with you this afternoon? I would hate for Miss Huxley and you to have to do all the work it takes to build two homes. That seems treacherous."

A cynical laugh escaped Cort's lips. "Oh, she's stronger than any woman I've met." His smirk turned into a full-on grin as he eyed the horizon. There was no trace of his landlady. "She thinks she's going to build her house all on her own."

Mrs. Hicks gasped.

"Impossible!" Mr. Hicks exclaimed.

"How can she build a home and care for her injured brother?" Mrs. Hicks began to fan herself. The thick heat was nearly visible as it rose from the hot earth and met the rays of sunshine.

"Good question." Cort rolled up his sleeves. "Don't worry, ma'am. I'll do my best to help her."

"That's good. And know that I will come care for her brother if she needs me."

"Thank you, Mrs. Hicks."

She nodded and began to clear up the dishes into a crate.

They continued to get their day started. Mrs. Hicks busied about the wagon and started on some mending while Cort took to the plow. It felt good to work. To sweat. To smell the rich dirt mixed with the sweet aroma of sliced grass. This was where Cort found his deepest contentment—labor that tired his muscles and worked up a well-earned ache come nightfall. This type of work kept him honest and gave him room to think and pray.

He began to pray for Aubrey. The Hickses' impression of his stubborn boss only bolstered a flame of admiration for the ebony-haired beauty. Bragging about her brought him more enjoyment than it should. He was almost proud of her in a way. Perhaps because he'd caught a glimpse of her misery back at camp with that pathetic man she'd called father. Reading her letter to him had given him a private peek into her sorrow. While guilt began to creep up in Cort's heart, a larger, more pungent emotion flooded him—his own sorrow from a broken life sprung from wayward roots.

Aubrey was escaping the weeds of her past. Cort had tried to escape, too. But what Cort couldn't shake off were the weeds that gripped his ankles and held him prisoner to all he'd witnessed and just kept quiet about before God met him on the plains. Even Ben seemed to sense the rot. Perhaps Ben wouldn't doubt him if he knew what Cort had really given up. A land title was nothing compared to giving over his life. One day, when the Stanton name was finally redeemed as honorable, it would all be worth it.

Lord, be with Charles now. Keep him strong in his word to change his ways. Let the Stanton name be redeemed at every breath I take.

Another lunge forward with the plow unearthed a thick cloud of dust. The sweet scent met his nostrils. Cort grunted with more effort, forcing himself into another, more fruitful motion. He sliced the ground, working the plow with every ounce of his being.

While the Hickses were concerned with a woman building a soddie on her own, Cort had enough energy coursing through him right now to build a whole town of soddies. He'd rather plow from Texas to Kansas, feeling nothing but the sweat dripping down his cheek and the shirt clinging to his back. He didn't want to feel any deeper than that. He didn't want the temptation of stopping the movement. It was in this toiling that the hours went by without being found. Each moment of his borrowed freedom was a blessing.

Like he told Aubrey last night, this was his second chance. Even if it might be his last.

If all he could do was work the land until his time was up, then he'd be satisfied. Working was what Cort Stanton did best.

By the time noon rolled around, Cort returned to Aubrey's property wondering if he'd missed seeing her return from across the prairie. Mrs. Hicks had grown worried for Ben and set out ahead to check on him while Cort finished up the last of the bricks. That was fine by Cort. Less chance of confrontation if he showed up alone.

When Cort returned to find only Mrs. Hicks and Ben, he was in a quandary. "She's not back yet?" He'd cost himself a sunburn and backache working for the Hickses all morning. Now his mind was set on cutting sod for himself that afternoon, but Aubrey was nowhere to be found and they hadn't discussed the matter of his plot yet. More than that, though, he worried that she'd found trouble. He couldn't shake the discomfort of being stuck without his horse to come to any aid that she might need.

Mrs. Hicks sat fanning herself beneath one of the few trees near Ben, her wrinkles drawn in a tired sag. "Mr. Stanton, this heat is too much. My Mr. Hicks okay?"

"Don't worry about him. Before I had a chance to leave, he'd already started snoring inside your wagon. How is Ben?"

"Poor boy. I fetched him water a few times. He refused at first, wondering who I was. At least he's in his right mind."

Cort thought about their earlier encounter. But before he could respond, the same little girl from this morning bounded across the patch of prairie and stood at Mrs. Hicks's feet beneath the meager shade of a mesquite.

"You're not Miss Huxley." The girl dropped both arms by her sides in a slouch, her doll dangling from her hand.

"No, I am not." Mrs. Hicks straightened and pushed her nose up in the air. "And that's no way to greet a person, young lady." Adelaide's blond curls spilled from the back of her bonnet. "Does your mother know you're here?" Mrs. Hicks asked. "I daresay a little girl shouldn't be running around in this heat."

"Maybe. I don't remember." Adelaide kept her attention downward on her small fingers stroking the doll's curls. An ache filled Cort's chest as the girl's sweet innocence reminded him of his nephew, Trevor. He hoped that the little boy was living the life that Cort had bargained for—that he had sold his freedom for.

Cort shoved his hands in his pockets and walked up. "Don't worry, Mrs. Hicks. I know this child."

Adelaide spun on her heel and leaned her head back to look up at Cort. "Why, you're the man who ripped my dolly's dress." Her little brow furrowed and her bottom lip stuck out farther than her button nose.

Cort chuckled. "I *saved* your dolly, if you'll remember." He squatted down eye level with the girl.

"Do you know where Miss Huxley is? She said she'd fix my doll's dress."

Cort stood up. "I'm wondering the same thing." He rubbed the back of his neck, searching the prairie once more for any sign of Aubrey.

The squeaking of a cart squealed across the plain and all attention turned westward. Aubrey led his horse pulling an old rickety cart. Mrs. Jessup strutted alongside her.

"Adelaide Jessup!" The woman hurried as fast as she could, her swollen belly causing her to struggle. "We've told you not to wander, child."

Aubrey walked up, her chocolate gaze timid like a doe's stare. "The Jessups loaned me this cart to carry a board for Ben's stretcher. I would've been here faster if I had the cart in town. How is he?"

Mrs. Hicks scampered up to standing. "Oh, dear. He's just fine. I just had to come by and help. I've made sure he's been drinking. He tried reading some. Said his head was fuzzy."

"Oh?" Aubrey stared at Mrs. Hicks. "Thank you." She bounced her eyes from Cort to Mrs. Hicks. Cort stepped up and offered Aubrey and Mrs. Jessup some water.

Mrs. Jessup spoke breathlessly. "It seems my Addie is persistent. She's been talking about Miss Huxley all morning." She loosened the ties of her bonnet. "She ran off just as Miss Huxley came around again." Her last words squeezed through her teeth, directed at her daughter. A deep red filled Mrs. Jessup's face. She began to fan herself and gripped Addie's shoulder.

"Ma'am, you don't look well." Cort rushed to her side. "Here, lean on me, and we'll go to the shade." He gave her the canteen for a second time.

"I s'ppose I should've waited until my husband could've come looking for Addie. But he was in town getting supplies. I let worry get the best of me." She brushed aside a stray golden strand and took a long sip of water.

Aubrey held out her hand to the child. "If you had had patience, I could've pulled you here in the cart, and your mama wouldn't have had to walk all that way." They jaunted across the grasses. "Come along. We'll find a pretty button for you."

After Cort returned from taking Mrs. Hicks home, the day baked along with everyone settled beneath a thin veil of shade. Aubrey chatted and sewed with Adelaide while Mrs. Jessup rested against a tree. Mrs. Jessup's tired face was enough to cause alarm. The woman seemed too fatigued to carry her own weight, let alone the addition of a baby's weight also. Before Cort got too close, he noticed Ben on the other side of the grove, glaring while he perched himself on his elbow. He'd seen that look in a man before. It was nothing but pure trouble. Cort didn't want any enemies out here. But as Ben's contemptuous stare followed Cort around the prairie, he wondered if it came down to one of them leaving, who would have to go first? An unsettled current lapped across his heart.

Cort quickly offered his canteen to the expectant mother, then took his horse to scope out the rest of Aubrey's land.

It was a fine acreage. One that he hoped to work for a good long while. Prayer filled his heart for the future, reconciliation with Ben and for Mrs. Jessup's fatigue.

At least he received an immediate answer to one of his requests when he returned. Mrs. Jessup was up and about, fussing over Adelaide's bonnet with a stern crease of maternal frustration etched between her eyebrows.

Ben was snoozing under the tented quilt again.

Cort approached the women. "Mrs. Jessup, how about I help you and Adelaide atop my horse and get you home before Mr. Jessup sends out a search party?" He held out his elbow.

Mrs. Jessup agreed with a nod, tucking her hand in his arm. While he helped the mother and daughter to a sidesaddle position, Aubrey's voice carried from beneath the tent. A singsong babble, the kind that a nurturer gave to their ill ward. She was a good sister to Ben and a deserving landowner.

The joy on Aubrey's face when he relinquished his claim was nearly enough to tamp down his regret for fighting Ben. It was a look he'd forever carry in his heart, no matter where his heart might beat its last beat. The dark-lashed brown eyes had been wide and dazzling, and her lips were slightly parted as if she would speak. But she had just stared at him without speaking a word, her ebony hair carrying upon the hot breeze of the prairie. Yes, Aubrey Huxley had outshone the sun that day, and he'd never forget it. No matter how much he should. Now, as she approached them from the tent in the crimson light of sunset, a new flood of awe swelled in his heart. She was just as beautiful, even more so, as he watched her stand tall with hope even amid all her hardship.

Aubrey spoke as she walked toward them. "Now, don't lose that button. It's one of my mama's." She smiled at the child then squeezed Mrs. Jessup's hand. "You take care of your mama, Addie."

"Why don't you join us, Miss Huxley?" Cort suggested. "Your brother's been well taken care of all afternoon. Do you think he'll mind?" Cort wanted to discuss the plot of land that he would lease. Strolling with a beautiful lady at day's end had little to do with it. At least, he tried to convince himself that the romantic notion had not one ounce of weight in his invitation.

Aubrey nodded with a gentle smile. "There is a matter I'd like to discuss with you, too." She nibbled her lip then turned her attention to tying her bonnet. This soft side of Aubrey only kindled more affection in him. He almost wished she had said no. If his confession about second chances last night had earned a chance from Aubrey, he worried that it would only make him lazy in keeping a good distance between his heart and his reason. She knew nothing of his dishonorable family, nor the magnitude of his uneasy future. He shouldn't fool her into becoming a friend. A twist of his gut told Cort to remember himself before it was too late.

"I have some business matters to discuss with you, as well. It will be nice to get it settled before daybreak tomorrow," Cort said. He clicked his tongue and led the horse toward the west. Aubrey followed close behind.

Good. He'd made it all about business.

His fanciful dreaming had no place on this trail toward a setting sun.

Chapter Six

"Thank you for lending me your horse again," Aubrey said against the relentless prairie wind that had carried dust all day long. The grit of the land settled in her teeth and on her cheeks and every inch of her, it seemed.

"Of course. Did you hear of any work in town?"

"No." She pressed her lips together and batted away frustrated tears. "I didn't have much time once the doctor found the board for Ben. I'll have to go back." She balled her hand. This afternoon, as she struggled to get the board across the prairie, taking not one step closer to building her ranch, independence seemed like a fairy tale. Perhaps it was the heat, or maybe her nausea coaxed by the stench of unbathed settlers and the taste of dust on her tongue, but she wasn't so sure she believed any of this was worth it right now. Ben must come first. And her frustration with that nicked her heart. How selfish. How unloving she was.

Her biggest regret now was turning down the shelter Cort had dug—for her. As much as she considered asking him for the shelter, she could not bring herself to do that. Even on this peaceful evening stroll beside the handsome cowboy with emerald eyes and a kind smile. Her face flushed at the ridiculous thought.

She blew away strands of hair from her face. Her own shelter must take priority now—something better than the ridiculous quilt flung over her shovel's handle and a worthless stake. "You wanted to speak with me about business?"

"Ah, yes." His face was covered by a sharp shadow, and his strong shoulders were washed in the pinks of the dying sunlight. "I'd like to speak with you about which section of land I might rent from you."

She squared her shoulders, drinking in the property ahead. It wasn't much as far as looks went, but it was broad and vast and all her own. They walked in silence except for the dry grass crunching beneath their feet and the occasional snort from the horse. Cort's long shadow stretched farther than hers.

Now, what parcel to give the man who may or may not be staying?

"It seems you have claimed a piece already with your dugout." Aubrey winced. Why would she bring that up? "Or the dugout you'd assumed would be mine." She spoke softer now. She could feel his gaze—or glare—on her left side. "What did you have in mind?"

He brought the horse to a halt.

When she glanced up at him, her heart surrendered its beat for a moment. His handsome face was so intent on her that she felt obliged to stare back. Her pulse returned at full force, pounding in her ears and drowning out the wind whipping through the grasses.

"I thought—" He cleared his throat, still trapping her

in an intense stare. She feared that he'd steal away every bit of her. "I might take the far northeastern corner." A smile crept along his sunburned lips, and laugh lines splayed from the corners of his eyes above his chiseled cheekbones. "Starting at *my* dugout?" His amused expression broke the strange enchantment and she grew embarrassed.

"I've already told you that I appreciated the sentiment—"

"I know. I understand." He tipped her chin up, unlocking a rush of heat. She believed he did understand her. Which frightened her even more. This man could see right through her, it seemed.

Aubrey hesitated then gently pulled her chin away. "You may lease the land on that side of the creek. I am hoping to build my ranch beyond the creek." She would need a bridge. And a fence. And so many more important fixtures that Aubrey felt as though she were the old horse burdened with a heavy cart.

Cort noisily gathered a stuttering breath and stared toward the darkening eastern sky. "Cutting twice as much sod will only fill my days with the work I need to keep my mind busy." He smiled faintly. His green eyes sprouted with more vibrancy than the dead brush all around. "Let me build you a house, Aubrey." Her name on his lips never failed to grab her attention, but she mustn't be needy. She was stronger than he seemed to think.

"I'd have started on my sod house tomorrow if it weren't for Ben's leg. He needs shelter now." She must remind him that her circumstance was not a reflection of her intention.

Cort ran his hand beneath his hat and blew out a long minty breath. "I am sorry for his injury, Aubrey. Wish he'd understand that...that—"

"That it was his fault?" Aubrey perked an eyebrow. "He'd never admit it. Did he speak with you?"

"More like growled."

"Oh, I see." She bit her lip. "I tried explaining what happened to him. But he's pegged you as untrustworthy."

"Do you believe that?" He stuck his hands in his pockets and rocked on his heels. Her heart skipped.

"No, Cort. Not from what I can tell." But his second chance might not be so firmly set, and she was afraid that Ben did have a point—Cort wasn't dependable in this whole predicament. "For now, I trust your word."

He curled his lip and looked away. "Wish you could count on me wholeheartedly." His jaw flinched. "I am at my best when I work, and I surely want to help you as much as I can. As long as I can."

An unexpected wave of compassion flooded every corner of her spirit. His secret, whatever it was, seemed to torment him. "If you wouldn't mind, I would appreciate your help, Cort." His face brightened. "It's what I had hoped to talk with you about this evening. I'm going to work on a dugout tomorrow. Would you help me carry Ben down when it's ready?"

"If he'll let me." He snickered, and the evening air grew lighter.

"Thank you. I'd better check on him." She began to walk away. Cort followed just steps behind, but Aubrey was relieved to part ways at the tree grove.

As she administered more medicine to her brother and offered him some bread and water, though, she couldn't shake the heavy feeling resting in her chest. Her burden was more than a cart filled with circumstances. There was something more. This cowboy weighed her down with his kindness and generosity. She'd prayed for this land, but she hadn't thought God might provide a partner in bringing Mama's dream about.

As much as she wanted to keep Cort at a distance, she felt herself wanting him nearby indefinitely. And with Ben and a big dream to tend to, Aubrey couldn't handle anything else, could she? Why did the thought of caring for this cowboy invigorate her amid such hardship?

Ben interrupted her thoughts. "I don't like that Stanton. He seems to be up to something."

"He's plotting his piece of this land deal is all." Aubrey rolled her eyes. "You need to stop worrying about him. Besides, he's going to help you get out of this silly tent and get to a proper shelter."

"I don't need his help."

"Well, I do." Aubrey scrunched her nose and looked away. She loved her mother, but she did not want to follow her needy, dependent way. "Mr. Stanton is a good tenant, Ben. He will help get this ranch going." Yes, he was her employee in a way. She must dissuade her heart from thinking anything contrary. She spied the fire flickering across the clearing. Cort was there.

"I could stay and help you start the ranch," Ben offered, jutting his chin out in a competitive way.

"You've done enough. Lost my horse and didn't help out with Pa one bit."

His nostrils flared and he tried to sit up farther, but then he clutched at his thigh and groaned.

She reached for his hand and steadied him as he took deep breaths. "I am sorry. I shouldn't argue with you. You just need to get better." A heavy guilt settled on her shoulders. He'd fought for her, hadn't he? And he was her brother. A part of her. A part of her mother. "Once you're better, you'll be itching to get back to Liza and Pa and your life. You'll see."

He gave a weak smile and then slowly lay back down.

She settled next to him and decided to sleep instead of eat. She was exhausted just thinking about the long day of work ahead. It was her turn to break her back on this land of hers. She needed to rest up for such a task. Digging was something she'd only done in a garden.

The morning sun came quickly, and she scrambled to get ready for the task ahead. It seemed she'd just closed her eyes on nightfall, and now it was a bright sunny day.

By late afternoon, she had only dug half the area of Cort's shelter. Between caring for Ben and stopping for meals, the task was more strenuous than she'd expected. At least she was wise enough to take advantage of the nook they'd slept in that first night. It saved some work. She rushed as best as she could, hoping they could move in by nightfall. Ben's countenance was nothing like yesterday's. His fighting spirit was gone. While in the past she would have considered it a good thing, she feared it was a sign of his declining condition. He'd hardly stay awake long enough to drink. Either the medicine was too strong, or he was weak from dehydration. As the day heated up, she offered him water more and more. There were people just two miles away paying and dying for water. He needed to get down in the cooler shade of the creek bed. And hopefully, she'd find Cort to help her when she was ready.

The cowboy was gone all afternoon. Probably to help at the Hickses' place. Every time she took a break to check on Ben, she would strain her eyes across the prairie but couldn't make out Cort or his horse.

When dusk fell, she began to worry about Cort. Maybe he'd left for good now? So soon? Loneliness began to overwhelm her. How did she ever plan to do this alone? The vastness of the prairie and the openness of the sky seemed to swallow her up.

Lord, I am never alone with You by my side.

She began to build a fire so she could heat the can of beans she'd bought while in town yesterday. It would be nice to have a fire to light up the growing darkness, although after the high temperatures she'd endured while digging all day, she didn't want to sit near any kind of heat.

Once she warmed the beans, she took her can and sat on the other side of Ben's tent, staring out into the land she had run through just a few days before. The stars speckled the sky. Had God hung a few extra tonight? She'd never seen so many stars before. The glitter mesmerized her and she thanked Him for giving her this gift.

God never did disappoint her. He really was the only person she could count on besides herself.

"Aubrey?" Cort's voice startled her.

Her knotted-up nerves collapsed, and she couldn't help but smile up at him. "I was wondering where you'd been all day."

* * *

By the look of hunger in her eyes, the smell of burned beans didn't seem to offend Aubrey. If he'd been here, he could have made them for her. After all the meals he'd prepared for hungry cowboys on the drive, he'd love to work up a meal for this pretty lady.

Aubrey scooped up some for him. After praying, she nodded to Cort with a sort of matronly permission to eat. He shoved his spoon in his mouth to halt the smile that she coaxed from him more often than he'd preferred. The crackling of fire and scraping of spoons on tin plates accompanied the song of a flycatcher, no doubt hunting for grasshoppers in the bright moonlight.

After they finished eating, Cort settled on his side. He pulled out his carving knife and a piece of wood from his pocket. It'd been too long since he whittled.

"I think Ben's dehydrated." Aubrey's voice hitched. "This would have never happened if he didn't steal my horse. Makes me wonder if Pa's going to come looking for us any minute."

"I doubt he will." Cort stilled his knife and looked up. Aubrey gaped at him. "I'm sorry. I just… I saw him at the camp the morning of the race. He didn't seem too upset about the letter or Ben's absence." He began to cower inwardly as her stare intensified.

"You know about the letter?"

"He had it with him."

"What did he say?" Aubrey waved a waft of smoke away with her hand.

Cort set his knife down. "He didn't say anything." He couldn't tell her he was sleeping. Would that hurt her as it should? Cort didn't want to inflict one ounce of hurt on Aubrey. "But he wasn't in any rush to come looking, so you don't need to worry."

She narrowed her eyes at him, then relented to a frown. "I hope you are right. I don't need him coming here and bossing me into debt." Her words sharpened with threat. He half expected her to wave a fist in the direction of her home state of Kansas.

"You are wise to get away." Cort sighed and continued whittling. He'd incurred an insurmountable debt from his own family. Maybe not financial debt, but emotional and criminal. A ludicrous amount that would no doubt follow him to the grave.

Aubrey cleared her throat. "I'm almost finished with my dugout."

Cort stopped for a moment. "Really?"

"Yes." She wrapped her arms around her legs, resting her chin on her knee. "Thought you were going to help me move Ben today." She scrunched her nose, opened her mouth, then clamped it shut.

"I'm sorry. I thought I'd get started on my own soddie, too. Our neighbors were in need of my help." Pride wrestled with disappointment as he thought about his day spent helping the Hickses and the Jessups, even though he had wanted to help Aubrey most. He tried to convince himself that he felt loyal to her because she was his landowner and not because she was the object of his growing admiration.

Curls of wood fell to the ground as he continued with his knife.

Aubrey slowly rose. "I hope everything is okay with our neighbors."

"They are fine. Just needed an extra pair of hands."

From the corner of his eye, he watched her boots inch

closer. He tried to concentrate on his whittling, but his pulse was too distracting.

"What are you making?" Her soft question halted his movement. This woman's gentle side cropped up again, just like yesterday. She'd whispered away the fortress around his heart, exposing it to a fierce desire to battle any future doom. But he had no control over whatever might come his way. So he must guard his expectations.

He sighed. What a conflicted life he might lead on this prairie. But there was nowhere else he'd rather be.

"Just getting started right now." Cort worked the knife. "I sit and think, and pray, and a shape comes to me."

"What are you thinking about, then?" She scooted next to him. Not too close, but close enough that he could smell faint lavender on the night breeze.

He nearly spilled the truth. *My heart, you, this constant turmoil your wondrous ways put me through.* "A fortress."

"Oh." She leaned on her hand and rested her head on her shoulder as she watched him.

He worked diligently on the piece, trying to resist the nagging urge to study her hair mingling in a long glorious wave among the tall grass.

"I often pray when I sew. Especially if I know the person I am sewing for," she said.

"Might get you to do some of my sewing." He chuckled.

Her chocolate-brown eyes snagged him with a straight shot of scrutiny. "And what would you have me pray for?"

Cort frowned at her obvious distrust. "Do you usually inquire about your customer's dirty laundry?"

Her mouth fell, and then she snapped it shut in a tight line. "I hoped to get away from dishonest men. Ran across the Cherokee Strip to do so." She bit her lip, widening her eyes.

"Have I been dishonest?"

"You've got secrets, Cort. That's all. I've told you mine."

His jaw tightened. "My secret will hurt more people than me if I tell it. I'm not being dishonest, just careful." He thrust his knife into the wood and tossed it to the ground. "I thought you said you trusted me?" Why did he care what she thought?

"It sounds like you don't trust me—with your secret, I mean." Aubrey's words stabbed him like his knife in the unfinished piece. She was right. He couldn't trust anyone with the truth, especially someone like Aubrey. She was an honest woman who'd feel obliged to tell the truth to the authorities if they found him.

"It's a burden you don't want to bear." His fortress walls began to rise around his heart again. *Keep it to business, Cort.*

He walked over to his pack and pulled out his wallet. He'd be a good tenant and build this business relationship.

"Here's my first payment for rent." He handed her money. "You can trust me while I'm here."

Aubrey blinked in surprise and took it. "Thank you, Mr. Stan—Cort." She held out her other hand and he helped her up. Her forehead was just to his chin. A silent inhalation of her flowery scent prodded him to step back.

"I will not ask of your secret again. You have my

word." She placed her hand on his arm. Her soft touch chipped away at his sound decision to remain business-like. He tried to ignore her eyes by scattering his attention across her cheekbones, her nose, her lips—no, not her lips. He ended up staring at her chin. The firelight tinted her ivory skin with its glow, tempting him to peek at its showcase caught in her brown pools. They danced with an amber shine.

His hand covered hers. Her unflinching face lured a rush of warmth in his chest. No. He mustn't let his heart control him. If this were any other time in his life, Aubrey would be the woman that would make his future bright again. He'd have never allowed the shenanigans of his family to jeopardize life with such a beauty.

Why would God give him the land and the woman at such a time like this?

A blush deeper than burning coals filled Aubrey's cheeks and her eyebrows tilted with uncertainty. Did she also wrestle with the same current that now pounded in his ears?

"Aubrey."

Her lips parted slightly, and she questioned him with a steeper tilt of her brow. He rubbed his jaw, trying to keep his free hand occupied. It seemed to have a mind of its own, wanting desperately to pull her face closer and feel the tenderness of her glistening lips. Her now-golden eyes danced with his own.

"Good night, Aubrey." He jerked away and forced his boots in the direction of his dugout. His face was red-hot, as was the blood in his veins. The torment of his past had won this time, but could he continue his resistance to an impossible hope?

Aubrey hadn't flinched or turned away. He must figure out a way to build the walls around his own heart taller.

For his sake, but mostly for the sake of his landlady.

Chapter Seven

Aubrey lay awake early the next morning, wondering if she'd imagined Cort's attention the night before. A man had never looked at her so affectionately, and yet it was deeper than that. Joy had blossomed with such fullness that she was anchored to the ground where she'd stood long after Cort had left. Perhaps that was the trap into which her mother had fallen when Pa first found her? Aubrey understood more clearly the ease of giving a heart away now. The danger of getting wrapped up in the attention of that cowboy could cause her to stumble into leaving all her ambition behind.

She released the curl from around her finger and sat up carefully, trying to not disturb Ben. She shuffled through her pack to find breakfast. When her fingers stumbled upon the cool tin sewing box, she swallowed the misery away. In the pale morning light she opened the box and feasted on a more dependable joy—memories of fine gowns and chatter with her mother and Maureen as they sewed. Aubrey scattered the many buttons she had upon her lap. Each one caught the sun with different intensities, painting a shimmering rainbow on her cotton skirt. Little Adelaide came to mind, and she picked up a fine scrap of linen from the bottom of the box. A perfect match for the deep pink silk dress of the little doll. She'd sew an apron for Addie's doll. Aubrey tucked it in her pocket, along with a smaller tin of needle, thread and a bit of ribbon. Delight relieved her spirit of all its turmoil by the mere fact that a sewing project awaited. She tidied up and crawled out.

"Good morning," Cort greeted her as she emerged. He'd steadied the board she had bought upright, leaning one elbow on its edge.

She scrambled to standing, brushing her skirt down around her ankles. "Hello," she said as she pulled her hair back with a ribbon.

"I'd like to get Ben situated now, if you don't mind. The Hickses are waiting for me." He lifted the board. "Besides, it will be much more comfortable for all of us to do this in the cool morning."

"If you can call this cool." A film of sweat tickled at Aubrey's hairline. "Any chance you need to go to town later on?" Aubrey lifted her hand above her eyes: the sun was already promising a scorching day. "I'd like a ride in so I can purchase a horse."

A cloud swept over Cort's expression, but then he livened with a grin. "If you promise to let me help you pick one out again." He winked.

She took the board, warding off ill feelings toward her brother, who never let her ride the horse she'd bought. "I wouldn't expect anything less, Mr. Stanton. You seem to have a mighty big opinion when it comes to horses." She begged the wild rush inside her to not flare upon her cheeks as she remembered his gentlemanly way at the camp. "But I'll do just fine picking one out on my own. And besides, I am going to look for work, too."

"I'll probably not stick around for that." He cracked his knuckles. His secret bound him to this piece of land. She'd forgotten that he was in hiding. A slight hook of his eyebrow revealed discomfort, and the confidence in the firm set of his lips seemed to teeter a bit. "My fingers are itching to get started on my house."

"If you don't want to take the time to go into town, I understand." Aubrey could walk it. She dreaded the heat and the thought of abandoning Ben for another long afternoon, though.

Cort sighed and swiped his hand beneath his hat. "No, of course I'll help you." The tension in his jaw was apparent.

Aubrey resisted worrying about his apprehension. But then again, Cort had proved to have a generous helping of compassion for her needs. Should she offer the same to him? "If it will jeopardize you, Cort—"

He opened his mouth to speak, but Ben called out, "Aubrey!"

"We're here." She rushed toward him. "Here, sit up and drink."

He leaned forward on his fist, pressing his elbow into his good leg. "It's so hot. Can't hardly breathe."

Aubrey took her handkerchief and soaked it with what was left from the canteen. She placed the luke-warm press around his neck. "Better?"

He shrugged his shoulders.

"The faster we get down to the dugout, the cooler

you'll be." Cort squatted at the opening, his broad shoulders blocking most of the view.

A grimace contorted Ben's face. "I don't need advice from you."

"Enough, Ben. He's going to help." Aubrey secured her fingers around his shoulders, hoping to suppress any sudden movements that might worsen his condition. His temper was too much like her father's, and his ability to hold a grudge was identical to the old man's.

"Let's get this over with," he mumbled.

Once Cort dismantled the tent, they tried to help Ben onto the board. He jerked his arm away from Cort and dragged his splinted leg across the board.

Aubrey snapped at him, "Ben Huxley, if you do anything to hinder your healing, well, I'll—"

"Have that cowboy break my other leg?" he seethed.

"Now, listen. I didn't intend to—"

"Enough, both of you." Aubrey battled a strange feeling of kinship here. And it wasn't with her brother, but with Cort. She knew the truth of the matter—Ben had forced Cort to fight.

But that didn't matter now. The only thing they needed to focus on was working together to get her brother to shelter. Cort carried one end of the board while she carefully maneuvered the opposite end by Ben's feet.

"Okay, let's carefully turn to the left." Cort directed them to the top of the ridge.

Sweat stung her eyes and slid down her cheeks. "How are we ever going to manage down the slope?"

"Don't worry about that. I've got it all worked out."

His white teeth gleamed, and he topped off his pleased expression with a wink.

Ben's gasping and groaning stole her attention away from the playful cowboy at the lead.

"What is it, brother?"

"You try being escorted on a board in this blasted furnace. It ain't too comfortable."

Cort began to go down the slope, but it seemed smoother than Aubrey had expected.

She did her best to keep her hands level. The wood cut deep in her palms, burning more than the sun on her shoulders.

"What in the world?" She craned her neck out to see where the path led. Just beyond Cort, a carved-out path snaked at a gentle slope down to the creek bed. It was void of all rocks and roots that had previously decorated the face of the embankment in a gnarled mess. "Did you do this, Cort?"

He grunted as he took careful steps backward down the path. "I did. Figured I could help since I was awake and ready to work. Used the fill from my dugout to level it."

This man insisted on taking matters into his own hands. Even if it was Aubrey's land, her dream and even her brother, Cort Stanton was unable to sit by and take care of himself alone. He cared for others—something she'd rarely ever seen in a man.

Her throat tightened. She wanted to cry in sheer gratitude—and from the grief of years void of such kindness. "Thank you, Cort," she mumbled.

His emerald eyes narrowed with a genuine smile

and he tipped his stubbled chin down with a quick nod. "You are mighty welcome, Boss."

Cort left Aubrey to tend to her brother, but she wasn't far from his thoughts the whole ride over to the Hickses' place.

Maybe it was a good thing for her to make residence on the other side of the creek. Out of sight, out of mind?

Not likely. Here he was in the middle of the prairie, thinking about that determined Aubrey, who'd insisted that she'd walk to town. Her grateful reaction to the path Cort had dug on her land yesterday only hooked him with that pesky hope again. She didn't scold him for touching her land without permission. Just days ago, she'd given up a whole dugout for that very reason.

He worked beside Mr. Hicks until midmorning, when they took their first break. The unrelenting heat teased that it was already quitting time.

"How's that boy, Mr. Stanton?" Mrs. Hicks was fanning herself as she sat in the shade of the wagon.

"He'll be better now. Transferred him to a dugout this morning."

"You tell Miss Huxley that I don't mind watching him when she needs help. It's nice to take care of a young man again. Reminds me of my boy. He's now about your age." A far-off look glazed Mrs. Hicks's pale eyes.

"That's kind of you, ma'am."

Aubrey appeared in the distance, trekking past the grove of trees. She was just now setting out to walk to Alva?

Cort hadn't acted too enthusiastic to take her when

she'd asked. A chill shook his spine as he thought about exposing himself to a whole town of people. One man in particular crossed his thoughts more than once—the surveyor from Amarillo. Cort had seen his own wanted poster. His missing beard wasn't enough of a difference. Surely he'd be recognized.

But Aubrey needed him. Even if she refused to admit it, a ride in town would be a lot quicker than walking. He couldn't hide forever, could he? Perhaps Mrs. Hicks's offer was a good excuse to offer Aubrey a ride to town?

"Mrs. Hicks? How 'bout I take it upon myself to accept your kindness to Aub—Miss Huxley?"

The older lady twisted her mouth in confusion.

"I see that Miss Huxley is on her way to Alva. It'd be much more efficient if I took her. Your offer to take care of her brother would certainly put her at ease, I'm sure."

Mrs. Hicks nodded enthusiastically. "Of course. I can mend over yonder just as well as I can here."

"Mr. Hicks, do you mind if I make a run to town? Any supplies you need?" Cort asked.

"Well, actually, I could use some lumber for a door frame." He took a swig from a canteen.

"Good. I can certainly do that for you." Cort untied his kerchief from his neck and wiped his forehead. He helped Mrs. Hicks up on his horse, and together they rode across the prairie.

Aubrey stopped when they were a few yards away. She planted her hands on her waist. "Is something wrong?" She was breathless. Her puffy eyes and stained cheeks gave away that she had been crying. Cort immediately brought the horse to a halt, wanting to jump down and comfort her. Why did he care so much about this woman's well-being?

"Mrs. Hicks offered to help with Ben," Cort blurted.

"Oh?" Aubrey gave a weak smile to the lady. "There's no need. I just sat with him for an hour or so. He's resting now."

"I certainly don't mind, Miss Huxley. You've got your hands full on this prairie. I'd hope to be as good of a neighbor as I can." She patted her bag. "And I brought some biscuits to share."

Aubrey bounced a stare from Cort to Mrs. Hicks. "If you insist, that will be a nice comfort knowing he's taken care of."

"I'll take her to the ridge." Cort clicked his tongue and the horse began to trot. "Oh, and Aubrey, I can give you a ride into town. Mr. Hicks needs a few things."

He never took pride in helping a woman. He had just expected to when times arose. It was the gentlemanly thing to do. Cort would rather be a gentleman than a coward hiding like a prairie chicken.

When he returned from dropping off Mrs. Hicks, Aubrey was sitting beneath a tree. He offered her his hand.

"What about being seen?" She shoved her hand in his as he helped her up.

He couldn't contain his smile, nor the frenzy of nerves at the mention of being noticed. "Are you trying to protect me, Miss Huxley?"

"No. I just thought…" She twisted her lips in thoughtful consideration. "I just figured it was about time that I get around without borrowing your horse."

"Oh, I see." He settled in the saddle in front of her,

unable to ignore the notion that she was protecting him. To feel that sort of care from a woman like Aubrey?

Cort nearly whistled.

Although the sun was in full force, he didn't mind the warmth of Aubrey's arms around his waist one bit. They rode quietly toward Alva, Cort being tempted to ride on past. He was held captive by this woman. He needed to be on guard as the pea-size tents and half-built buildings sprang up on the horizon, but all he could do was breathe in the delicate lavender and lace his fingers around hers. She would have none of it, pushing away from him. "Cort Stanton. That's enough. We're nearly in town."

She was right. He squared his shoulders and rebuked himself for getting caught up in a daydream that had no business rolling around in his mind.

"I'll get off at the start of the wooden walk. I need to purchase a horse and find some work," Aubrey said.

"Fine by me. I'm heading over to get some lumber for Mr. Hicks." As he brought his horse to a hitch, he noticed the land office south of town. His teeth clamped together. An ache stretched wide along his jaw.

The dust had barely settled from their ride in town before he spotted the surveyor entering the land office. And he looked familiar. A seed of dread sprouted a strangling weed in Cort's throat. He fingered his collar and pulled it away from his sweating neck.

If the surveyor from Amarillo seemed familiar to him, would Cort be easily identifiable? Had to be. He was a notorious Stanton, wasn't he? And an outlaw. Even if it wasn't by his own doing.

With his head low, he tied up his horse. "Meet back here in an hour?"

"Are you okay, Cort? You're pale." Her concern would've melted him at any other time. "Is it that surveyor?"

"I'm fine. Meet you in an hour." He turned and bulled his way across town. He came to the train depot where piles of lumber and crates were sorted, and townsmen picked through the merchandise. Cort kept his head down and looked through the merchandise. He found the beams Mr. Hicks would need, and then some for his own home—and for Aubrey's. His insides twisted with torment for his love of work and his love of working for her. Denial was his close friend, assuring him that he only enjoyed filling an obligation to his landlady.

"Howdy, Mr. Stanton." Adelaide Jessup came up and tugged at his shirtsleeve. "I'm here with my pa." His name aggravated his ears. He should've changed it. But his conscience had got the best of him when he first found freedom. Living a lie was not honorable in the least, was it? And if Cort wanted anything more in the world than freedom right now, it was to redeem his family name from trouble to honor. He couldn't do that hiding behind falsity.

Cort's anxiety lessened a bit at the sight of the round-faced child peering up at him. Her tall, lanky father loomed from behind her. Dave Jessup had kind pale green eyes framed by permanent laugh lines. His hair poked out from his hat—the same blond as Adelaide's.

"Good morning, Dave." Cort stretched his hand out to the man he'd met yesterday while working at the Hickses' place. He'd asked for help turning his wagon upright, and of course, Cort had obliged. No matter how many acres lay between the landowners, there was a neighborly feel across the plains.

Dave gave a firm shake. "Cort Stanton. I was just talking about you to Gerald Patterson over there."

"Oh, really?" Cort chuckled to loosen his nerves. Exactly what had they talked about?

"Gerald! Come here," Dave hollered across the crowd in a booming voice.

A heat hotter than the Oklahoma sun no doubt shone from beneath Cort's skin. Wonder who *wasn't* looking in their direction? He cleared his throat and adjusted his hat to settle it just above his eyes. A broad man, with a starched shirt and a fine hat that certainly didn't ride in the race, approached. His cordial smile seemed kind enough.

"I told you about this cowboy neighbor of mine?" Dave placed a firm hand on Cort's shoulder. "I think he's the man for the job."

Gerald measured him up and down with a thorough look. "You've moved cattle before?"

Cort rubbed his jaw, not sure what would give him away now.

A hearty laugh erupted from Gerald. "Pardon me for nosing around a man's business before a proper introduction. I am Gerald Patterson." He offered a strong, confident handshake. "We're trying to muster up some help for a chuck wagon dinner in a couple weeks. My men just drove our cattle from down south but the cook's heading back tomorrow for a family predicament. Hate that I promised a good meal to my new neighbors and might not deliver." He rubbed the back of his neck and adjusted his hat. "Dave said you're a cookie?"

By the eager way these men looked at him, Cort entertained the invitation. It'd been a long time since he'd cooked for a large group—a few years ago on the drive up to Wyoming. And only under the watch of old Jerry Lankin, the best cook in West Texas.

"I'm hardly a cookie now. It's been a while." He shifted his weight.

"If you know your way around a chuck wagon, Mrs. Hicks and some other fine folk would help you out, I'm sure," Gerald suggested. "It would certainly give me a chance to keep my word, and for that I'd be ever grateful." He seemed to be a gentleman through and through. Sincere eyes with a hopeful glint. There was nothing more honorable to Cort than the ways of a gentleman. He hoped to adopt such chivalry before it was too late.

But, as tempting as it was, Cort would be cooking for who knew how many people, his face for all to see.

How could he say no, though? There wasn't any reason to make sour relations on the plains. Even if it was a risk to be known when there were Texans around. Cort glanced over at the land office south of the town square.

Cooking at a neighborly dinner would hardly put him at danger of being discovered. And making friends out here would be wise for someone whose secrets might turn everything noble upside down. With the ease of new friends, and a particularly beautiful landlady, Cort felt like he might just change his opinion about himself. Or at least muster up enough opinions from others that he felt worthy of this newfound freedom. It seemed the here and now could draw him further away from a life of regret.

Aubrey was much more prepared to take on the hustle of Alva this morning. Especially with Cort's rent payment and a good talk with Dr. Mills. He promised to give Ben a proper cast soon. And with her replenished purse, she'd finally buy a horse. Things were looking up—as long as she wrangled away thoughts of the rugged cowboy who'd nearly lassoed her senses. Independence had found her overnight, yet she was reckless with her heart around the handsome Mr. Stanton.

In their quiet moment last night, Aubrey understood more clearly why her mother might have fallen for a man like Ed Huxley. Although Cort was nothing like her father, he had that secret which might just make him as unreliable as Pa in the long run. At least she had resisted Cort's hand-holding attempt on the ride into town today. Enough was enough. It was as if God was warning her to not give up on her pursuit of freedom so quickly.

She wove through the tents and framed-in storefronts, trying to find the tailor Mrs. Jessup had told her about. An assortment of colors splashed in and out of her vision as the canvas flap of a tent wrestled with the breeze. She worked through the crowd and peeked into the tent. A small wood sign leaned up against a chest. It read, *William Caldwell, Tailor and Shoemaker.*

"May I help you?" A voice traveled from around a wire mannequin adorned with a pin-striped waistcoat.

Aubrey followed the neat seams to find two beady eyes peering at her from around one shoulder.

"Actually, yes." She swept a hand across a particularly rich-looking swatch of velvet. "Your inventory is wonderful."

"Aye. It is." His Irish lilt was as obvious as his hint of pride, even with a pin clenched in his teeth. "Didn't expect so much of it to arrive before having a store to stock."

"My mother had a dress shop back in Wichita." The mention of it swept Aubrey back two years. The hum of her Singer, the smells of lavender sachets and the lingering perfumes of affluent customers. She fiddled with the buttons of a neatly folded shirt upon a trunk. Mr. Caldwell rattled on about his opportunity as a gentleman's servant traveling from Ireland, and how his boss allowed him to apprentice under a tailor back in Pennsylvania, and now he'd ventured on his own with many clients to call on. Aubrey suddenly grew envious. A successful story of dependence to freedom.

"You'll sew for the rest of your life," she muttered, entranced by the fine needlework on a crisp handkerchief.

The busy tailor laughed. "Of course. Unless my hands fail me before my heart." He winked.

"It must be lovely." Aubrey sighed. She straightened the shirtwaist upon another mannequin and then mustered up some courage. "Do you sew gowns?"

"Nay. I am a tailor, not a seamstress."

Aubrey browsed through the rest of the fabrics. "Have you had any inquiries about dressmaking?" She tried to calm her insides while making such a business proposition.

"Nay. I suspect pioneer women are quite able to care for themselves."

"But certainly there are some who'd need the service, even occasionally?"

"None of my concern. I've enough work with the gents."

Aubrey straightened her shoulders and approached the tailor. "Sir, I would like to propose a business opportunity."

The spindly Mr. Caldwell, with his puff of red hair at his brow and his thin glasses slipping down his nose, gave Aubrey a once-over. "And you are?"

She blushed at her lack of professionalism. "Forgive me. I am Aubrey Huxley. I own land east of here and would like to find work in town. My expertise is dressmaking." And horses, but that hardly seemed appropriate to mention. "Would you consider my working in your shop?"

"What good would that do for me?" He looked around the tent and threw his hand up in the air. "I've done all the work to establish my business. So out of the goodness of my heart, I will let an eager seamstress use my equipment?" He snorted and returned to his waistcoat.

Of course, she wouldn't expect to use his supplies without a price. Aubrey doubted she'd ever like this man and swiveled on her heel to leave without even a farewell. He was rude and arrogant.

Mr. Caldwell added, "Besides, you will not find enough clients around these parts. Like I said, the women are quite self-sufficient on the prairie."

Aubrey stopped. She winced at the knowledge that she was nothing of the sort. How often over these past few days had she depended on those around her—Cort, Dr. Mills and Mrs. Hicks? Was every other woman out here more able than she? No, she knew of at least one who had mentioned the need. Sarah Jessup. Surely there were others.

"If I find the need, will you allow me to work in your space? For your own cut of the profit, of course."

The tailor smirked. "You are persistent, aren't you?" He stood and hooked his thumbs in his own waistcoat pockets. With one long stride he stood in front of her. "A chance at more profit? You make quite a bargain, Mrs. Huxley." He rubbed his chin. "If you find a woman in need, I wonder what husband she might bring my way?" he muttered. Staring over his spectacles, he said, "You must find six customers for me to consider taking you on. That would hardly pay for the cost of my next shipment of buttons."

Aubrey scoffed at Mr. Caldwell. He was either a joker or a narcissist. Perhaps both. But her pulse sped up at the thought of how close she was to securing a steady income and indulging her passion to sew.

"Six?" Aubrey fiddled with her gloves and then clasped her hands together. She gave Mr. Caldwell a pointed stare. "If I find six clients of my own, we will have a deal, Mr. Caldwell?"

He scratched his head, then held out his hand. "Consider this my act of kindness." They shook.

After they discussed his percentage of the profit, and she had negotiated him down from an absurd number, they shook again. The chance to make dresses overshadowed the fact that it all depended on the skeptical Mr. Caldwell. And six frontierswomen.

Lord, lead me to six women quickly. And may Mr. Caldwell's word be more appealing than his character.

Aubrey stepped out from the tent, squinting in the bright late morning.

"Thought I'd find you here." Cort leaned against a barrel outside a makeshift general store. His hat was tipped low, barely above his vibrant green eyes. Just like the first day Aubrey met him at the corral, his hair curled at his neck and he wore a melt-worthy grin.

She looked up and down the aisle of tents, then crossed the path. "Did you get what you needed?"

"Yes, ma'am." He winked. "All waiting at the hitch. Can't wait to get started on building. How 'bout you?" He rubbed his hands together and they began to walk to the center of town. "Did you get a horse?"

"No, not yet. Guess I should head that way."

"Well, I think I'll get back to the ranch. Mr. Hicks is waiting on me." They had come to the half-built-up town square. "Unless you'd like a second opinion on a horse?" He raised a brow. A smirk seemed to tug at the corner of his mouth. She lingered her gaze, waiting for that dimple to appear.

"If you remember, it was my second opinion that bought you your horse." Aubrey tipped her chin up and playfully batted her lashes. "I am just fine picking out my own horse."

He gave a hearty chuckle and shoved his hands in his pockets. "Very well. Got more lumber than I expected. It's going to be a long haul. You might catch me before I even get there."

"Oh? Mr. Hicks is building more than a soddie now?"

"Nope. Just picked out some beauts for my own door frame and windows." He started walking off. "And some for you." He continued on, clearly pleased with himself as she spied that dimple appear before he completely turned away.

Aubrey tried to convince herself that he was just the hired ranch hand, albeit a generous and thoughtful one. But her common sense was losing its hold on her well-guarded heart, and she was frantic to calm its erratic rhythm. Was there any moment over these past few days that Cort Stanton didn't think of her in this great venture to build her mama's dream?

It seemed he knew better what Aubrey needed than she did.

Maybe Cort was a godsend more than she'd care to admit?

Chapter Eight

Cort spent a couple of hours with Mr. Hicks, all the while anxious to begin staking out his soddie. His dugout was comfortable enough, but a house of his own? Well, it was the next best thing to owning land. Aubrey had agreed to his suggested location with her matter-of-fact nod, then set up a midday meal for her brother. If only Cort didn't have to work with Ben glaring at him from beneath the mesquite trees. If Aubrey wasn't there tending to him, Cort wondered what sinister words would accompany Ben's threatening stare?

Instead, Ben just complained to Aubrey that the doctor was taking too long to arrive. Finally, his sour attention dissipated as he settled back to nap.

Aubrey brushed off her skirt and strode over to Cort. "I've been thinking. You've had all this experience helping Mr. Hicks, so maybe I should stay close and build mine just over there? Learn as I go?" She pointed eastward beyond their usual nightly fire spot and his own half-cleared fourteen-by-sixteen-foot plot.

"Oh? You want to be neighbors, then?" He tried to

contain a beaming grin, reminding himself that this was business only. Perhaps he should sway her from such close proximity?

Aubrey rolled up her sleeves and retied her hair ribbon. "Show me what to do."

She was determined. No messing with that.

He wiped the back of his neck with his handkerchief. "First things first." He grabbed her hand. She shot a glance in Ben's direction. He was sleeping soundly. All tension melted away from her grip, and she allowed him to guide her to the corner of his freshly cleared ground. He took her other hand, his shadow angling across her petite frame. His chest pounded with the fanciful thought that they were plotting out a future—together. It couldn't be so. Even if it did pan out that way, he'd never be sure when life was his own again. His mind was at war with the exhilaration coursing through him. "How far apart do you want our houses to be?"

She looked up at him, one eye squinting away the beaming sun, the other, brown and gold, sparkling and attentive. "Far enough." She gave a smile, one that did nothing good to keep his thoughts in their rightful place— unattached and unaffected by a treasure that he didn't deserve. She squirmed away from him, pacing eastward and stopping about ten yards away. While she began to take small, measured steps to stake out her plot, Cort forced himself to work instead of stare.

As they cleared their plots, they did their best to preserve the sod for the initial base of their house walls.

"Make sure you place the sod-side downward. Before the grass dies, the roots will attach themselves to each brick and then the whole wall will stay strong."

"How do you know all this?" Aubrey questioned in a raspy voice as she put her whole self into working the plow.

He shrugged his shoulders. "Just do. Seen enough sod houses built in my time."

By sunset, they'd cleared two large rectangles and got started on the walls, only stopping when Ben demanded to be taken down to the dugout. The doctor failed to arrive, making Ben's sour attitude worse.

Cort and Aubrey returned to survey their work, tired and sunburned.

"Are you sore like I am?" Aubrey rubbed her shoulder, collapsing beneath the meager shade.

"It's a good sore, isn't it?" He sat beside her, plucked a piece of grass and stuck it in the corner of his mouth. "I'd take an aching back from honest work, any day."

"You are better than me, then, Mr. Stanton. I'd rather have sore fingers from sewing than this kind of pain." She took a sip from her canteen. Cort diverted his eyes from her lips. Her new horse grazed next to his own. He had admired her pretty mare all day. Long, strong legs and a healthy coat. Nothing like the horse that her father had tried to sell him.

"Did you find any work back in Alva?" he asked.

"I found a challenge." Aubrey untied her bonnet and placed it in her lap. She gathered up all the loose strands of hair and tucked them into her braid. "Seems like I'm going to have to prove myself to Mr. Caldwell. He doesn't think there's a need for a seamstress in these parts. But I hope to find six customers to show him. Going to get some ideas from Sarah Jessup. Maybe Mrs. Hicks would be interested?"

"Six?" He whistled. "I'll pray for that. You have a lot on your hands besides starting a business."

"Thanks for the confidence, Cort." She stood up and straightened her skirt.

He leaped to his feet. "Building a house is not an easy task. And then to make six dresses?" He lifted his hat and scratched his head. With the Cherokee Strip ablaze in a drought and her brother practically bedridden, he couldn't stand the idea of sitting back and witnessing Aubrey buckle under all the pressure. Funds for a far-off horse ranch could wait. She needed to build a home and give her brother a proper place to heal.

Why was he so determined to protect this woman? Was it because of his guilt for breaking Ben's leg? That would dissolve with Ben's recovery. He'd not credit his natural attraction to such a beautiful, strong woman. No, there was something else that urged him to help her succeed. Perhaps it was the same thing that drove him to prison? The same determination to secure a hopeful future for his nephew and family name. Cort wasn't sure if his desire to promote others was a blessing or a curse. So far, he'd only seen consequences. No fruits.

"I can handle it all, Cort. It's something I've dreamed of. If my mama could save as much as she did amid a broken marriage and raising a family, then I can certainly care for my land and my pocketbook." She sipped from her canteen then hung it across her torso, wiping her mouth with her sleeve.

"All I'm saying is build your house first, Aubrey. Worry about your ranch later."

Her cheeks reddened. "If only you knew how many times I've heard that before. *Wait and worry about the ranch later.* Pa used to say the same thing to my mother. And look what happened. He took advantage of her and sold her horses. He didn't care about the ranch."

"I am not saying it to hold you back, Aubrey. There's so much to be done, but priorities can help you—or destroy you. I've seen that happen with my own brother. He put everything above his family. And it nearly crushed them in the end."

Her eyes wobbled with moisture. "I...I didn't plan on Ben coming along and needing my help...but I'll do that. And I'll get work."

He reached for her elbow. "Aubrey, let's do one thing at a time. You'll wear yourself out—"

She shook his arm away. "I've got to do it all, Cort. For my mama's sake and for mine."

"I was just trying to give you some perspective." He kicked at the dirt. "Believe me, I know how to manage a ranch, and once it gets going, you aren't going to have time for sewing or broken legs or anything else."

A gust roared through the grasses and rattled the crisp tree leaves. Aubrey gazed across the prairie toward the spot where Cort had first staked land. But her chestnut eyes lifted higher, resting on the far horizon where they'd journeyed from just days ago.

Her chest heaved with a deep breath, and she wiped her eyes with the back of her hand. "I didn't realize that your opinion came with the land that you *chose* to give up. Perhaps I'm not the foolish one with a loss of perspective?" Aubrey bit her lip. Regret carved her brow in long creases. She opened her mouth to speak then grimaced as if thinking better of it.

All he could do was stare at her. His nostrils flared

and he tried to tamp down the humiliation that burrowed through his chest. He tossed his sweaty handkerchief next to his empty canteen and walked away.

"It seems the sun has gotten to that pretty little head of yours." Cort's ears were on fire, and he could hardly think straight as he stomped away.

"Pretty little head?" she called from behind. "How dare you, Cort? I am not just a silly woman to brush off. I am your landlady, and I do not have to put up with this."

He raised a hand up, not looking back. "Fine. Don't. I am going to skip supper tonight."

"Well, me, too."

"Good night." He plowed through the tall grasses and didn't take a breath until he made his way down the carved-out path along the ridge.

He really shouldn't have talked like that to a lady, but she just knew how to irritate him with her sharp tongue. His fingernails dug into his palms. Even if she was partly right, he didn't need to be reminded of his folly. Aubrey's sharp retaliation stung, and the word *foolish* bored a hole deep in his heart. Everything about the Stanton way was fool's folly.

After watching his father sit in a jail cell most of his childhood, Cort had tried to do good. Especially after a few years of schooling under the pretty Mrs. Parsons. He'd pretend she was his mother. For the first time in his ten-year-old life, he'd felt like he understood what it meant to be honest and respectable.

When she moved away, school just wasn't the same. And since his brother had dropped out the year before, Cort eventually did the same.

Mrs. Parsons's kind but firm words were never far from him, though, when his soul seemed thirsty for goodness.

"Stay away from a fool, for you will not find knowledge on their lips," she'd said the day she left. Took him by the shoulders and stared him straight in the eyes. Mrs. Parsons knew that he'd grow to be a fool. At least she'd tried to postpone it a little.

But when he'd followed his brother's unruly ways all over West Texas, he was tightly knit to everything that defined a Stanton—and there was nothing wise about it. If a brawl was going to take place, then the Stanton brothers were there to get things started. If a softy was coming into town, well, may as well take advantage of his naïveté and swindle a few dollars for the next adventure. *Foolish* was definitely a good word to sum up everything about the Cort Stanton of those days and his kin that he despised.

The only good thing that came out of that foolishness was the accidental run-in with a cattle drive when they had planned for him to be a distraction while his brother stole a horse. The drive's cookie had needed a hand, and Cort needed an escape from a lifetime of mistakes.

Oh, how Cort prayed that the Stanton foolishness died that night he took the blame for his brother's crime.

He filled his canteen before heading to his dugout. The crimson rays of the setting sun were cut off by the rising embankment along the creek bed. No more light followed him, just the gloomy shade of dusk.

"Lord, remind me who I am in You." Right now, Cort felt as big as an ant beneath a giant sole. He may have been noble during his days on John Buford's Wyoming ranch, but he had relapsed to his cowardly ways just a few days ago, when he'd given away his own land.

Aubrey had every right to disrespect him. There was nothing noble or respectable about giving up all this land. It was foolishness.

He ran his hand through his hair and tossed his canteen into the back of his dugout. At least she'd tried her best to take the noble way, working from the ground up. Even trying to earn money to do so. So what if she'd taken it on all at once? The fact remained that she was walking in perseverance. He was blessed by her. Her example reminded Cort that honest work was all that he had now. It'd be right to spend the rest of his days working honestly. However many days he had left.

He set his hat down and put his hands behind his head before lying back on the packed earth.

"Stay away from a fool, for you will not find knowledge on their lips."

If Aubrey took Mrs. Parsons's advice, she'd be a wise woman.

Stay away from this fool, Cort thought.

He'd belittled her hard work after she'd finally started giving him a chance to help her.

He had to make things right. There might not be an ounce of wisdom to be found in this cowboy, but at least he knew how to offer an apology.

Aubrey helped Ben wash up before daylight slipped away with twilight. They settled in their small space while crickets began to chirp.

"I don't want any more of that medicine," Ben muttered through chapped lips.

"Why?"

"I'd rather deal with the pain than feel like my head is heavier than the whole prairie on top of us. Besides, my senses need to be sharp with that cowboy about."

Aubrey nearly grunted. "Ben Huxley, do not worry about that man. He is harmless." Except that he seemed obliged to express his opinion without invitation.

"Why do you stick up for him? He broke my leg."

"And why did he? You were relentless," she snapped.

"I did it for you. It was for your land." A flicker of hurt crossed his gaze.

"Well, you weren't supposed to be here, were you?"

"But I am. You care more about this land than about me."

"What?" All the steam Cort had stirred up in her earlier billowed now. "Why does everyone have an opinion about my priorities?" She threw down the ribbon from her braid. "I am trying my best, Ben."

Aubrey tried to storm out of the dugout as best as she could. There wasn't much room with Ben lying across the entrance, and her threadbare quilt was hardly slam-worthy. But she needed to clear her mind and her conscience. She stepped into the creek bed and swiveled around, nearly running into Cort. She stumbled backward.

He reached out and steadied her by the elbow. "Aubrey, I need to speak with you."

Standing tall and lean, the man was just a shadow piercing a soft swath of moonlight. No matter how straight she kept her spine, Aubrey's whole self was eclipsed by his height. For a slight moment, she felt dainty and feminine, unwillingly thrilled in the presence of this strong cowboy.

And then she remembered his insult. Her pretty little head was keeping her from making wise decisions.

"What is it, Mr. Stanton?" She refused to be affected by his good looks any longer. She turned her chin up and surveyed the speckled skyline above the embankment where she'd hoped to build her home, if only she had a bridge. She'd consider turning her present house into a barn after winter and build a bridge. There had to be a more peaceful place to build a permanent structure than right next door to the nosy cowboy.

"I wanted to apologize for discouraging you from your efforts." He leaned his elbow up on the rocky wall beside them. "The Big Man upstairs wouldn't let me have one wink until I settled with you first. Your determination is inspiring, Aubrey." He cast a look across the shadowy creek bed toward the rest of Aubrey's acreage. She suspected there was a storm in his silvery jade eyes, one that swept away her own animosity and sparked a curious awe for her tenant.

"That's thoughtful of you, Cort," she said, then swallowed hard. He'd once again spoken like a faithful man. A rugged, on-the-run, faithful cowboy. "I've hardly ever received an apology." She sighed and crossed her arms. "Seems my quick tongue provokes me to give them on most occasions."

He tipped his hat back. The night sky's glow washed over his chiseled face.

They were caught in this strange arrangement together, and while it sometimes felt like a trap, right now it seemed like a divine plan. Cort's kindness was like a salve to the blisters of Aubrey's own heart—wounds that toughened her and inspired her to work harder toward Mama's dream. They'd hurt so bad, only growing her determination to strive. But now God had placed in her life this man who'd turned her skepticism of others upside down. How could anyone be this honorable?

"I've not received many apologies in my time, either," he said. "Seems that's something you and I have in common." He studied her in a serious way. "After some time away from troublemakers in Texas, the man who'd led me to faith told me to always admit when I'm wrong. He said that it was a safeguard to fewer mistakes in the future." He let out a soft chuckle. "He was my boss... before you."

"That's fine advice." She wanted to engrave it in the dry earth of the rocky bank and ponder it every morning before her words got the best of her. An owl hooted in agreement.

Cort scuffed the toe of his boot back and forth in the dusty earth, not seeming to go anywhere anytime soon. She should say good-night but her soles were firmly set. Nothing but her good sense told her it was time to go. A whisper in her heart urged her to know more about this man. "Where'd you go after Texas?"

"Clear up to Wyoming. Part of a cattle drive. Those were good times." A reminiscent smile tugged at the corners of his mouth. "I'd never seen so many stars in my life."

They both cocked their heads up toward the heavens. Shiny sequins decorated the sky. Cort shook his head. "Nope, not near as many as on that drive. I think God was prepping me for His introduction in the spring of '92."

Her breath caught in her throat. She let it out with discretion as she remembered her own encounter with a star-filled sky. "I remember a particularly starry night under which God met me, too." It was when she'd lain on her granddaddy's porch after a long day of revival at church. "God shows up in His creation, doesn't He?" She continued to stare upward, trying to ignore Cort's attention across the small space between them.

"He showed up all the time in Wyoming. My boss never let a moment go by without recognizing the blessings around us. I try to follow suit."

She couldn't look up any longer. Before succumbing to his gaze, she searched the blackness beyond him.

"I've never been surrounded by so much…blessing," Aubrey whispered. Finally, she locked eyes with the handsome man before her. If she was brave enough, she'd acknowledge him to be a blessing. But to show such vulnerability to him? That wasn't brave at all.

No, this wasn't about courage, was it? It was about weakness. She couldn't give up this venture for the softening of her heart. Take her eye off the prize? Well, even though she was trapped in a staring contest with Cort Stanton, she had to remember that the true prize was hers—on the title of the deed. Cort might not stick around, but what she'd won was permanent.

"Aubrey, you've been such a blessing to your brother. And to me."

"How have I been a blessing to you?" Aubrey could hardly blink. He'd gone and said what she'd dared not say. Yet she had many more reasons to speak up. Everything about Cort's way with words made her feel needy. She'd won the hundred and sixty acres. Why did she feel in want? It was something he had that she didn't. Faith, not only in God, but in others.

The space between them shrank to inches, and Cort held her hand. This time, she didn't wriggle it away. This time, she was frantic to hear any justification for him to think so well of her. She wouldn't let go until she was certain his explanation was deserved.

"You've given me a home, Aubrey. A place to call home until…"

"Until?"

"Until it's time for me to go."

She stiffened, remembering another reason she must guard herself from growing an attachment. He was running from the law. He could be snatched up any moment. She had to brace herself for that. She'd felt loss before. Her mother's death had crushed her heart to the fine grains of prairie dust. She must only focus on the ranch. But when he released her hand, her heart lurched as if he'd stolen whatever heart dust she had left.

"Cort, you've proved to be a good man, regardless of the fact that you might leave." Her mouth went dry. "I wish my brother could see that." He'd made her dream come true and continued to prove himself worthy of gratitude. "You don't know how much your consideration has meant to me."

He slid his hands across her arms. Warmth filled every corner of her soul. He lowered his head closer, their noses barely touching.

She gathered her remaining fragment of courage as she melted in his arms. "You will be missed."

His brows tilted and his eyes widened with surprise. "I don't want to be missed, Aubrey."

"Well, I don't want to miss you, either, believe me." She tried to pull away, realizing she might have been too vulnerable. But he tugged her close again. She should protest, but the only place she wanted to be was in his arms. His lips pressed firmly against hers, soft and strong just like Cort. His mouth's delicate caress rewarded her for speaking her heart and not her mind. If ever there was a chance to taste strength, it was in his firm, determined lips. He drew her in and she indulged deeper in their sweetness, in the gentle touch of this ever-surprising cowboy.

When he pulled away, disappointment met her—but only for a second. He brushed his mouth across her cheekbone and her uncontrollable smile grew.

"Aubrey, you can't miss me," Cort muttered against her cheek.

Her eyes fluttered closed as she leaned her cheek against his. "Well, then, don't kiss me like that."

His dark face filled up every corner of her sight and he kissed her nose. With a half-cocked smile he whispered, "Fine. I won't," and began to step back.

"Wait." She tugged at his collar, picked herself up on tiptoe, brushed his lips with hers once more and managed to finally admit, "You're a blessing to me, too."

She slipped away, not daring to look back on the face that tempted her too much. Ducking into the dugout, she carefully stepped over Ben, who let out a steady snore. Nothing about Aubrey was steady. Her heart was erratic, and her stomach filled with a stampede of butterflies. But it was her mind that she couldn't escape. And it wasn't frantic with excitement, but crumbling with disappointment.

One more distraction to contend with on the prairie, and it was the man who promised he wasn't sticking around. She'd never cared for any man before, and now, when God seemed to place this helping cowboy in her path, she'd gone and kissed him. Tying her heartstrings to his was only securing a future bout of mourning when he'd leave.

Perhaps a good night's rest was all she needed. The hard work and heat of today had made her weak in the presence of a handsome man, just like those kinds of women she despised.

Aubrey drifted into a deep sleep and woke to the gray light of dawn, ready to start the day on a different foot. She busied about making breakfast for Ben, beginning to feel like herself again. As she walked up the path along the ridge, she noticed Cort heading toward the Hickses. By midmorning, she set out to explore the extent of her land now that she had a horse.

Galloping in the open prairie enlivened Aubrey's passion for the ranch. She sliced through the warm wind, dreaming of the place she'd create for Mama and redevoting herself to the plan she'd carried across the Kansas state line to the camp at Kiowa. With empty pockets worrying her and cowboys stealing her attention, this ride into her dream-come-true was a good reminder of the prize she'd set out to obtain.

But by the afternoon, Cort's suntanned arms as he stacked the bricks of his home in the Oklahoma heat threatened to distract her good sense again. She galloped past him, averting her attention as much as possible. He waved, then continued building the first wall of his soddie, placing the chunks of sod on top of each other grass-side down, exposing the wiry root structure to the elements.

The lingering scent from the early morning fire was reminiscent of a wintry aroma and a season when darkness fell early. She'd be alone with her sewing then, if she could gather customers, and behind her own four walls to separate her from this cowboy.

Cort dragged his arm across his forehead then stretched his back into a strong arch. He started to walk toward her. A flash of knowing caught the glint in his eye as he stood opposite her. Did he regret their kiss last night? She was trying to, as well. But it was a difficult thing to regret. "Priorities, right? We've got a lot of work on our hands." He spoke like a schoolteacher. She understood his meaning now. And it had nothing to do with work or Ben or Aubrey's dream. No, they couldn't focus on last night, just on the work ahead. Was it as difficult for Cort as it was for her? After all, she'd never been kissed by a man. Quite like that, anyway. He gave an assuring smile, frightening away any insecurity.

Cort thumbed his suspenders and said, "Want to get going on your plot?"

"Sure," she declared as confidently as she could, trying to borrow some of his unwavering work ethic.

Aubrey began to plow the clearing between their homes. There would be a flat dirt yard once the sod was used. Much more practical than wading through the tall prairie grasses.

The heat was torturous. Whenever she needed to check on Ben, she was thankful for the creek. Dipping her handkerchief in the warm water, she'd pretend it was cool then place it on the back of her neck. But more than refreshment, she took these moments to clear her head from the racing on to thoughts of the man she worked next to. Aubrey tried to convince herself that he wasn't worth her thinking time, but it was difficult. Especially since he'd turned her criticisms about men roots-side up, just like the sod bricks he'd been stacking all afternoon.

Chapter Nine

Over the next two weeks, noon became a coveted time. Cort would finish up helping the Hickses and then continue working on his own house. Building his own home was like molding his heart outside of his chest. This house was a symbol of the weathered past becoming a useful and humble present. And building it alongside a beautiful landowner wasn't so bad, either. Together, Aubrey and Cort cut sod. He forbade his mind to wander, focusing only on the bricks of earth that began to form the kitchen wall. Even though that kiss haunted him with a large measure of joy and a heavy brick of regret.

His emotions were taking his reason hostage. A cowboy like Cort knew the danger in that. If his reason didn't wrestle free soon, more than his own heart would suffer. Aubrey's happiness was at stake, too.

He squatted down on the opposite side of the row she'd just plowed. "How is it coming?" The sun baked their patch of homestead, and he slung back his canteen.

"Fine. Too bad we can't get the plow in the morning. The sod wouldn't crumble so."

"True." He offered Aubrey a drink.

"Did you speak with Mrs. Hicks about a dress?" She fidgeted with her apron and nibbled her lip.

He still thought she was taking on a whole lot of responsibility, but he also admired her for it. For some reason, when he pitched Aubrey's business venture to Mrs. Hicks, his pride swelled for his landlady. He'd seen Aubrey's work ethic over these past weeks and knew she was good for it. And her eagerness to work and thrive resonated with Cort's own desperation to toil and survive. "How long have you been wanting to ask me about Mrs. Hicks?" He narrowed his eyes, smiling wide.

Aubrey snapped her vision in line with his. She straightened up and stuck her hands on her hips. "Well, I'd just assumed you'd mention her answer on your own."

He stood. "You're right. Not considerate of me in the least."

Her mouth opened then shut. "Well?"

"Of course she'd hire you. Said she can only manage small projects with her arthritis."

"Really?" She clasped her hands together.

Cort laughed forcefully, pushing away the wildfire sparked by her excitement.

"Oh, thank you for asking," she said.

"My pleasure." If he was forced to leave by winter, that might be a good thing. Would the warmth of his soddie ever keep him as content as when he found himself by Aubrey's side?

They worked diligently with little words for the next few hours. Just as the sun began to slide down the western sky, they both dragged their feet to the shade near the horses.

"It's been a long, productive afternoon," he said.

"Yes, it has." Aubrey frowned as she eyed her one-foot sod walls. "Wish I'd done more."

His home was a little further along than Aubrey's. He clenched his teeth. He'd work until midnight if she'd let him help her. But that would only bring them closer together and farther from his vow to avoid attachment. He swallowed hard, scolding himself for that reckless kiss.

Rummaging through his bag, he found the last of his provisions. He'd have to get more. The thought of going into town and risking being recognized spoiled his appetite. He returned his attention to Aubrey. "How's Ben doing?"

"Fine. The new cast makes it easier to move around, but he still has some pain. He doesn't care for the meds, though." She rubbed her shoulder.

"I wish he didn't hate me so much. I feel like I'm being glared at every time he's around."

"Oh, that's the Huxley way." Aubrey rolled her eyes. "Don't expect him to shrug off the fact that you broke his leg anytime soon."

"But—"

She placed her hand on his arm. "Don't worry, Cort. I saw what happened."

"You'd stick up for me?" He arched a playful eyebrow.

She stood up and giggled. "I'd stick up for the truth, yes."

Cort began to stand up, too. "Well, I wish things were

different with Ben." He headed for the fire. "Guess I'll get supper on."

"Maybe I can convince Ben to eat with us? He could get to know you better?"

"That's an optimistic idea." He tipped his hat, resisting a wink. He barely had enough for one person, but now he'd feed three. The old cookie inside him couldn't think of a better way to call a truce than with a meal, even if he was running out of supplies. "I'll convince him that I'm not so bad. Some conversation in the open air might just clear things up."

Aubrey hurried down the ridge.

He'd nearly finished cooking by the time they joined him. Ben just stared into the flame, hardly speaking a word. It didn't take long for Cort and Aubrey to finish their share of the meager meal they'd prepared, but Ben just pushed the food around on his tin plate.

"Ben, I've said it before, but I am sorry about your leg. I didn't want to fight you."

Ben's brow pulled lower over his eyes, but he didn't look up. Aubrey poked her brother with her elbow. He just jerked away from her. Aubrey blew a piece of hair from her nose and slouched in defeat.

Crackling embers filled the quiet. Cort gathered up the plates and set them aside for washing.

"I don't know where you learned to cook, Cort, but those biscuits were amazing," Aubrey said.

"Thank you. I was taught by the best—an old cookie named Jerry Lankin."

"Cookie?" Ben scoffed.

"The cook for a cattle drive. I've spent many nights

around the fire after cooking a meal for hungry cowboys."

"It seems you might have many more miles on your boots than Ben and me," Aubrey sighed. "I'd never been out of Kansas until we crossed into the Cherokee Strip. And even then, it was only for a handful of days."

"Looks like you are full of adventure now." Cort gestured to the land around them. He winked at her.

Did she blush? He shouldn't care, but his heart stuttered against his will.

Ben just sat there with his head hung low.

"Ben, did you know that Cort not only cooks but whittles, too? Maybe you'd like to learn." She raised an eyebrow Cort's way.

"It's an old hobby of mine. Might do you good to get a hobby out here, Ben." He pulled out his latest project. It was a half-formed castle.

Ben slid his attention away from his plate and over toward Cort's hands. It was the first time he'd looked over his way.

"Whittling's not hard. Just takes patience…and care that you don't slip and nick a finger." Cort spoke while he worked. The smell of mesquite and fire-baked biscuits was the perfect setting to whittle. Always after a meal. Same as when he was on the drive, and when he was on the ranch up north. The only difference was, instead of a circle of dirty, spent men, two sets of large brown eyes watched him intently.

"Want to try? I have some fresh wood," he said to Ben, holding out his knife by the blade.

"Dunno." Ben lifted his shoulders but seemed to consider the offer.

"Go on. It must be downright boring to heal with nothing to do." Cort pushed the knife and wood into Ben's hand and patted him on the shoulder.

He struggled to position himself without disturbing his leg. Remorse crept into Cort's conscience. Even if Ben was relentless in the fight, he was only trying to help his sister. Would his own brother have fought so hard for him? Cort was the sibling always backing up Charles. Not the other way around.

"There you go, brother." Aubrey encouraged him, then gave Cort a curt nod and mouthed, "Thank you."

Cort settled back on his elbows and plucked a long piece of grass. He tucked it into his mouth and gazed at the glittering sky. No matter how grim the past and the future might be, God had blessed him with another star-filled night to ease his sorrowful thoughts.

"You just let me know if you have any questions, Ben. I am always here to help." Cort laid down his worry. He just soaked in the evening and appreciated the company, kicking up his well-traveled boots, hoping he could stay put awhile.

It had been nearly a week since Aubrey'd spoken to the tailor about finding customers. And between caring for Ben, learning how to work the plow and building a soddie, her excitement about making a profitable living as a seamstress had dampened like the soggy bed of her meager creek. At least there was Cort. No matter if he didn't agree with her priorities, he'd asked Mrs. Hicks on her behalf.

Gratitude filled her heart at the thought. Affection washed over her when the cowboy crossed her mind.

She prayed for God to give her a steadfast spirit and a practical heart, especially when it came to her relationship with the ranch hand.

A laugh escaped her lips as she considered the word *practical* describing such an unreasonable thing as the heart. She might be a determined landowner, but she was human after all. Cort's effect on her had proved that she was not above the fancies of a courted woman. It was becoming more and more difficult to ignore his attention.

The cowboy galloped off toward town while Aubrey kept her horse at a steady pace behind him. At least she had her mornings apart from his constant presence. How many mornings would it take to build up enough resistance to be completely unmoved when he was around?

Her thoughts dissolved with the sight of a near-completed soddie appearing in the distance. A couple of piles of sod bricks sat where the Jessups' tipped-over wagon had once been. Mr. Jessup, two of his daughters and a couple of unfamiliar men were hard at work.

"Hello there." She rode up beside them.

Mr. Jessup wiped his hands on his trousers and offered her a hand. "Good morning, Miss Huxley." She dismounted and one of the girls led her horse to a post that served as a hitch. The two Jessup horses were attached to a fine plow. Better than the grasshopper plow she'd been using by hand.

Aubrey shaded her eyes, admiring the home. "My, you have worked long and hard. Your house looks perfect."

Mr. Jessup laughed. "Perfect? Hardly. But we have at least one room walled in with a temporary roof. Sarah feels a whole lot better now with the baby's arrival so close."

"I can imagine. Is she around? I'd love to speak with her."

He motioned for her to follow him around the corner of the home.

It seemed a family of six with one on the way knew the urgency of establishing a home in an efficient manner. Sarah appeared in the open doorway, holding a bowl of porridge against her large belly. Little Adelaide emerged just below Sarah's elbow.

"Good morning, Aubrey," Sarah greeted her while her husband returned to work.

"Good morning to both of you. And how is your dolly?" Aubrey knelt down, pushing her bonnet back. "I have something for her." She reached into her basket and pulled out a miniature apron. She'd sewn it yesterday while keeping Ben company.

"Oh, thank you!" The little girl squealed and disappeared inside.

Before Sarah and Aubrey could exchange words, Adelaide reappeared, holding her doll out to Aubrey.

"Here you go." Aubrey tied the tiny ribbon around the waist. "Perfect."

"Thank you, Miss Huxley." Adelaide and her mother spoke almost in unison.

"You're very welcome."

"Come inside, dear. We were just finishing breakfast," Sarah offered breathlessly, stepping aside.

The partially built room was quite large. Its dirt floor

was swept clean and four neat pallets lined the western wall. A feather mattress sat in the far northern corner. A few chests separated the sleeping area from a kitchen space already furnished with a small iron stove and a table and chairs.

"How nice it must've been to bring a cart full of possessions on the run," Aubrey said.

Sarah sat at the stove, stirring a pot. "We are very blessed." She smiled. "And I am so glad you came for a visit. Pull up a chair and I'll pour you a fresh cup of coffee."

"Thank you, Sarah." The comfortable home assured her that beginning her own was a wise decision. "Your home is lovely."

"Dave and the girls promised to finish before the baby came. They seem to be holding true to their word. The two Patterson boys have been a godsend, too."

"You have a fine family." Aubrey swallowed away any distress that came with speaking such a word. Family was hardly a comfort in her mind. Except for Mama. She was the only reason family seemed valuable. But the Jessups certainly gave new meaning to the arrangement. "I am certain your girls are also helpful with mending and sewing." Her nerves prickled. She didn't expect a mother with three capable daughters and a soon-to-be capable child to be in need of a seamstress. However, besides the Hickses, she had no other contact on the prairie. She must find a way to spread the word about her business plans.

"Jolene has already fashioned two gowns for the baby." Sarah pushed away a golden strand then set a steaming cup of coffee before Aubrey. "You are quite the seamstress yourself, Aubrey. Adelaide is your most faithful customer." A playful grin grew on her pretty round face. "Did you ever speak with the tailor?"

"Actually, that is what I came to talk with you about." Sipping the coffee, Aubrey explained her venture. Her enthusiastic friend listened and squeezed her hand in encouragement. "Have you made any acquaintances around here?" Aubrey asked.

"We've made a few." Sarah's sapphire eyes rounded. "Oh, there's that chuck wagon dinner tonight. Have you heard?" Sarah leaned from her chair and gave the pot a stir. Aubrey shook her head. She hadn't seen a soul besides Cort and Ben in the past week or so.

Sarah carefully laid the spoon across the pot then sat back, resting her hands on her lap. "The neighbors to the north are hosting it. The Pattersons. We buy our milk and eggs from them. They're trying to get acquainted with the folks around here and invited us a couple weeks ago. All are welcome. I am sure you'd find many women who would consider your business. Especially with all the work it takes to make a homestead. If it weren't for my girls, we'd be in quite a mess trying to establish a home, feed mouths and ward off the heat. There's hardly any time for mending, let alone making dresses for the winter."

Aubrey couldn't contain a smile. "That sounds like a fine idea."

"Why don't you walk with us? Mr. Stanton is welcome to join us, as well. Didn't he say he was a cookie once?"

"Oh, I hadn't thought of that." She nibbled her lip. Cort was leery of going into town. Would he care to be around a whole gathering of strangers? "I am not sure about Mr. Stanton, but I'd love to join you." She might as well make friendships that would last for the long term. And next to the home-making Jessups, Cort was only the good-looking visitor helping for a season.

By the time Aubrey returned home, the sun had grown relentless again. The cloudless sky offered nothing but bright blue kindling for flaming rays. She dreaded getting to work with the sod. How much lovelier it would be to sit in her cool dugout and work with silk and pretty buttons. She trekked down to the creek bed. Ben was up and asked for help to wash.

Afterward, she offered him some muffins and butter that Sarah had made. The butter was lovely and smooth. Aubrey hadn't savored such richness in weeks, it seemed. Once she could make an income, she could afford the simple tools like a churn for a functioning kitchen. A wave of anxiety swept over her as she examined the crude mud walls and crooked quilt hanging as a door.

"Are you okay, sis?" Ben wiped the corners of his mouth.

"Just a little overwhelmed."

Cort's unwanted advice floated to her mind. *Priorities can help you—or destroy you.*

Ben grimaced. "If I hadn't stole your horse, you'd be in a whole different situation, wouldn't you?"

"There's no use looking backward, Ben Huxley." Aubrey swatted his good knee. "You just need to heal and I need to work. That's all we can focus on right now."

Ben sighed. "Wish I wasn't such a burden."

Studying his face, she felt the Jessups' sense of family come to mind. She doubted that they'd consider any member a burden. Shame threatened to release the tears pulsing behind her eyes. Ben was a burden. She may have never said it, but when she searched herself, she knew her perspective to be true.

The Huxleys weren't worthy of such a title as family. It seemed the living Huxleys were all in for themselves only. Was she included in such an assessment? Maybe before, but now she'd witnessed a different type of people out here on the prairie. God had surrounded her with all these giving people—the Jessups, the Hickses and, of course, Cort. Could she learn anything from their generosity?

"Stay as long as you need, brother." She swallowed hard and scrambled to her feet. "I am going to go build a nice home. Maybe you will have the chance to enjoy it, too."

"Do you think I could come up with you? Maybe sit in the shade and whittle some?" He scratched his knee, just above the hard plaster.

She couldn't help but grin. Cort's enthusiasm for his hobby was transferring to Ben. That cowboy was something else. He'd reached out and given Ben something to think about besides his broken leg. And he'd given Aubrey something to think about, too. It wasn't necessarily the best use of Aubrey's thinking time, but she had to wonder one thing: What in the world would life be like without Cort Stanton on the Cherokee Strip?

Cort cut through the tall grasses, rushing to help Aubrey with Ben. They were struggling to make their way up the ridge. Ben leaned into Aubrey as he apparently tried to keep his cast from bearing his weight. This heat was treacherous, and Cort could see its effect on Aubrey's reddened cheeks and distressed frown.

"Here, take my hand," Cort said. Ben managed to hop up the last few steps with Cort's help, while Aubrey kept him steady on his other side.

"That was not what I expected." She crumpled to the ground, swiping her face with her apron.

"You need to get to some shade, Aubrey." No matter how much he must keep a distance from this woman, his concern would not be contained. His last venture to town had shown him the results of this torrid heat. Many lay ill with heatstroke, and word was going around about the latest death from the relentless drought.

Aubrey took his hand, allowing him to lead her to the shade. He then assisted Ben and sat him next to his sister.

"You'd better drink, both of you," he commanded.

"Cort Stanton, you are acting like an old mother hen. We are fine." Aubrey unscrewed her canteen. "Ben just forgot his crutch up here, so I had to help."

"Sunstroke is taking Alva like the plague. Heard about at least three people who almost died from it. One funeral is being planned for an unfortunate townsman." He spoke quietly as he wet his own bandanna and placed it on Aubrey's neck. She looked down at his hand from the corner of her eye, then up at him. He brushed her cheek as he pulled it away.

"Well, thank you for caring about us, Mr. Stanton." Aubrey slid a sharp look in Ben's direction. Would he offer a retort to Cort's affectionate gesture? But her brother didn't notice and was starting to whittle.

Aubrey extended her hand, and he helped her up. To his surprise, she didn't let go immediately but discreetly tugged him away from Ben and toward the plow. "It's time to get to work now." She threw her voice loudly. When they were a good distance from her brother, she let go of his hand and turned to him. A softness pervaded her face like rain freshening a thirsty flower bed.

"What are you thinking, Boss?" he mumbled, stepping closer. A magnetic pull grew strong and unavoidable.

"I'm just curious about your trip to town, that's all." Her eyes rounded with expectancy. "Has anything changed?"

A warmth filled his chest. "You mean, my secret?"

She lowered her eyes. "Well, yes. I mean, your secret keeps you from town, doesn't it? And it keeps you from promising to stay?" She bit her lip and her hand flew to her mouth.

"You want me to stay, don't you?" And she shouldn't. And he should take every precaution to protect her from the inevitable.

"Cort, maybe if I knew more about your secret, I could help you. I am your..." She loosened her bonnet ties. "I am your friend, Cort."

"You are?" His throat tightened as his heart sped up.

"One of my only out here." She crossed her arms. "At least, I think you are." She raised an eyebrow and pursed her lips.

He could tell her everything right now. She was trustworthy. Why shouldn't he? But there was something nagging his conscience. It had nothing to do with Aubrey, but his own flesh and blood. If he shared his innocence with her, then if the time came for him to serve the sentence, there'd be a chance she'd spill the truth to the authorities. Charles would never forgive him, and his nephew would miss the chance of having a father.

"Aubrey, my secret isn't just mine to tell. It could ruin innocent people."

"What about you? It could ruin you, and you're innocent, aren't you?" Her eyebrow hooked in suspicion. Or was it desperation? She appeared anxious for assurance that he was innocent. The only thing that stopped him from admitting it was his allegiance to his brother. He must be loyal to his word. And by his word he was guilty, even if he was innocent by his deed.

He tapped her chin and said, "I am glad you are my friend, Aubrey Huxley. I've never had such a pretty one before."

The bloom on her cheeks was definitely not from heat, he thought.

Instead of feeling guilty for encouraging her affection, it gave him good reason to focus extra hard on working this afternoon. For now, he would enjoy the unlikely hope that their friendship might be a long one.

Chapter Ten

Aubrey looked around for Cort, but he and his horse were nowhere to be found. She should at least tell him about the chuck wagon dinner. Pushing fret aside, she tried to remember her place out here, and Cort's. Especially since he obviously had avoided admitting his innocence. The thought of him being guilty of anything dishonorable soured her stomach. She couldn't imagine it...but she had little sure reason to believe that he wasn't.

Her effort to convince Ben to go with her was futile. She'd offered to borrow the Jessups' cart, but his itchy cast made him irritable, and he didn't want to see anyone.

The scorching heat still baked the air. A wall of clouds hid the sun's glare, but fortunately a persistent breeze lapped through the plains. The Jessup family was ready to go when she arrived. For most of the walk over to the Pattersons', Adelaide swung Aubrey's hand to and fro. Aubrey tried to enjoy the moment, even though the evening ahead would be more of an attempt to promote herself as a dressmaker rather than participate in a social engagement.

"Looks like we're tardy." Mr. Jessup strode ahead and Adelaide abandoned Aubrey's hand to run up with her pa. He scooped her up onto his waist.

"Come on, sugar. Let's go see what's cooking." With an armful of giggles, Mr. Jessup disappeared into the socializing neighbors. A silver thread of smoke evaporated in the sky above a dozen or so hats and bonnets.

"Just like him." Sarah hooked arms with her. The expectant mother shook her head and leaned in close. "He is more of a social creature than I am." She smiled, a bit wearily for such light conversation. Aubrey steadied her arm. The woman seemed to need all the support she could get with her unbalanced midsection causing discomfort. "I appreciate you joining us, Aubrey."

"Thank you for the invitation." Her eye caught on nearly every woman in the group. Prospective customers chattering all around.

She led Sarah and her daughters to a couple of benches near the rear of the chuck wagon. A savory aroma coaxed a ferocious growl from her stomach. "My, it smells delicious. I haven't eaten a full meal since—" Aubrey's breath caught as she spied Cort Stanton with an iron skillet and a spatula, transferring biscuits to a basket held out by Mrs. Hicks. "I had no idea Cort was cooking," she exclaimed under her breath.

While Sarah was busy with her girls, Aubrey slipped away, skirted around some barrels and approached the cookie. "Hello there, Mr. Stanton." She pulled her shoulders back in confidence, yet the smile on her face would not be contained. "Full of surprises, I see."

Cort cocked his head and a flash brightened his emerald eyes. "Surprises? Well, you've had a taste of my cooking. This won't be much of a surprise to you. Except I have a few more items on this menu." He winked.

Dear God, I must not fall for this man.

But her heart refused to ignore his playfulness. He released his iron skillet, then leaned his shoulder on the wagon frame, giving her his full attention. Her pulse skittered away, only to return with a great thud in her stomach as he clearly waited for her to speak.

"Um, you're the cook?" she stuttered.

"Seems so. They wrangled me into this jig a while back." He rubbed his jaw. "Sorry I didn't tell you." He wore his signature look of compassion—furrowed brow and lips slightly tilted downward.

She couldn't find words. Why did he apologize to her? They weren't accountable to each other. But deep down, she knew—she'd come to depend on him as her closest confidant. Hadn't she already admitted that he was her friend? She also felt a twinge of guilt for not inviting him.

"It's okay. Sarah Jessup suggested that I might find customers here." It would be difficult to do so, as her heart was perfectly content to stay put by his side for the rest of the night.

"I'm sure you'll meet plenty of ladies here who're looking to have gowns made for winter," he affirmed, his adorable dimple making an appearance.

She could get lost in his wide grin, a new source of encouragement in her life. Perhaps her only source of encouragement besides the Scriptures. Yet old aggravation crawled into her thoughts at the near contentment with this new friendship. Her mind had wandered into territory unbefitting for a mere friend—or a business-woman wanting nothing to do with depending on some-one. She mustn't get carried away with silly emotions when so much was at stake.

Mrs. Hicks breezed between them and cupped Aubrey's elbow. "Hello, dear. I was just telling some women about you taking on some mending for me. They seemed mighty interested in your services."

"Thank you, Mrs. Hicks." She cleared her throat. "You sure are a godsend." A prayer of thanks crossed her heart. With excitement for her mission rekindled, she left behind the distraction of Cort and allowed Mrs. Hicks to whisk her away.

After Mrs. Hicks introduced her to their gracious hostess, Mrs. Patterson did nothing short of guiding Aubrey to each gal who might be in need of a seamstress, including three of her daughters-in-law.

Mrs. Patterson stated, "Trust me, I have raised my boys to find beautiful women, but I fell short in urging them to find practical ones."

Most of the women were truly delighted by the fact that they could hire a dressmaker instead of squeezing one more task into their busy lives. By the time every-one's plates were filled with second helpings, Aubrey had secured enough accounts to bring to Mr. Caldwell if he'd still have her. The perfect timing of this chuck wagon dinner assured her that God was on her side. Her heart spilled with thanksgiving. She couldn't help but think of her mama and the ranch that didn't seem so far off now.

She savored the robust beef stew with tender potatoes and carrots. Cort's signature biscuits were even better with fresh butter, thanks to the Pattersons' dairy cow. The evening promised to be near perfect after such a delicious meal.

A band of orange settled on the horizon like turned-up sun dust. Mr. Patterson's ranch hand strummed a guitar amid the children's laughter and the settlers' chatter.

Aubrey sat beside Sarah. The tired mother squeezed her hand. "I am so happy for you."

"Thank you. I would not have had the opportunity if it weren't for you." Aubrey squeezed back.

Mr. Jessup held out his hand to Sarah. "Come on, dear. We should get you home to rest." Aubrey declined to walk back with them and said she'd wait awhile. It would be faster to cut across rather than walk down to the Jessups' and over to her land, anyway. The couple gathered their daughters, thanked the host and quietly said their goodbyes.

Aubrey's gaze lingered on their shadowy figures growing distant on the plains. How different a father that Mr. Jessup appeared to be compared to her own! What was his flaw, if any? she wondered.

She sighed and glanced over at another man who'd jostled any previous notions Aubrey had formed. Cort's sleeves were pushed up, and he sat on a barrel across the fire pit, whittling away. She couldn't see his face beneath his wide-brimmed hat. Mr. Hicks and several other men had their backs to Cort. He may as well have been in a different county.

And then it occurred to Aubrey. Maybe he wanted to be ignored.

He was in hiding, wasn't he?

"Miss Huxley?" Mrs. Patterson approached, fanning herself as if it were the heat of day. "Have you met Mr. Swanson?" She turned to see a lanky man with his hat pressed to his chest. The last glow of embers bounced their reflection on his balding head. Aubrey gave a timid smile.

A booming voice carried across the yard. "Swanson! Glad to see you here." Mr. Patterson barreled across as if he'd seen a long-lost friend. Every eye was on their interaction now. Aubrey spied Cort's own face from beneath his hat. She was confused by his expression. Was he angry or afraid? Even in the dimming light, he seemed pale.

"Thank you for the invitation. I'll be heading back south before too long. Seems Alva will prosper just fine." Mr. Swanson placed his hat on his head and hooked a thumb in his suspender.

"Only thanks to you, sir," Mrs. Patterson gushed. "You've surveyed this new town of ours in record time, no doubt."

Cort's hat was now low over his face, and he whittled quickly. Her suspicion, first roused on the day of the race when the scout mentioned the land surveyor, was correct. This man before her had something to do with Cort's secret. It seemed her tenant was squirming like a mouse caught by his tail beneath the paw of a large cat.

"Miss Huxley, I wanted to introduce you to our Texan guest," Mrs. Patterson said.

Texas? Cort's old place of residence. From what Aubrey knew, Texas was mighty big. Surely big enough that one man wouldn't necessarily know another?

Mrs. Patterson yanked Aubrey by the arm to turn her squarely facing Mr. Swanson.

"Hello," she murmured, trying to stuff the anger of being forced into introductions. After all, she *did* owe this woman much for gathering her customers.

"Good evening, ma'am." Mr. Swanson's nasal twang matched the wisp of a man that he was. Mrs. Patterson continued doting on the surveyor. It was hardly deniable that Aubrey was part of some overt matchmaking scheme. All that delicious food began to sour in her belly. She fiddled with her kerchief and caught Cort's look just as he glanced up. A pleading filled his eyes, but not necessarily meant for her to see. His gaze roved around the party in a paranoid frenzy. Aubrey longed to calm him in this moment. He had proved to be a good tenant, a man of his word. In all this world, he was the only man to whom Aubrey had given her trust. And in all this world, he was the only man who'd given her so much—land, work and help with Ben.

But what had she given him in return? The chance to rent land that he had once rightfully won? Perhaps she owed him more than one deed to even the score, so to speak. If she could get close to calling it even, then maybe her ridiculous notion of swooning into dependency would flee. Was she willing to aid in hiding him for a secret she knew nothing about, though? A secret that he'd admitted could hurt others?

Cort curled his lips inward, taking in a visible breath. If she knew any better, she would think he was gathering up the courage to walk over and make himself known. The defeat in his face bulged. As he rested his chin on his chest, his face was concealed from her view once more.

Aubrey swiveled around. "You say you're from Texas, Mr. Swanson?" She bustled between the chatty hostess and the land surveyor. "I've always heard the sky is bigger there." With a hearty laugh, she took the arm he offered, but only half listened to his response as they strolled to the nearby benches. She would do her best to hide Cort from this man, and maybe one day she could discover how such a twig could frighten the strong, bold cowboy.

He may as well just keep on going. Kick this horse to a gallop and head east. He'd never been past the Mississippi. What was holding him back?

Certainly not Aubrey Huxley. She'd lied about trusting him, it seemed. First chance she got, she went prying into his past with that surveyor from Amarillo. And she seemed to enjoy it, too—taking his arm and chattering away. All the while, she peered at Cort after every mention of his home state.

Cort ground his teeth and groaned. Hadn't he warned himself to not get attached to anyone? Especially a woman? If he'd only kept his heart to himself, this wouldn't sting so bad. But right now, the image of Aubrey and the Texan burned worse in his memory than the day he'd found his brother amid the gunslingers who'd tried to take over the ranch up in Wyoming. It was bad enough that his mind was burdened by his past, but then to be exposed by this woman, no matter how pretty, ripped Cort's spirit in two.

He steered the horse to the back side of his soddie and circled it twice, wondering if he'd ever see it finished. If Aubrey found out that she'd rented her land to an outlaw, she'd kick him out for sure. Or she'd promptly bring her new beau to the dusty threshold of Cort's unfinished home. It was only a matter of minutes, maybe hours, depending on the mixture of business and pleasure in their seemingly entertaining conversation.

Cort dismounted, situated his horse and walked along the ridge above the creek. The moon was bright tonight. A coyote howled in the distance, prickling his skin with uneasy nerves. He stomped down to the creek bed. Snores came from Aubrey's dugout.

If Ben didn't hate him, he'd go check on him. But the young man had every right to grumble against him. No matter how much Cort tried to stay clear of trouble, it found him.

Guilt tightened Cort's throat. He could barely swallow past a lump that had formed over this past hour. An old prayer spilled from his very soul: *Lord, I just wanted more time.*

"Cort?" Aubrey's voice slid on the air like a cool winter wind. Soothing in the muggy night, but a chilling reminder of her tête-à-tête with the surveyor.

Cort met her at the bottom of the path. Her black hair shone silver, and in the dark night, her eyes held captive all the light they could gather from the small lantern in her hand.

"Didn't realize you were going to show up so soon." He stepped around her to head to his dugout, hoping she'd not yet confront him. Give him a night's rest. Allow him the pleasure of freedom these last hours.

He followed the creek. Aubrey rushed up beside him and grabbed his arm before he ducked inside his dugout.

"Do you have nothing to say to me?" She was breathless and stern.

He bored a look into her searching eyes. "If only words meant nothing, Aubrey. But it seems you've no doubt had your fill of words tonight." He shook off her hand. "Did your curiosity about my past not find satisfaction in interrogating Mr. Swanson?"

"What?" Aubrey's mouth remained opened while she just stared.

He didn't permit himself to look too long, but he assumed her hands had taken their usual position—on her hips. How could he admire such a willful creature? No, he must excuse his emotions once and for all.

"Do you believe I was being a snoop?" Aubrey's voice lilted on a high note.

Cort chuckled. "And do you want to concoct a story that would prove otherwise? Come on, Aubrey. Sometimes curiosity gets the best of us. And who'd blame you for wanting to know the dirt on a man who's sleeping just down the crick?" It didn't make sense that, when she began to boil, he delighted even more in her steam, but his heart sped up at the furious passion in her face. This woman was strong and beautiful and determined. Always ready and willing to prove herself just and worthy. If he could prove himself the same, he would. But there was no use fighting for an ideal.

"Do you think I would sit right there, with you staring your fool head off at me, and question another man about your secrets?" Now she leaned in, glaring enough to melt the moonlight from her eyes and wash her face in its glow. But he doubted there would be tears from this woman. Not with angry fire pursing her lips, knitting her brow and burning in her pupils.

"You're telling me that you didn't ask him about me? You know that he's the reason I gave up the land in the first place. You guessed it on our first trip to town."

She gaped, then huffed into a slouch. The crickets and shushing sound of the wind in the prairie swelled in the silence.

Aubrey shifted her weight and dropped her hand from her hip. "Well, I might've considered it, for the briefest moment." Her head hung low, and she shook it slowly. "I am so sorry," she whispered. "But all I wanted to do was help you tonight. Promise."

"I thought you were spiting me with every look as you talked with him," he said.

"I was only talking to him—" She looked away, her hair floating on the breeze and caressing her cheek. "For you, Cort. To keep him away from you."

"Why?" The word tumbled from his lips before he could even think. The rich aroma of soil from the dugout scented a new breath of hope. And with it came an irresistible urge to lift her head. He inched closer, his pulse pumping in his ears.

"To pay you back." She faced him with a look of determination. "You've done so much."

Cort pulled his hat from his head and ran his fingers through his shaggy hair. He'd never considered that Aubrey was distracting the man. For him? His torso trembled with his effort to keep his emotions under control.

"Cort?" Aubrey placed her hand on his forearm. "Do you understand? I wasn't snooping. I just saw how upset you'd become—"

He placed his finger on her mouth. *Hush, Aubrey. I understand.* The gift she gave him not only secured him more time, but fanned the flame of what he sought in the opinion of men like Mr. Hicks and Mr. Jessup. Could Cort Stanton truly be considered a man worthy of such help? A man whose landlady would aid in keeping him anonymous because of trust and goodness? Was he a man who'd be defended by his neighbors when trouble came sniffing around?

Now this woman brought to life his hunch that second chances might just be ready to bloom on the prairie. She'd given him her allegiance as a friend, by word and deed.

He fought against the nagging in his soul. No attachments. It would only hurt in the end. Yet this woman had protected him with full knowledge of the possible danger behind his secret. Surely she knew there was risk in what she'd done. Perhaps she was willing to take the risk for him? Perhaps it wasn't his job to protect her from himself when she so diligently displayed her loyalty?

Her lashes lowered across her eyes—a subtle curtsy. He cupped her face in his hands, holding her like a treasure. As he pulled her mouth to his, he inhaled her sweet fragrance, drinking in the hope she offered in her kiss. He should pull away. Step back and run from the trust he didn't deserve. But her gentle lips caressed his own.

Yet, as his grasp grew firm, Aubrey pushed away from him.

"We can't keep doing this." She gathered in a jagged breath. The corners of her mouth tipped downward. "I just distracted that man because I owe you much, Cort.

But I need to stop myself from being distracted. Spending our evenings like this is exactly that."

Cort stuffed his hands in his pockets, forcing himself to step back. "You owe me much?"

"You've helped me. I wanted to repay you."

"Aubrey, when will you realize that my helping you is not a form of debt, but because there's nothing more that I would rather do."

"Why?"

"Because—" He clamped his mouth shut. The answer was sprouting on his tongue but he couldn't release it into the night air. The fragile declaration of his heart would ruin both of them. Suddenly, the wrestling inside him surrendered and his good sense prevailed. No attachments. No pursuit. The past wasn't through with him yet. No matter the hope that grew from Aubrey's considerate attempt to keep Texas away.

Not yet being caught by the authorities offered him a deceiving prospect of a future of freedom. But this wasn't based on truth. Just feeling.

"Because you want to accomplish too much too soon." He winced, anticipating the nerve he might've pricked with such an answer. It was only partly true. There was a lot more to helping Aubrey than assisting her to fulfill her excessive ambitions. He desperately wanted to see her succeed. There was a heartstring undeniably attached to this woman. He must do his best to not let it become a thread of destruction when the time came for his departure.

In Aubrey fashion, she grimaced and backed away. "Mr. Stanton, let's not talk about priorities again." But then her face softened. She brushed away the hair from her cheek. "Please, know that my intentions tonight were from friendship as much as obligation."

A mixture of pride and dread set in as he watched her slip into darkness, only the small light of her lantern bobbing in the black. Aubrey's favor toward him was delightful but frightening. He'd seen the damage done to those he cared for in the past, and now his heart swelled. But the disappointment that surely lay ahead was larger than any fancy, and the hurt was something he didn't want to bestow upon anyone.

He made his way after her but hesitated.

Lord, thank You for Aubrey, but protect her, protect both of us.

His dugout was the safest place to be. No matter the wall he begged for God to put between their feelings, a vine of hope seemed to climb into his thoughts. Hope had been a stranger to Cort all these years, creeping in only since this wild prairie journey. Aubrey had kindled hope in his heart again. Even if he was quick to snuff it out.

Why'd he always have to assume the worst was ahead, instead of enjoying the best in the here and now?

Chapter Eleven

"You're awfully intent on fixin' that dress." Ben adjusted to an upright position as he rested his back against the dirt wall.

"Be careful with your leg." She barely lifted her eyes but could tell Ben was scowling. His near snort told her so. His attitude had steadily declined over the past month.

"You might be perfectly content down here sewing away. I'd rather be on a train to Kansas." Ben flicked a stray button across the swept dirt floor. "Shouldn't you be working on your house?"

"I am only able to work on the house in the evenings now. Mr. Caldwell is adamant that I get my first orders finished if I want to have access to his supplies indefinitely. He was stingy with his machine for the first couple of dresses. I have to do most everything else by hand." It'd been a month since the chuck wagon dinner, and she had finished only two orders to completion. The last thing on her mind was the unfinished house. She'd rather sew than cut sod any day. "Cort doesn't even get the plow until noon, and he needs it for his own house. How about you come with me to Alva? I am sure Cort will let you borrow his horse."

He tossed a stick across the dirt floor. "Who knows where he got that horse? Probably stole it."

"Ben Huxley, I was with him when he bought it fair and square." Aubrey set aside her mending and gave him a hard look. His lips were hooked in a sneer. "Hasn't Cort proved himself trustworthy to you? He's helped you, and he's been a friend."

"Isn't he the same cowboy who disrespected Pa's horses?" His brown eyes were a thin slit.

Aubrey rolled hers. "Oh, please. He just spoke the truth. You know it."

"Seems you're more allegiant to that cowboy than your own flesh and blood." He pulled out his own bag and took out some parchment. "I'm going to write Pa. It's not right that we haven't contacted him."

Flesh and blood. How much did that truly mean when it was a breeding ground for bitter betrayal? Pa had betrayed her mother when she was alive, and in her death, and he'd cared more for his own business than loving his daughter. "He hasn't come looking, Ben. I left him a pretty penny. I am sure that's more precious to him than flesh and blood."

Ben laughed and wagged his head.

"What?"

"For someone who's so bitter against a man you've known all your life, you sure do trust a practical stranger."

"Who, Cort?" Aubrey's throat tightened.

"Yeah. The man who broke your own flesh and blood's bones."

"That's not fair, Ben. He proved to be a perfect gentleman and a hard worker in only a handful of days." She'd not seen that from her father, or Ben, in all her years.

Cort had been slowly unwrapping the dark cloak of cynicism given to her by her years with her father. While she still kept her promise to avoid any distraction to grow this ranch, she also prayed for God to work on her heart. The prairie was becoming ground for not only a new venture, but also a new perspective on life itself.

"Think what you want. But I feel like I'm lying in a grave. Cort may as well have dug it." He took another stick and stuck it in his cast. The plaster was a nuisance. Even with the weather cooler than their first few weeks on the prairie, he often complained about his leg being hot and itchy. At least he got around on some crutches he'd fashioned with wood scraps they'd found in town. But the young man was restless and irritable.

Aubrey held her tongue. The quicker he'd heal, the sooner he'd leave, and then she wouldn't have to prove herself to Ben.

"Hello?" Little Adelaide's voice rang like a tiny bell from beyond the quilt.

"Come in." Aubrey set down her work. A mess of blond curls sprouted from beneath the child's bonnet, and a cool breeze accompanied her.

Ah, thank God for October.

Aubrey stood, bending her head slightly below the ceiling. "Does your mother know you are here?"

Adelaide nodded. "Yes, ma'am. Jolene watched me

get to the curve of the crick. I just wanted to show you somethin'." Her blue eyes filled with excitement as she held out her dolly. "Look, I stitched an *A* on her apron." She pointed a small finger to a very rudimentary letter *A* composed of three crooked stitches. "I did it all by myself. Mama told me your name starts with *A*, just like mine."

Aubrey laughed. "That's right. And what a fine seamstress you are becoming. Come. Let's allow Ben to rest." Aubrey carefully put her work in her basket and scooted the girl out of the dugout.

"Can you bring your button box? I just want to look," Addie said.

"Of course." Aubrey reached across Ben, grabbing her tin. She also gathered up his knife and half-whittled piece of wood and plopped them on his lap. "At least Cort taught you to whittle." She kissed his forehead.

For a brief moment, his rounded eyes held a softness about them, almost remorse. He turned his head away.

Aubrey sighed. Doubt wormed its way into her heart. How could she choose a friend over flesh and blood? How could she not? The shining example of the Jessups' tight-knit family crept into her mind. It was as unfamiliar to her as her first push of the plow.

Lord, give me wisdom.

She joined the little girl up the path. Adelaide enjoyed spending time amid her sewing things. Her own mother had a nice sewing kit herself, but an attachment had formed when Aubrey became Addie's doll's exclusive dressmaker. Sarah had mentioned it was a relief to know that her youngest daughter wasn't completely distraught by the lack of attention she received with this pregnancy coming to an end.

They sat beneath the shade, sorting through the buttons. From the corner of her eye, Aubrey spotted more progress done on Cort's soddie. While the child was intent on ordering the buttons from largest to smallest along her apron's hem, Aubrey was drawn out from beneath the tree's canopy. Clouds streaked above, streaming by with the wind. Yet they moved against the direction where she was headed. In her contemplative state she wondered if it was a sign that she might be going in the wrong direction. After all, she'd crept closer to her hired cowboy's soddie a few yards from where Adelaide sat.

His past lurked in the shadows. The mention of it was the one thing that turned Cort pasty white. There might be some sense in Ben's skepticism. She'd seen firsthand how a man could bring a good woman to a life of misery.

While she inched closer to their houses, the swiftness of the sky also reminded her of the speed with which Cort's secret could catch up and leave her all by her lonesome. Being alone was her plan all along. But was it still her heart's desire?

She stopped amid the whipping grasses. The roof of Cort's home was intact, and she admired it from where she stood.

Can I truly establish all this on my own?

Aubrey scoured the racing heavens. *God, You will provide for me, no matter what Your plan for Cort is, won't You?*

172 · *The Outlaw's Second Chance*

A ray of sun pierced a cloud and startled her eyes to a close. She turned and began to walk away.

I'll only go where You lead, Lord.

Cort may have taught her to trust and shown her what compassion could be, but she felt like a tumbleweed tossed about by the prairie's breath when it came to this growing dependence. She scolded herself. Another ranch hand would come along to help if he went away.

But there was little comfort in that.

She peeked around the corners of each house. He wasn't there. Shortly after she returned to Adelaide, the rumble of hooves and a wagon grew near. Cort was coming up from the west, heading straight toward them with a wagon full of timber.

"Whoa!" He brought his horse to a halt and dismounted. His grin sparkled as he approached. "Good afternoon, Boss." Cort winked at Adelaide. "And pretty little lady. Looks like you found what you were looking for earlier."

"Did she come by before?" Aubrey watched the child stack buttons carefully atop the box.

"She did. Proud as ever to show you a few stitches she'd sewn." His emerald eyes searched Aubrey's face, as if she were his own sought-after find. If any other man looked at her that way, she'd slap him. But with Cort, trust encapsulated every feature.

She breathed deep, turning her attention to the cart. "What's the timber for?"

He pulled off his hat and ran his fingers through his wavy chestnut hair. The curl against his collar distracted her for a moment, and then she turned completely away, walking over to the merchandise.

"Now, hear me out, Aubrey." He came up behind her, a hint of apology in his voice. "I couldn't help myself. Now that my house is nearly done, I've got to have something to occupy my time. This timber is perfect for a fence."

Aubrey spun around. "I need to make my own purchases, Cort. I don't want any debt."

"You can pay me back. But I'll go crazy without something to keep my mind off..." He bit his lip.

"Off what?" Aubrey tried to shoo away the dread that filled her every time he hinted toward that secret thief coming to steal him away.

Cort's mouth parted and he stepped closer. "My mind's always reeling. Especially with a beautiful boss around." Her heart stuttered when his flirtations crept into their conversation. "Aubrey, your friendship means the world to me. If the ranch is important to you, it's important to me, too."

"Do you think you'll be here to finish the fence?" Desperation filled her heart. They'd found a sweet rhythm together. Each evening they shared a meal and enjoyed the peace of the prairie after a long day of work. Aubrey's work was less laborious than Cort's, as she had let her soddie sit unfinished to create smartly trimmed dresses.

"I am praying. Praying that my second chances are lifelong." He winced. "Pray with me?"

"Of course." Aubrey dropped her gaze to her fingers, which fiddled with her apron. She didn't budge when Cort grew closer. He swept away a strand of her hair and brushed her cheek with the back of his hand.

Lord, prepare me for our goodbye.

The land surveyor left town without crossing Cort's path. The confrontation Cort had fabricated in his mind would never happen. He tried to convince himself that he would never get caught, hoping some relief would lift from his burdened soul.

He tamped the fence post into the hole as his brain reeled. Aubrey was just across the creek bed, on the higher ground, reluctantly finishing up the last of her sod walls.

He chuckled to himself. It had taken a good long while to convince her that starting on the fence before she could pay him was necessary. Who knew what winter would bring? If the ground froze, that could set her back a few months before she could keep horses. After considering it, Aubrey had given in.

"Got to do something to move my plan forward," she had mumbled, tossing aside a dried-out sod brick that broke into pieces when it hit the ground.

This afternoon, she appeared frantic to finish her house. Her cheeks were red, and her dress disheveled with streaks of dirt that matched those on her face.

"You doing okay over there?" he yelled across to her as she fumbled atop a ladder.

"Fine." Her answer pierced the air like a venomous arrow. He imagined that she grew more red as she threw her voice.

He should help her, but he'd committed to this fence now. Building it across the creek bed was a twofold decision by Cort. Aubrey would need a fence in the long run, but Cort needed the distance for his heart and hers. Still, he hadn't planned for the pleasant surprise of watching her as he worked.

The day drew to a close, and after washing up, he began to cook the evening meal. Now that Aubrey had partaken of his cookie talents, she refused to cook for him. Burned beans were no longer on the menu.

The sky blushed with the setting sun. Aubrey appeared from the creek bed after eating with Ben. Her tiny silhouette grew closer. Yes, he could live like this for the rest of his life. And he almost believed he would. He flicked that thought away and focused on this moment as if it were his last on the prairie—a safer way to keep his heart from tangling with Aubrey's.

"Keep that fire bright. I've got plenty of work ahead of me tonight." Aubrey settled on a blanket, placing her large sewing basket between them.

"You don't seem to be fretting much." He leaned on his elbow.

Aubrey shrugged. "It's my own doing. I love to sew."

"You've accomplished a lot, Miss Huxley, in a short period of time. Obtaining land and a small business." And even more that he dared not mention. "Perhaps I was wrong about your priorities after all. You amaze me."

He focused on the fire, but from the corner of his eye, he saw her cheekbones lift with a smile.

"My accomplishments have left me sore and tired." She straightened her spine then rolled her neck back and forth. With a sigh, she began to pull out her sewing.

"Your house is almost complete. In record time for

a seamstress." He shifted away, ready for her to strike at his jest.

"I might remind you, Mr. Stanton—" she spoke with a pin between her teeth and her attention on her work "—I am the landlady. I can kick you out whenever I please." Her eyebrows were arched high. If it weren't for the smiling eyes and the past month of intermittent affection, he'd have taken that as a sinister warning. She shook her head and resumed with needle and thread, studying the stitches as she made them.

He just watched her. Her face filled with peace and joy as she toiled. He'd not seen her like this since the day she'd chatted with the ladies at the chuck wagon dinner. From what he could hear at his skillet, the conversation had been all about her sewing. Sewing was certainly a different kind of work than what he enjoyed. Those tiny stitches would have frustrated him as much as sod-laying brought the anger out in her.

The evening was quiet except for Aubrey's soft hum and the crackling fire. He began to whittle, shaking away his growing suspicion. But it wouldn't budge from his wondering mind. Was Aubrey's dream of a horse ranch more of her mama's dream than her own? Striving so hard for something that might bring her more toil than triumph, like an entire ranch, might just break her spirit in the end. Hadn't Cort walked away from his old life with a scar inflicted by a similar strife? He'd struggled with his ownership of it all as he sat in prison for another person's crime. While he trusted that it was worth his surrender for the future of his family name, he couldn't shake the sliver of resentment toward his brother. Charles had spit in Cort's face just moments before he was caught, cussing him for fighting opposite his gang in the ranch wars. He realized Charles had been selfish in forcing Cort to take the blame out of guilt. But at the time, all the shame of who he was, and who he was expected to be, had led him to accept the death sentence as his own. No matter how much Cort's boss had told him salvation was free, he wanted redemption in the worst way.

Yet would he have chosen to take the blame now, with the prospects of life out here on the prairie? He dared not look over at Aubrey for fear that the answer to that question would slice his heart with a double-edged sword.

He continued whittling, concentrating on getting out of his head and into the stroke of each movement. His eyes grew heavy by the time he figured out that his latest piece would be a horse—maybe Aubrey's mare. What a beauty.

"I'm going to call it a night." He tucked his knife and block into his shirt pocket. "You heading down soon?"

Aubrey kept her nose down as she continued to sew. "Maybe. Going to finish this hem." She didn't look up.

He half smiled and shook his head. She was so consumed with her sewing that he wondered if she really knew what he had asked. Cort traipsed across the grass and headed to his newly finished house. The air was several degrees cooler inside, even more so than the dugout. He'd sleep well tonight.

He wasn't sure when he fell asleep, but he slept hard and woke with a start. He'd had a nightmare. Charles was trying to fight him and all Cort could do was whittle. He felt a little sick as he sat up on his bedroll. Like he'd just been punched in the gut. A mixture of regret and anger stirred in him.

Why was he angry? The thought of his brother usually brought about remorse, not anger. But Cort was fighting more than just his own past. He was also battling the hope of a future. Was this new perspective a temptation from the enemy or a promise from his Maker?

Oh, how he prayed it was the latter and that the future would throw the past to the ground.

A silver fray glowed from his ragged cloth door. The early morning offered enough light to read his Bible and ease his spirit. He gathered up his bag and tin kettle to start boiling some water for coffee, then headed to his usual spot by the embers from last night's fire.

Mornings were finally starting to cool off. The moderate temperature was nearly enough medicine to usher in a fresh start. Today, he'd open to Psalms for assurance.

Cort stopped midstep. "Aubrey?"

She sat in the same place he'd left her, only with a different colored fabric sprawled across her lap. When she looked up, her bloodshot eyes were framed by dark circles.

"Good morning," she rasped then cleared her throat. "My, that came quick."

"You worked all night?"

She set her needle down and cracked her fingers. "I suppose I did." Yawning, she gathered up her basket and carefully folded her current work. "I'll be fine. Just need a couple of hours to rest."

"Aubrey, you have so much sewing." He helped her up. "Why don't you let me finish your roof?"

"No, I said I am fine. I can do it all. It's what I was meant to do." Her weary words slurred.

"Meant to work yourself to death?" He shook his head. "Nobody is meant to do that."

"You don't understand, Cort," she said with more vigor. "It's perfect in a way. Mama sewed to save for her ranch, and Pa stole it. But he couldn't steal my ability to sew, which Mama had passed on to me. Little did she know that it would be *my* sewing that establishes her ranch." A giddy laugh blurted from her chapped lips. "Look at the Jessups. My mother would have turned green with envy at such a love like that. Look at you." She laid her hand on her chest, tears brimming in her eyes now. "Your care for the land and for my well-being is more than a whole twenty years of Mama's marriage to Pa." She looked as though she would spit northward. "But she did love horses, as much as I love sewing these dresses." She walked toward the ridge, calling out, "She worked hard for her horse ranch. My horse ranch."

Cort rushed up and escorted the exhausted woman down, settling her in next to Ben. She didn't refuse but fell fast asleep as soon as her head rested. Cort still held her hand. He slid his fingers over hers, feeling the calluses from sewing and noticing the scars from needle pricks. He gently kissed her finger and placed her hand beside her.

Stubborn seamstress. Aubrey was stuck working for another woman's dream because of the torment of sad memories.

If he could stick around and encourage Aubrey to

step out of the shadows of her mother, perhaps she'd find peace. Cort drew in a deep breath, realizing that the rest of his days were in another's shadow—his brother's.

Aubrey might have the chance to find joy on the horizon regardless of a selfless burden. Against his will, Cort was jealous of his landlady's freedom even in the midst of her strife.

Chapter Twelve

Aubrey woke up to an umber glow crawling across her dirt floor. She was alone. Her neck was sore as she sat up, and her knuckles ached. From the corner of her eye, the periwinkle dress that she'd been working on caught her attention. She reached for it, but then stopped when she remembered this morning. Cort had met her by the fire after he'd left her the night before. She'd worked all night. Had she slept all day?

She gathered herself up and went to wash off, not just the grime of the day before but the embarrassment of being caught indulging in her work. Cort had reprimanded her like she was a child. She felt irresponsible. Trying to stir up anger against the cowboy was futile because she knew he was right. Aubrey would work herself to death with this much sewing. But she loved it so.

The tepid water slid down her neck and around her collar. She took her apron and dried off quickly. Now that she was fully awake and ready for the day, she had to at least try to finish her home. Today was a new day, and she would work on the roof and get more sewing done this evening. She was determined to do it all, just like Mama sacrificed so much for a good life, no matter the circumstances. Aubrey could accomplish much if she followed her mother's footsteps toward a dream.

The rhythmic thud of Cort's mallet carried across the creek bed. She continued up the path to the houses. When she reached higher ground, she spied him working diligently on the fence along the southern stretch of land.

Aubrey sighed. If only she was as determined to work the land. It seemed her motivation was waiting for her back in the basket of thread and fabric below.

Please, Lord, give me the perseverance to complete this task.

The long shadow of her house stretched halfway across the land between hers and Cort's. It was later than she'd thought. Yet, as she began to work, exhaustion crept from the corners of her elbows to the lids of her eyes. She moved at a snail's pace. The sound of hooves was a welcome chance to step away from her work. But when she saw who was atop the horse, panic eclipsed her exhaustion.

"Benjamin Huxley, what in the world?" She rushed over as he gingerly dismounted and began to tie the horse.

His face beamed. "Doctor came by today, said I was healing nicely, so I decided to get out and see the place." He pulled off the crutch situated across the horn of the saddle then hobbled to the shade.

"I don't think that's very wise, Ben," she scolded. "Going out in this heat without telling a soul? What if you got hurt?"

"It's not that hot anymore. And I told your cowboy." He nodded toward Cort, who was heading from the creek bed. "He thought it was a fine idea. You trust him, don't you?" He sneered.

Her face grew hot, and she glared at Cort. "You thought this would be a good idea for him?"

Cort crushed the grasses as he plodded toward them. His half smile didn't waver, only making her more angry. "I didn't see the harm. He broke his leg, not his back, and he seems to get around better each day."

"This really isn't your decision, Cort," she said. "Ben, you should've at least waited until one of us could ride with you."

"Well, I whittled half a chess set waiting for you to get up," he scoffed. "Else you'd have had a say before I left."

Aubrey opened her mouth to speak, but between her jeering brother and the cool, unmoved cowboy, she could only groan and spin back toward her house.

She called over her shoulder, "Fine! Be reckless." Not like it wasn't in his blood, anyway. Maybe it was good that he was getting up and about. Didn't she want him to leave so he could keep Pa from coming around? She took a few deep breaths and began to work again. This time, more energized than before. She was so worked up her ears rushed with her pulse.

"Aubrey?" Cort's baritone voice carried over her shoulder.

"Yes, Mr. Stanton?" She raised a threatening eyebrow in his direction.

"Now, now." He held up his hands wide. "No need to be mad at me. I am not your brother's keeper. I just answered him when he asked for my opinion. It might have lessened his soreness toward me, too."

"I just assumed you were more levelheaded than that." She squirmed inwardly. Her late night and early morning sewing marathon was hardly levelheaded.

His palm cupped her shoulder. "Aubrey, why don't you come sit down, and I'll heat up some biscuits. You haven't eaten since yesterday."

Her stomach instantly grumbled, but she shook his hand away. "Are you trying to change the subject?"

"I am trying to offer you a meal." He lifted his hat and ran his hand through his hair. His emerald eyes sparkled intently. "Come on. I think you'll feel better if you eat."

"You don't think I should be upset with Ben?"

"I think he's a grown man. Let him make his own decisions. You've taken good care of him, but now it's time that he did things for himself. Don't you agree?"

Her throat tightened. She wanted desperately to release a lashing. All she could do was shrug her shoulders. With a huff of reluctance, she followed him to the fire, unable to come up with a retort. While he began to unwrap some biscuits from a cloth napkin, she repeated all that he had said in her mind.

Suddenly, she wanted to cry.

Even though he was correcting her way of thinking, he was also complimenting her. She *had* taken good care of Ben. And that was something she'd set aside as duty. But now the worry she felt for him riding today reminded her that she really did love her brother. And love was what made a family, wasn't it?

"He's my brother." She tested the ownership in it.

"Yes, he is." Cort grinned. "And you are a good sister to him."

"Thank you," she whispered.

"It's good to protect our own. I know exactly how you feel."

"You do?"

"Yes. My brother and nephew are the reason I'm..." Cort's jaw tightened beneath his stubbly cheek. "I would do anything for them." His brow furrowed as he kept his eyes on his task at hand. She hadn't seen his cloudy disposition in quite a while.

"Would they do the same for you?"

He curled his lip. "Good question. Doubt it. My brother's not the kind to look beyond himself. Or at least he wasn't." Cort shoved the coals of the fire with a blackened stick. "I tried my best to get him to change. Even when he didn't stand up for himself, I tried standing up for him."

"Ben and I never had much of a relationship like that. He wouldn't do much of anything for me."

"Except fight the cowboy trying to take your land?" He hooked his eyebrow and gave a half smile.

"Yes, guess he did do that." But she'd pushed him into it, hadn't she? "You think your brother would do that for you? Would he have fought for your stake of claim?"

Cort's face darkened even more. He just shook his head. Seemed like Cort might understand a broken family, too.

"Then why would you do anything for him?"

He stood up and shoveled in the smoky air. "There's more than just reciprocity when it comes to blood, Aubrey. There's responsibility for the future. His little boy deserves a father like we never had. My brother had the chance to change his bad ways and give his son a future. There's little I wouldn't do for the chance of a Stanton legacy."

Aubrey bit her lip. He'd mentioned that his brother was the only one who knew his secret. Did it have something to do with his legacy? She couldn't ask now. She had said she wouldn't pry anymore.

After they had a quiet meal, Cort went down and filled up their canteens while Aubrey continued working on her house. He tried to keep his thoughts straight and not think too much about her or his brother. It seemed both subjects filled him with agony. He'd never felt resentment toward Charles until Aubrey walked into his life. And he had never felt…well, whatever it was that triggered such a wild beat in his chest at the very sight of his dark-haired landlady.

By the time the sun neared the end of its western crawl, Aubrey met him halfway down the ridge, dirty and sunburned.

"I finished," she declared, showcasing a dazzling smile.

"You did?" Cort scratched his head, wondering how she could've completed the roof so quickly.

"Well, it's good enough anyway. Now that Ben's up and about, he fetched the materials as I worked. We have shade and a partial roof on the western side."

"So you let him help you, huh?" He quirked his brow.

"Stop it." She swatted at him with her handkerchief then wiped her forehead. "He owed me. Stealing my horse back at camp." She pushed past him, using his arm to steady herself. He couldn't help but place a guiding hand on her back as she walked. She seemed to relax beneath his palm, letting out a quiet thank-you. When she turned to him on level ground, he noticed those dark circles again.

"I am going to get our things," she said. "I have some sewing to do and need to go into town first thing in the morning to use Caldwell's machine."

"You needn't worry about that. Take this week to finish the house—" He stopped himself when she narrowed her eyes. "Just get a good night's rest tonight." He rocked back on his heels.

"Yes, it will be nice to start making home up yonder." She leaned her back against the packed dirt of the embankment. "You've gotten a head start. Is it nice?"

"It is. Cooler and better air up there."

Her eyes fluttered closed and she hid a yawn behind her delicate, dirt-stained fingers. "It'll be a good change to not breathe in all the dust down here. Can't wait to get furniture. Maybe we could actually eat at a table."

"I don't mind our fireside suppers, personally." He swept damp hair away from her cheek. Did she lean into his hand? He crammed it into his pocket.

"It has been nice. This prairie makes a great dining room for two." She smiled.

Prairie life sure had its perks—like spending evenings with Aubrey Huxley by their own private fire. She was too familiar. If he'd allow this admiration to grow to its full potential, they'd both end up devastated. The downside to this arrangement was how isolating their life had become. If they were in town, this strange dance of theirs may have never started. This whole situation would've been different if she'd depended on more people than just him. He'd leave her behind with nobody to take his place.

An idea formed in Cort's head. He needed more than just a fence to keep his mind occupied. They should surround themselves with more people to give Aubrey the chance to secure relationships once he was gone. Especially now that Ben was mobile and returning to Kansas sooner than later. "What do you say we have the Hickses over after church on Sunday? I'll return the plow, and they can see our hard work."

"That's a fine idea. Maybe the Jessups can come, too?" She pushed off of the wall and started to her dugout.

"Sure. I'm used to cooking for a whole herd full of cattle drivers. Think I can handle it." He chuckled.

"I'll try to help as best as I can," she called over her shoulder.

Cort headed back up, and Ben joined him at the fire as he began to cook supper. He watched Ben from the corner of his eye.

"That's a fine piece you are whittling there."

Ben continued without looking up. "Thanks. My pa used to whittle."

"Really?" Cort exclaimed. "Aubrey hadn't mentioned it."

"She was with Mama more than Pa. Pa didn't have use for a daughter. Me? Well, we had some wild adventures." Ben chuckled. "Surprised he hasn't come lookin' for me." A crease carved in his brow, and he frowned.

Cort focused on the flame below his kettle of coffee. Seemed Mr. Huxley wasn't living up to either of his children's expectations. His absence was a relief for his daughter but a wound for his son. "Some men don't realize how much they have." *Believe me.* Cort hoped that was not the case for Charles anymore.

Ben continued whittling, his motions getting harder and faster. "I don't get you. You had all this land, but you gave it up. What's in it for you, Cort?"

"I get to work and breathe and live."

"I don't think that's it." Gray dusk dulled his brown eyes. They just stared at each other.

Cort's spine crawled. "You don't?"

"Nope. See, I did the same thing as you. Just got caught." Ben continued whittling. "I won Aubrey's trust. She had it all set up for me to stick by Pa while she ran away. If only she knew that she'd given me the idea to find land of my own."

Aubrey admitted that she didn't trust her brother anymore. Whatever trust he'd earned was gone. "How is that like me at all?"

"She trusts you, Cort. What are you planning on doing with that? I mean, you gave up the land, won her trust. Now what?"

"Nothing. I am doing what I set out to do. Work the land and live a peaceful life," he declared, releasing a long breath. Admitting that out loud brought him closer to peace. He didn't have an ulterior motive. He was trying to live the rest of his life by the Good Book.

"There has to be a reason that you gave up the land," Ben persisted.

"Maybe there is. But that's my business," Cort muttered. The peace was escaping him, just as the steam rose from the kettle.

"I've learned a thing or two about secrets, Cort. They'll eat at you until you finally tell," Ben said, his mouth hooked in a sneer. "I've got a whole slew of them that Aubrey don't know about. Kills me slowly inside. Wonder if yours will, too."

"Maybe. But they won't hurt anyone else, and that's important." At least, he was trying to make that so. Giving Aubrey the chance to deepen her connections out here was a start. But could he protect her from Ben? "Will yours?"

Ben gave a bitter laugh. "They'd make my mama roll over in her grave."

Cort winced. "I don't think your sister needs to know about those." The cry of the kettle pierced a quiet interlude. Tension seemed to rise as quickly as the kettle spouted.

Ben focused on his knife. Apparently he was lost in thought. His brow rose and fell as if he were arguing with himself. At one point, a groan slipped out. "Have you ever wronged someone and they didn't even know?"

"Maybe. But I try to stick to admitting my mistakes now," Cort said.

"I can't ever admit it. I—I...don't want Aubrey to know I am just a petty thief."

"Thief?" Cort bristled.

Ben nodded and continued on his wooden piece without looking up. "What's that saying—once a thief, always a thief?"

Cort set the kettle down and sat back down. All he could think about was Ben's ride today, and how he lost sight of him over the horizon. Was this self-proclaimed thief up to something more than healing his leg?

Cort tried to dig up some grace. He'd been given a prairie-full of it, but his defenses were up. He tried to push aside assumptions, but he knew better. His whole family line could take that title of "thief," and when the opportunity arose, temptation overpowered a weak-willed offender. Cort had always felt it was wrong deep down, and until he was up in Wyoming, he'd ignored his conscience.

Now this man was confessing and all Cort could do was clench his fists and get ready to fight for justice. There'd be no wrongdoing around here. First, he wouldn't allow any hurt to come Aubrey's way if he could stop it, and second, law-breaking meant attention from the law. They didn't need any audience of the sort around here. He didn't need it.

"Have you stolen something here, Ben?" His words rolled low and deep. He demanded a straight answer.

Ben widened his eyes. "Oh, no." He frowned. "There are things I stole from Mama." His Adam's apple bobbed with a hard swallow.

"Have you stolen anything from Aubrey?"

He shook his head. "No. I only did it for Pa. He put me up to it."

"It's a dangerous life to live, Ben." He stood, grinding his boot heels into the earth. "Believe me. I've seen men throw their whole lives away with such dishonest living. You'll be wise to stay clean from now on."

He stomped toward his house in need of some more supplies but mostly wanting to sort out the uneasiness brought about by their conversation. Cort prayed that God would protect them. He then prayed that God would protect his nephew. Was Charles leading his own son astray just as Mr. Huxley had coaxed Ben? He hoped that Charles was good on his promise to put all that evildoing behind him.

That was all Cort had asked when he'd sacrificed his future for his family.

By the time Sunday rolled around, Aubrey and Ben had slept in her home for two nights. Or at least, Ben had. Aubrey hardly slept more than a couple of hours at a time. She had three more dresses to complete, and her money was gone. She desperately needed to deliver these dresses and collect payment.

After church, she took a small nap then joined Ben and Cort outside.

"Where'd you get that skillet?" She yawned into her linen sleeve. A cool breeze balanced out the ever-shining sun.

"Borrowed it from Mrs. Hicks." Cort was preparing supper on a makeshift workbench constructed of a board and some crates. "Did you get some rest?"

"Hardly." Even when she tried, her body was tense and she couldn't sleep for long. There was too much to think about. Sure, her house was somewhat finished— more like a shell than a home yet—but she was dragging her thread and needle to get these dresses complete. She wanted them to be just as pristine as her mama had taught her. Aubrey really did pour her heart into her work. Yet the only one pouring anything into Mama's ranch was Cort. The more she glimpsed his progress on the fence, the more anxious she became to work the land instead of the fabrics. Although, if she dreamed at all, silks, linens and taffeta were what piqued her fancy. Not a single horse could be found in any of her thoughts unless she was atop hers to go use Caldwell's supplies.

She did what she could to help Cort prepare the meal. He put her in charge of chopping up potatoes and onions. They worked side by side until she couldn't take the burning in her eyes anymore.

"Those are some of the strongest onions I've ever cut." She wiped her eyes with her apron, careful to avoid the onion juice from her fingers.

"They are." He wiped his eyes on his sleeve. "They'll taste good tossed in some butter from the Pattersons. Offered some shoeing in exchange for cured meats, cheese and fresh butter." He tapped a crock that sat on the bench.

"You must have shoed all day for such a fine meal as this." Aubrey sniffled, feeling like she'd just had a good cry.

Cort shrugged his shoulders, keeping his attention on preparing a cornmeal mixture. "Eating with friends is worth it, don't you think?"

She thought back on all the meals they'd shared together. "That's something I didn't realize until a month or so ago."

"It's been a good month of eating and talking, hasn't it?" Cort captured her with his emerald stare.

She gave his forearm a squeeze. "Thank you, Cort." Aubrey could say that without fear of him taking advantage of her situation. He was a man she could trust.

His chest heaved upward. He studied her face, her lips. Turmoil grew deep and wide in her belly. It warned her that sweet kisses and strong embraces would only tie her to a passing-through kind of cowboy more than she should allow.

"I need to check on Ben." She slipped aside and hurried around the house.

Lord, give me strength.

In her mind, she should be satisfied in her friendship with this cowboy. In her heart, she wrestled with hoping for more than just the here and now with him. And in her body, exhaustion warred over her thoughts and her strength to be wise and independent. Weakness would be her demise. Just like her mother. She was weak-willed when it came to Pa's ways. Maybe because he'd finally exhausted her with disappointment? Aubrey needed to be strong. Even if every part of her screamed otherwise.

She settled in the shade next to Ben, who was now starting a new piece of wood. His coyote figure sat in her window.

"Going to tidy up the place soon," she said, more to get out of her head for a while. "Just going to rest awhile."

"Okay, sis. Do what you've got to do." He continued whittling, not offering his help at all.

Aubrey rolled her eyes. "Just a few moments and I'll set out some blankets for everyone to sit on. One day, maybe you could whittle me a table?" she jested.

"That would be quite a feat. I'll just send one down on the train from Kansas."

"I'll be waiting." She grinned.

Her brother and the handsome cowboy had not been

part of her vision in Camp Kiowa. What would life be like without either of these men on her ranch?

Before she could stick to her plan, the Jessups arrived in their wagon. Mr. Jessup hopped down along with all the girls and gingerly escorted his wife across the prairie.

"Sarah, you look more exhausted than I am." Aubrey rushed up to her. Sarah's cheeks were flushed, and the lines around her eyes probably matched Aubrey's own dark circles.

"It's close now, dear." She patted Aubrey's hand as they made their way to the clearing where they'd dine. "Dave? Can you bring out the chair for me? I need to sit."

Her husband ran around to the back of the wagon and brought out a small chair. He placed it under the shade. Ben was now over by the fire, leaning on his crutch while he watched Cort cook. The four Jessup girls were attracted to the fire like flies to honey. Little Addie tried propping her doll up on the ground to admire the flames.

"Be careful you don't get too close," Aubrey warned as she walked by. "I am going to get a blanket so you have a more comfortable place for your dolly."

The little girl beamed.

Once the Hickses arrived, everyone settled beneath the shade and Mr. Hicks led them in a short prayer. They all filled their plates and began to eat. Aubrey relished the constant conversation. This was more intimate than the chuck wagon dinner, more like a family gathering that she'd only witnessed from a distance back in Kansas.

"Cort, you've done it again," Mrs. Hicks cooed. "Delicious meal."

"Why, thank you." He tipped his hat to her. "If only I could whip up a fence as easily as that." He nodded toward the other side of the creek bed. The fence posts were barely noticeable beyond the grove of post oaks along the embankment.

"We are so happy that you finally have your houses ready," Mrs. Hicks continued.

"So am I. I've spent the last month living in a hole," Ben blurted, rubbing the back of his neck. Everyone laughed.

"Dave, why don't you get the muffins from the wagon," Sarah said breathlessly. She cast a twinkling gaze in Aubrey's direction. "I made those muffins you raved about. Thought they could pass as dessert— Ah!" She clutched her midsection and the entire Jessup clan moved toward her in one swift motion.

"What's the matter, Mama?" Their oldest, Jolene, asked.

"I think it's time, dear." She looked up at Mr. Jessup and patted his hand. "Mrs. Hicks, do you still want to help with the labor?" Their mutual neighbor clapped her hands and jostled over, offering a hand while Sarah stood. They took a couple of steps, and then Sarah stopped, seizing her belly and breathing hard.

Mrs. Hicks rubbed her back. "Take us home, Mr. Jessup," she commanded.

"Home?" Adelaide yelped. "We just got here. Mama!"

Mrs. Hicks took Sarah by one elbow while Mr. Jessup got the wagon ready. All the girls surrounded their mother and chattered away with excitement, except Adelaide.

Aubrey stroked Adelaide's curls. "Your mama wants to have the baby in her own house, Addie. That's why you worked so hard to get it up."

Her blue eyes swam. She clutched her doll and Aubrey's arm. "Please, Miss Aubrey. I don't wanna go."

"You'll want to meet your baby brother or sister, won't you?"

Sarah called out breathlessly from atop the wagon bench, "She's been looking forward to our picnic."

Aubrey hid a yawn behind her hand, then knelt down face-to-face with the girl. "Addie, we will have picnics all the time, but your baby sibling will only come just this once. It's an exciting time."

She shook her curls furiously. "I want to stay."

Mr. Jessup strode across and planted his large hands on Addie's shoulders. "Adelaide Jessup, you are not being polite to Miss Huxley or your mama."

"I'm sorry, Pa," she muttered, then swiveled around and wrapped her arms around his legs. "I'm—I'm scared."

Mr. Jessup bent down and kissed her forehead. He brushed his finger across her cheek and took her button chin. "Darling, it's not scary. It's life at its finest." Aubrey's heart skipped.

"I don't wanna see Mama hurt." Little sobs bleated from Addie's lips.

"I know. I know." He kissed her again then stood up. Aubrey tried to keep from gaping at the sympathy and concern evident in Mr. Jessup's actions. "Miss Huxley, how about Addie stays just awhile? I can send one of the girls to get her in a couple hours or so."

A few blinks and she pulled herself together. "Of course. We can make her doll a new dress for the baby's arrival."

Adelaide jumped up and down, squealing, "Thank you, Daddy! Thank you!"

Before the Jessups left, Cort and Mr. Hicks shook hands with Mr. Jessup. They all stood together while waving goodbye to the family. Aubrey gathered up Addie's hand and gave it a squeeze.

"Your pa is pretty nice to let you stay with me," Aubrey said as they walked to finish their food.

"I know." Adelaide smiled. "I love him."

What a blessed little girl to have a father like Mr. Jessup. Aubrey tried her best to remember that even though she'd never had a father care for her, her Heavenly Father did. "Those Jessups are paving the way for a mighty fine legacy. Don't you agree?" Cort said as he sat beside her.

She could only smile. Cort hoped to do so for his nephew. Children had a way of softening the hearts of even the toughest of men.

She wished she cared about the Huxley legacy. But it was hard to care for something that had been left to the wayside long ago. Although Mama's ranch would at least break away from the ill course the Huxleys had set. But she couldn't credit the Huxleys with such a legacy as Mama's ranch. Pa didn't deserve any part of it. Did he?

Chapter Thirteen

Once Mr. Hicks left, Cort tried to keep busy down in the creek. He washed the pans and plates, leaving Aubrey and Addie to tidy up the picnic area. A swarm of emotions crowded him more than at any other time. There was just something about a woman nurturing a child. Aubrey's ways with Addie reminded him of how, deep down, he would love a family of his own—perhaps have a chance to grow the Stanton name into a noble one himself.

Why had he given up his life because of his brother? Regret wormed into his conscience.

Father, forgive me.

But how could he expect God to forgive him, when he could hardly forgive himself? Wasn't that what had made him weak in the moment when he was caught for his brother's crime? He'd lived numb to a life of crime before, but he'd felt it was about time it caught up to him. He'd needed to reconcile it. Seeing the fear in Charles's eyes and thinking about his little nephew without a father had transformed Cort's weak moment to one of his own personal redemption.

He scrubbed off the crusty corn bread from the cast-iron skillet. Taking his time, he gathered the dishes in his crate and headed back up to the houses. When he placed them in the corner where he'd eventually put his kitchen, he spied his Bible. Just this morning he'd read Hebrews. The sacrifice was done. Nothing left. Why couldn't he believe that for himself?

He wanted to believe it, but it was too late to allow that freedom to settle in his spirit. The mess of trouble would catch up with him, eventually. Or else, he'd live this life wondering when it would and holding back from all life's joys because of it.

His mood soured, and he had a whole afternoon for it to fester. Great. He'd go for a ride. That would help. He strode across the prairie, anxious to mount his horse and clear his mind. Ben snoozed under the tree, and Aubrey was nowhere to be found. He'd heard her calling Addie's name earlier. They must be off playing a game.

When he headed east to go over to the other side of the property, Aubrey ran around the corner of her house, frantic.

"Cort! Have you seen Addie?" Her face was pale. "I—I—I fell asleep…and—" Her lip quivered and she began to weep. "I've looked all over the creek bed and up here. What if she's lost in the grasses? Or worse, what if she's hurt somewhere?"

He'd never seen her like this before. Her shoulders shook. He flung himself off his horse and folded his arms around her. Cort tried to push away the memories of men in town who talked about run-ins with rattle-snakes out here. He'd never seen one around these parts.

He cleared his throat. "She probably went home. Don't worry."

"How could I do this?" she screeched. "She was my responsibility. I couldn't keep my eyes open, and she seemed content playing with her doll." She pushed away and ran over to Ben, shaking him awake. "Have you seen Addie?"

Cort hollered, "I'll go to the Jessups' and see if she's there—"

"No!" Aubrey stumbled toward him, twisting her hands together. "If she's not there, then poor Sarah—" she clasped her mouth with a trembling hand, mumbling "—she has enough to think about."

"How 'bout I go and not say anything. Just look for her. If she's not there, then I'll come back and you and I will go search around. She couldn't have gotten far. If she did head home, I'll meet her on the way."

Aubrey nodded. Tear trails crossed her cheeks. "Please hurry."

"Of course." He kissed her forehead. "Pray, Aubrey. God knows where she is. He's with her." Cort hurried off. He tried to take his own advice, but Aubrey's fear singed his throat and burned behind his eyes the entire ride along the ridge. He searched below as he galloped, praying that a mass of golden curls would snag his eye. Nothing but the murky creek and the packed earth.

When he came up to the Jessup place, only the three older girls were outside.

"Hi, Mr. Stanton." They spoke in unison.

"Is the baby here yet?" he asked.

"No, sir. Pa went over to the Hickses to gather some more towels. Mrs. Hicks sent him," Jolene said.

"We think it's because Pa was nervous." Beatrice, the one closest to Addie's age, burst into giggles.

"Nobody else is here besides you three?" How could he be sure Addie wasn't around somewhere?

"Nope. Just us. Mrs. Hicks said she's done this plenty, no need for a doctor."

"Okay. Well, I guess I'll be heading on, then." Cort began to steer his horse back toward the creek bed. What if Addie was in the house? He couldn't ask.

"Mr. Stanton," Caroline, the second oldest, called out. "Can I come back with you? I'd rather be playin' with Addie than sitting here all day."

His heart plunged into his stomach. They thought Addie was still back with Aubrey. So they hadn't seen her.

"Uh, no. Not right now. I think it's best for you to stay with your parents." Before the child could argue, he turned his horse and galloped home.

His teeth ground against each other. By the time he arrived back at their property, his jaw ached with tension.

Aubrey ran up to Cort with wide eyes. "Was she there?"

It was torture to shake his head, and even more painful to hear the groan come from the tiny woman. Her face screwed up, and she fell to her knees, sobbing into her hands. Ben hobbled about on his crutch, his hand over his eyes as he looked out into the prairie.

Cort yanked his horse around. He'd go into the creek

bed. The child couldn't be far. Rocks tumbled as the horse slipped down the steep embankment.

"Addie!" His coarse voice boomeranged around the miniature canyon. Silence returned his cry. He wiped the sweat from his eyes. He checked both dugouts. Empty. What if she was hurt somewhere and couldn't speak? The thought iced his veins.

Aubrey descended down the path. "Cort, let me search with you. Ben said he'd wait by the houses for her."

"I think we should go to the back of the property." He held out his hand and helped Aubrey up. She wrapped her arms around his waist. They splashed through the creek and found the most shallow path up the other bank.

Slowly, Cort steered the horse along his half-built fence. The pat of hooves smashing the grasses and their jagged breathing interchanged with the blood pumping in his ears. As they turned past the last post he'd secured southward, Aubrey gripped his arm.

"Look!" She pointed back toward the grove of post oaks near the creek. A small lump of blue gingham was huddled in the shade of the trees. "Hurry, Cort!" As they galloped, he spotted blond hair poking out from beneath a bonnet.

"Addie." Aubrey squealed. But the child didn't move. Cort stopped the horse and helped Aubrey down, imagining venom coursing through the child. He balled his fists, bracing himself. Why was the girl so still?

When they reached her, she appeared to be sleeping. Her dolly was wrapped in her arms, and she was curled up with her head resting on an exposed root. He checked her limbs and her arms for any bites or wounds. Everything seemed to be fine.

"Addie?" He gently lifted her head. Her little lips pursed then relaxed. A flood of relief overwhelmed Cort at the small movement. He looked up at Aubrey. "I think she's okay." He gathered her into his arms and rocked her gently. "Adelaide?" Her peaceful face was round and creamy. He brushed a finger on her soft skin. "Wake up, sweetheart."

They just sat there, Aubrey at his elbow, gripping him firmly. He rocked the child, trying to wake her. This was what his brother had. A woman and a child to share life with. From deep within his spirit, jealousy sparked.

"Here, Cort. Let me try." Aubrey stole her from him in a quick motion. He sat back and took a moment while Aubrey awakened the child.

Addie rubbed her eye. "You're done with your nap, Miss Aubrey?"

Aubrey gasped, clutching the little girl tight against her. "Oh, Addie. I am so sorry."

Cort reached over and slid his hand over Aubrey's hair, comforting her as she cried quietly in the child's curls.

"Look what I found!" Addie wriggled away and held out an old arrowhead. "I was going on a scavenger hunt and found it." She rubbed the side of her head, staring at the root. "Guess I got tired, too. Shade's nice, but that's not such a comfortable pillow."

They all laughed. Cort wiped his eyes at the same time as Aubrey. They shared a tender, wordless exchange while little Addie scrambled to her feet.

"Thank you, Cort. I would have been lost without

your help." Aubrey squeezed his hand, then slipped past to catch up with Addie as she ran toward the creek.

It was nightfall by the time Mr. Jessup came around and announced the birth of yet another little girl. Her name was Polly. Aubrey loved the name and couldn't wait to hold the baby. She'd never held a baby before. Addie fell asleep on her daddy's shoulder as he spoke quietly about the new addition to the family. While the moon made its entrance in the night sky, they rode away into the indigo horizon.

"Well, that was quite a day." Cort leaned back on his elbows. Aubrey settled in her usual spot with her basket. "You're going to sew now?"

"Got to." She smiled brightly, trying to ignore the tugging guilt. If she hadn't worked so much on these dresses, then she would have never fallen asleep while caring for Addie. She could feel Cort's stare across the fire. What did he think of her? This once-responsible, independent landlady couldn't even care for a child for more than an hour. She shuddered at the thought of who she might have taken after. Certainly not her mother.

Cort's inhalation was audible. She managed a glance. He was handsome as ever. Sparkling green eyes cast a gaze toward the jumping flames. He seemed to be lost in thought. She couldn't help but admire him.

"You're her hero now, you know." She began to sew, trying to divert the attention from this joyous work that also seemed to be a curse.

"Hero?" He scoffed. "We both found her. Thank God above."

She scrunched her nose and continued sewing. "I got

lost once." Should she open that window to her past? She continued to sew in silence.

"Well?" he prodded.

"Well. I didn't have a hero find me," she said, trying to keep her emotions at bay. "He never came looking."

"I'm sorry." He leaned forward. "Did he know you were lost?"

"Yes. But he had other things to take care of." She rolled her eyes. "I was so scared. He'd sent me to collect firewood, and I forgot which way I went. I spent a night in the woods. When I got home, Mama gathered me up in her arms. But Pa was too drunk to even notice." She stopped sewing and tilted her face to the starry sky.

"Sounds like you weren't the only lost one."

"What do you mean?"

"Your pa's lost in a different way. I've seen men who just can't find themselves. Sounds like he's one of them." Cort pulled out his whittling. "I was lost like him once. Not in drinking, just in trying to survive life down the wrong path. It's hard to find yourself when you get too far away from goodness."

Aubrey furrowed her brow. She tried to think of her pa in a different light and tried to think of Cort in wayward shadows. "I can't imagine you being lost. You are one of the strongest men I know." Actually, the strongest. She'd never been around a man who was so strong, yet gentle enough to care so deeply for a child who wasn't his own. She'd seen his tears.

Cort gave her his full attention. She could only look down.

"What made you change your course, Cort?"

"God found me. Or at least, I opened my mind enough

to let Him in. Then He worked on my heart, and I realized how lost I was without Him."

"Don't know if Pa knows how to listen. He never listened." A foreign wave of compassion suddenly lapped across her thoughts of Pa. "You're right, Cort. He's lost. All these years I've resented him. But now I feel pity for him." A small whimper escaped her lips. "Just wish Mama got more while she was here. Don't know what God was thinking, bringing those two together."

"Well, Aubrey Huxley. You're here, aren't you?"

"Yes, I guess I can at least bring my mama's dream to fruition."

"No, I mean, he brought those two together and made someone beautiful from their union." His chiseled face glowed from the fire. Speaking of getting lost, she could jump into those green pools and lose herself in that warmth and affirmation. Cort continued, "Don't you think you're enough?"

"What do you mean?" She resisted the intrigue of his conversation and fiddled with the sewing in her lap.

"I mean, your mama had your love. Sounds like she was blessed by you while she lived." He sat up. His jaw flinched. The clicks and crackles of the fire filled the space. He opened his mouth then snapped it shut.

"What is it, Cort?"

He rubbed the back of his neck. "Is a ranch something that she would have wanted you to take on?"

"What are you saying?"

"It's just that you've enjoyed sewing so much this past month. It seems like your passion more than—"

She stuffed her sewing in the basket and rose to her feet along with her rising anger. "Not this again. You're making me wonder if Ben is right about you. What do you want from this deal, Cort?"

"You know I would never take this ranch from you. Your brother just wants a reason to justify his hate." He stood with her. "I want you to know that I understand what it's like to give up your own dream for someone else's."

"Oh, you do?" She dug her knuckles into her hip. An ache wrapped around her throat like squeezing fingers.

"Yes, I do." Confidence emboldened every inch of his steeled face and seemed to expand across his broad shoulders. He stood to his fullest height, looming over. "Aubrey, I gave up my dream a long time ago. And now I am living with the consequences of it."

"What is your dream, Cort?"

"I am just saying that life's too short to turn your back on what you love. One day, time'll run out, and you'll never forgive yourself." He curled his lips. A deep crease etched between his eyebrows. Her anger dissolved. He was speaking from that giant heart of his, and deep down, the truth in his words planted a seedling in her own heart. But why couldn't Cort Stanton forgive himself—this man of faith and second chances?

She reached up and ran her hand over his stubbly jawline. "What is it that you gave up, Cort?"

His jaw tightened beneath her hand. "The chance to love, Aubrey." He moved away and disappeared into the dark.

Did he leave love behind? Aubrey's heart grew heavy at the thought that all this time she'd been right to resist her affection for a man who may be someone else's. As she sat and sewed by the firelight, she thought on all they'd said. Maybe, just maybe, Cort was right. The ranch wasn't her dream anymore. But it was her duty. And it was a fine one. Yet she couldn't imagine completing it without Cort by her side. As much as she didn't want to admit her reliance on him, she tried to convince herself she'd miss his work, and not a chance to love a man who would never truly be hers.

It was time she forgot the mysterious hold Cort Stanton had over her and established herself as she'd always imagined: an independent, business-oriented landowner carrying out a dream—or maybe two.

Cort continued to work on the fence, keeping his distance from Aubrey as much as he could. A fear iced his heart at the memory of their last conversation. Not because he'd muscled his way into her plans, suggesting that her dream might not be out on this prairie with horses and ranch hands—that needed to be said. She was wearing herself thinner than the shavings from his last whittling session.

No, that was not what sparked his dread.

While he had held his breath, figuring a "mind your own business" might escape the lips of his beautiful landowner, instead he saw a softening in her expression, so much so that he had nearly spilled his heart in a way that he could never take back. If he shared everything he felt about Aubrey, he would never forgive himself in the end. Her affection was obvious, and if he voiced his, he would be a thief, stealing her heart without the ability to return his in the full.

After his midday meal, Aubrey headed over to her horse. She gave a nervous glance down to the basket she held against her waist then up at Cort. "Would you like to visit the Jessups with me? I have a bonnet for the baby and a dress for Addie's doll. Going to Mr. Caldwell's afterward." She pressed her lips in a thin line, as if challenging him to try to sway her.

"No, thank you. I'll go by on my next trip to town," he said. "I—"

She cut him off. "Very well. See you tonight." She swiveled around and continued to her horse.

How could he explain himself more? It wasn't that he judged her for her dream, but he cared for her well-being. Maybe he cared too much.

Her cool demeanor had him wondering if she'd digested his words and was protecting herself now. So be it. The truth had been spoken, and she could do with it what she wanted. He wasn't her keeper. If he was meant to just work her ranch so she could indulge in her dressmaking dreams, then he was fine doing that. Seemed that they were both living their dreams, side by side.

Thank You for this work, Lord.

The weeks tumbled by into a temperate November, one where he no longer woke up damp from sweat, but found himself reaching for a blanket.

Aubrey's coolness never left her. She had become quiet and businesslike, no longer meeting him by the fire at night and only speaking with him out of necessity. He'd notice her lantern burning from inside her house in the late hours. Working on dresses, no doubt. But she didn't seem as tired as she used to be. Each morning, bright and early, she'd meet him along the fence with a cup of coffee and her shawl wrapped around her shoulders. They'd discuss the property and the location of the stables. Everything revolved around the concerns of a landowner and a ranch hand. On occasion, he'd want to break this strange discard of familiarity, and it seemed Aubrey considered it during awkward hesitations before leaving him to work. He reminded himself it was for the best.

In fact, this was what he'd wanted all along. To work the land and enjoy his hiding until the time came to serve his sentence. The unplanned distraction of beautiful Aubrey Huxley had only brought Cort to a stormy discontentment—a roaring, emotional tornado that had him second-guessing everything he'd committed to set out and do.

The third Sunday came around, and Cort set up his worktable to cook for their neighbors. They'd all decided that their first meal together had been a fine start to a monthly tradition, what with baby Polly's arrival. This was exactly what Cort wanted, more neighbors around to ensure that Aubrey had a community to lean into once he was gone.

"Are you making biscuits?" Aubrey was out of breath as she lugged a pail of water for boiling.

"I am." He continued stirring in the flour. "Where's Ben? I thought he might want to set up the chessboard."

"He's with Dr. Mills. It seems he might get his cast off soon." She tucked a strand of hair behind her ear.

"Oh?"

"He might leave on next week's train and try to make it home for Thanksgiving," she said quietly, keeping her attention on her finger as she traced the grain of the workbench.

He grimaced at his desire to comfort her. "You'll

miss him. That's to be expected." He gripped his spoon tighter.

"Yes, you're right. Guess I had more family ties than I realized." She sighed. "I think I am going to write my pa a letter."

"A letter?" Cort continued to stir, ignoring his delight in Aubrey's breakaway from business-centered talk.

"I'll have Ben take it to Pa when he leaves. You opened my eyes to something I'd never considered before. Pa's lost. He has nobody showing him the way. Maybe I could at least point him in the right direction."

His heart leaped, an old habit. He tried to tamp down his emotion. "You've got a good heart, Aubrey."

She beamed. He gave an internal sigh and allowed himself to admire her—for just a moment.

"Don't know if I'll forgive him anytime soon."

He returned his attention back to his work. "Forgiveness is a hard thing."

"Have you forgiven yourself, Cort?"

"Myself?" He stopped stirring. His teeth clenched. Why was she making this about him?

"Yes. You said you gave up on a dream and warned me not to do the same."

She'd listened to him. Had she spent these past weeks dissecting his advice? He'd probably said too much.

"I am no better than your pa. I've sown a whole prairie full of mistakes. It's too late for me now." He tossed aside the spoon, flinging batter on the bench.

Aubrey flinched but didn't drop her gaze. She just narrowed her eyes. "That doesn't sound like the Cort I know."

"Oh, really?" he challenged. She knew nothing of

his past. And he'd kept it that way on purpose. To speak it? He might as well bury himself in a grave as deep as the shame he felt. It would be more bearable than living another moment with it out in the open.

"The Cort I know gives grace and compassion more than a whole army of angels. Surely the same man can afford some forgiveness for himself."

"I've followed a wayward path for so long, I guess it's time I pay up." The shame began to rise. He could feel it starting at his boots. Where was his shovel?

Aubrey rounded the bench. "You're a man of much faith, Cort. Don't give up on yourself because of the past."

"Why do you care, Aubrey? I thought we'd reached an agreement. Business only. This whole getting into each other's business just makes a mess of things."

"I know." She knit her brows together as she stared over at the shade tree where Dr. Mills met with Ben. "No matter what you've done, or who's waiting for you, I'll never take back my friendship. You're my friend, Cort. I want to keep it that way."

"I don't want to hurt you, Aubrey." Cort's lip trembled. He was a miserably weak cowboy. This woman brought him to a place he never wanted to go, but he might be fine never leaving.

"You'll only hurt me if you continue to be so hard on yourself," she said. "You've changed my opinion about how to treat my pa. Now it's my turn to tell you something, Cort. Stop living your life with regret. Just live."

Chapter Fourteen

❧

As Aubrey folded the last of the linens into the chest,
her skin prickled with a thrill of accomplishment. Last
week had started with a sealed deal with Mr. Caldwell.
She'd finished another dress today, and she eyed the
bare mannequin that stood in the newly framed window
of Mr. Caldwell's shop. She'd come a long way since
that first day in Alva when the Irish tailor had doubted
her ability. If he were here, she wouldn't be able to resist asking him to display the soft woolen dress with
pretty puffed sleeves. But he had gone to the depot to
meet the afternoon train. Several yards of fabric and
embellishments were aboard from the west.

Aubrey flung her shawl around her shoulders to ward
off the recent chill that kissed the Oklahoma prairie.

"Are you ready, Aubrey?" Cort filled the doorway of
the shop, holding his cowboy hat over his heart. His rich
voice and humble stance sent her stomach in a tumble.

"Yes, Cort."

They'd agreed to be friends, even after those quiet
weeks of conversations confined to business. And she'd

hoped Cort was starting to take her advice to not be so hard on himself. During their silence, she'd asked God to help her understand all that Cort had said about her pa being a lost man. She'd also prayed that God's will for her next step in forgiving her father would be clear. And as she prayed, she had realized Cort's need for a bit of grace for himself. He was not only running from the law, but lost love. He needed a friend and some kindness. She could give him at least that. He deserved so much.

"Did you pick it up?" She clasped her hands together, anxious to hear.

"Yes, I did." He stepped into the dirt-packed road and crushed his dark curls with his hat. "You now own a wooden table. It barely fit on my cart."

She squealed. The sturdy table stood in the general-store window. She'd bought it with the profit from her first dresses, and Cort promised to pick it up with his newly purchased cart.

"Imagine eating at a proper table now. I'll never picnic again," she said.

He winked beneath the shadow of his hat's brim. His emerald eyes were a familiar elixir of comfort and home. Aubrey bit her lip. She should not think such things about a friend, should she?

She hooked her gloved hand in his arm and they began to walk toward the hitch. Whatever thorn lay in his past, her desire to be the one person who showed him God's grace in second chances grew every day. After all the second chances she'd been given, she could at least do that.

A whipping breeze lifted some dust from beneath

the wooden walk. She leaned her face into Cort's shoulder to shield her eyes. It was a strange thing to feel the prairie winds change along with the condition of her heart. These past days, she had begun to picture herself in a rocker on a swept porch, sewing the next batch of aprons for the women of Alva and listening to the hum of Cort working on the fence around her ranch. She'd be a seamstress, and he'd oversee the ranch. The vision suited her passion to sew and would mean Cort became a long-term resident. It was a dream that could replace her old stubborn one—the one she'd sought in desperation to escape the man who'd destroyed her mother, the man who was destroying himself. Her strife was dissipating with her need to reach beyond herself, giving grace as Cort had illustrated. Life was changing with the season from fiery fury to cool surrender.

"I see your new boss over there." Cort nodded toward the depot where Mr. Caldwell was removing crates from a train cart. A whole bustle of townspeople crowded Main Street between them and the depot.

"Do you mind if I meet you at the hitch? I'd like to tell him that I finished the dress for Mrs. Patterson." She gave a wry smile. "He didn't think I'd get it done before Christmas."

Cort gestured with a wide sweep of his arm for her to pass by. He smelled like peppermint and fresh leather, another scent of comfort.

Remember, he's just a friend.

She tried to heed her self-imposed warning and immersed herself in the crowd. Several women wove along the wooden walk as she pushed through. They smiled and ushered young children this way and that. One little boy crashed into her and fell back, landing on his sack that was tied around his wrist.

"Excuse me, ma'am." He scratched his head then grabbed his hat from the walkway and scrambled to his feet.

Aubrey looked about for a chasing mother, but everyone seemed focused on their own whereabouts.

"Are you lost?"

"I'm runnin' away," he announced. He was only about six years old but had a determined brow.

"I see." Aubrey crossed her arms. "Why are you running?"

"My mama cares about my new daddy more than me." His plump bottom lip stuck out.

"I am sure that's not true." Aubrey carefully knelt down. "And I'm certain you won't get very far without a mama. I wish mine was still here. You'll miss her something fierce, promise." She patted his button nose with her finger. Beady blue eyes peered up at her through long eyelashes.

"Trevor!"

His eyes widened, and he stiffened like a soldier. A woman approached from across the street dressed in a ruby-red shirtwaist, fashionable leg-of-mutton sleeves and a matching skirt. Her wide-brimmed hat shadowed a mass of blond curls resting on one shoulder. She jostled toward them with a carpetbag banging against her fine dress. "Trevor Jeremiah Stanton. You had me worried sick."

"Stanton?" A relative of Cort's? Here, in Alva?

The woman paid no attention to Aubrey's exclamation and grabbed Trevor by the arm. "Thank you, ma'am, for stopping him. He threw a fit on the train and stormed off when it stopped." She glared down at him while he wiggled his arm in her grasp. "This is not a good start to our new life, child."

"Did you say your name was Stanton?"

"Why, yes. Mrs. Cassandra Joselyn Stanton." She gave a dazzling smile. "We've come up from Amarillo." She pinched her cheeks and smacked her lips together. All she needed was a mirror. "Seems my sweetheart's hiding out in this godforsaken place."

Aubrey couldn't find words. A sudden dread pressed heavy on her heart. Was this the lost chance of love that Cort had spoken about? Surely he wouldn't hide a wife?

"You are...?" Cassandra's manicured eyebrows arched high.

"I'm...I'm Aubrey Huxley. And your sweetheart is?"

"Oh, perhaps you know him." She squealed. "There he is!"

Aubrey spun around, and dread split her heart in two. Cort was at the corner across where she'd left him, his face as long and blanched as hers felt. But his eyes weren't on Aubrey. They were soaking in the beautiful Mrs. Stanton, who then rushed past, dragging her child beside her.

Was this part of his secret past? A beautiful wife? By the looks of her, Aubrey doubted an entire hundred and sixty acres would be big enough to share with this woman. She felt like a scrawny schoolgirl, one who'd been tempted by a handsome cowboy. He'd not only come to her rescue more than once, but given her reason to think there was more to their relationship than a business deal.

While Cort's attention was completely stolen by the

two newcomers, Aubrey slipped around the newly constructed bank and hurried across town.

She would rather walk clear to Kansas than join in this family reunion. Hot tears coursed down her cheeks. Ridiculous. There was nothing to cry about. Hadn't she wanted to be left alone from the very beginning? Perhaps her original plan shouldn't be discarded so quickly?

But why did she despise the fact that loneliness consumed her with every step she took upon the familiar dirt path through the prairie grasses? How could this place of freedom and dreams be so colorless? Aubrey had little doubt in her mind that all the color in Alva was wrapped around the shoulders of that Mrs. Cassandra Stanton. Her crimson dress outshone the very hue of the setting sun.

"Cassandra?" Cort's voice cracked. He thought he was losing his mind when his brother's wife barreled toward him, dragging his little nephew down the main street of Alva.

"Oh, Cort. It's been too long." She clasped her gloved hands together then reached out and brushed Cort's cheek. "My, you've only gotten more handsome than I remember." Her glassy blue eyes swam in a mixture of joy and sorrow. "And I'd forgotten how much you look like…him."

Cort squatted to level with the youngest Stanton. "My, my, Trevor. Last time I saw you, you were half that size." He tousled the boy's hair. "You still look like your pa, even more so."

Trevor narrowed his eyes and tugged at Cassandra's waistcoat. "Mama, is this my new daddy?"

Cassandra let out a tinkling laugh.

Cort's heart plummeted to his stomach as he stood up again. "What is he talking about, Cass?"

"Oh, Cort. He's a child." She snaked her arm around his, leaning into his side. "We've got so much to catch up on."

"Where's Charles?"

Cassandra began to babble about her train ride, clearly avoiding a straightforward answer. Before he could drag any worthwhile information from the woman, Mr. Caldwell approached with a large crate in his arms.

"I'm losing my grip!" Mr. Caldwell declared.

"Here, let me help." Cort escaped Cassandra's hold and took the crate from the tailor. He craned his neck to see if he'd spy Charles down the street. He remembered Aubrey. She'd stood just across from Cassandra, hadn't she? A fog had fallen on Cort's conscience when he'd seen his sister-in-law. He hadn't even thought to wave Aubrey over. But she was gone. A deep, disconcerting pain crossed his chest. How could he ignore the most important person in his world? Even in the face of his debilitating past?

"Where's Charles?" He seethed in Cassandra's direction, but she and Mr. Caldwell were making acquaintance, shaking hands and introducing themselves.

"Pleased to meet you." Cassandra beamed her usual dazzling smile and Mr. Caldwell's own face lit up by it. Typical of Mrs. Charles Stanton. Able to get the most dull of men to brighten in her presence.

"I do appreciate your help, Mr. Stanton. My back isn't what it used to be." The tailor sighed, pulling out a handkerchief to wipe his brow. "I apologize if I interrupted you."

"Not at all," Cort mumbled. "I'll take this to the shop and then we'll get you settled, Cassandra. Wait here. My horse is the chocolate stallion with the cart over there." He nodded across the square, refusing to look at Cassandra directly. He swiveled on his heel and stormed down the street.

Something was terribly wrong. Why else would Cassandra be here without Charles? But more than that, how in the world did she know to find him in Alva? A dark cloud invaded every corner of Cort's soul as he imagined the worst. Apparently, the news of his whereabouts had traveled down the Oklahoma plains across the Red River and out west toward Amarillo.

"I thank you kindly, Mr. Stanton." The tailor fiddled with the lock and then opened the door. Cort placed the crate on the floor. "Ah, Miss Huxley has been hard at work." He raised his spectacles to his forehead as he inspected the seams of a dress.

If Cassandra could find her way to the Cherokee Strip, then who else was looking for him? Cort had to leave and find out.

"Well, I better go tend to my...uh, family, sir." He tipped his cowboy hat, but Mr. Caldwell only gave a distracted goodbye. The tailor continued to inspect Aubrey's work as Cort left the shop.

Cort was ready to get a straight answer from the woman. Cassandra and Trevor waited by Cort's horse. His little nephew was whining and jumping up and down. "Please, Mama. I just want to sit on him for a minute."

Cassandra just swatted at the air and looked in a small hand mirror. "You hush." She spied Cort from under her obnoxious hat, pushing her son aside. "Now look, Cort. You don't treat a visitor like that—shoving us to the hitchin' post to leave us by our lonesome?" Her notorious bottom lip plumped forward, and she batted her eyelashes. He had never allowed her flirtations to get to him before, and now, with Charles nowhere to be found, Cort bristled at her brazen charm. He wondered why exactly his brother's wife stood here without him.

"Where's Charles, sister?"

She blew away a golden curl that slipped from her hat. "Oh, Cort, don't call me that." She patted his chest. "You know I've never liked that about us. Brother, sister? So strange to think of you as my brother."

"This is not about us, Cassandra. I'm asking about my brother. Where is Charles?"

She crossed her arms and looked down at her little boy, who was drawing in the dirt. "He's gone, Cort. And Trevor and I are all alone." For the first time, she gave a sober look his way. "Your brother is dead."

The journey back to the ranch was a blur for Aubrey. She tried to prepare herself for the life she had first expected when she'd fought Cort for the land—to ranch by her lonesome, without help. He deserved a fair price for his help and then she should send him, and his young family, on their way. He'd warned her that the time would come when he'd leave. Why had she foolishly allowed herself to grow attached to the idea of a permanent tenant?

She approached the clearing between their houses. One soddie would certainly become a barn this winter.

"Hello, Aubrey."

Startled, she froze in midstep. Ben stood there, leaning on his walking stick without a cast.

"Ben!" She ran up to him and flung her arms around his skinny frame. "Your cast is gone! I can't believe it."

"Dr. Mills came by this morning."

"I am so happy for you, brother." After the miserable walk she'd just spent stewing, she welcomed a reason to be happy.

"You stuck to your word and helped me get better." His Adam's apple bobbed as he swallowed. "I realized how I'd messed up everything you dreamed of, sister. It wasn't right for me to take your horse. It was my own fault for getting injured. I never even planned on staying out here, really. Just wanted to make a profit off the land and take my earnings back to Kansas." He wagged his head. "You wanted to start new. Make something of yourself. And I took that from you."

A smile crept on her face and her heart skipped. "Oh, Ben, you haven't taken one thing away from me. I still got my land anyway."

"I wrote a letter to Pa. Going to see if he can meet me in Wichita." Ben shifted from one foot to another. She hugged him again. "And there's another thing." He disappeared inside her house, then returned with a small, but bulging, sack in his hand. "This is yours."

"What? What is it?"

"The rest of Mama's savings. Pa may've never found it on that day of her funeral, but I did." He grimaced.

"I am so sorry, Aubrey." He shoved it toward her then turned away, squeezing the bridge of his nose.

Her mouth fell as she stared at the lost money. All this time, he'd kept it from her. Anger crawled up her neck. How dare he? They'd nearly died from heatstroke because of her desperate, penniless state.

"Ben Huxley, you turn around this very minute."

He obeyed. She'd never seen him so broken, so close to shame. "Sis, I am sorry—that's all I can say. Guess I'd been hoping Cort would mess up before I had the nerve to give you the money. Then maybe I'd look like a hero." He kicked the dirt. "There's just something about him."

Ben wanted to be a hero? Maybe that was why he'd fought so hard for the land in the first place. Maybe he cared more than she'd thought? But she knew another side of him—the one who stole Mama's savings. Was his confession enough? Cort had given her apologies time and again, and he meant them from the bottom of his heart. He'd trained her well to spot sincerity, and right now, no matter how much her brother looked like Pa, she was certain his apology was authentic.

"Thank you, Ben." She wrapped her arms around his neck and he returned a hug. When they pulled apart, a silent truce filled the space between them.

"Want to see me walk without the crutch?" He wiped his eye with his palm.

"Of course I do." Aubrey stifled her tears. This was all happening so fast. As Ben took slow but determined steps in the colorless dusk, she couldn't believe how everything was coming into place. A life to herself, one she'd sought out that day in September, was now finding her at the onset of winter. Ben would return home, and Cort was leaving. That was how it should be. The cowboy was nothing but a temporary ranch hand—and the man who'd given her the deed to the land.

"Good job, Ben." She came up alongside him. "Let's get supper going, shall we?"

Together, they started the fire and began heating up some beans.

"I'm glad you saw the place, Ben." She began to doubt sending him off. It was not like their father had come looking for them. But she must get herself established in case he did. "I want you to come back one day, when I am all set up."

"One day. Who knows what Pa's got going on back home. I'm sure he needs me there." Ben stirred the beans, glaring at them as if he might see the future if he looked hard enough. Or maybe trying to convince himself that he was needed by a man who seemed to use people more than depend on them. There was a bond between a father and son that she dared not try to sever. She feared it would hurt Ben worse than a broken leg.

"And Liza's waiting. Hope she's taking care of that dress." She patted his shoulder. "Going down to gather some water, and then we can get those letters ready." She gathered up the pail and headed to the creek bed.

The rudimentary path Cort had first carved out for their many trips to their dugouts was proof of all the life she'd lived on the prairie already. They'd worn it out in their journeys to the creek and retiring from hot days to sleep beneath the very earth that was hers. As she crossed along the dried portion of the creek bed, she spied the dugout that was first a gift to her and then a returned gift to Cort. He'd worked so hard—for her.

Not because of anything but his need to help. Nothing like her father. Or any man she'd met. And now her ranch hand, and her friend, would leave. The day had finally come.

She looked up at the twilight sky and spotted the moon far to the west. One day, she'd hire help. And a family man, one whose wife and children would also live on the ranch, would be the most dependable person.

What if Cort asked to stay here with his family? They were friends, after all. Their friendship was one that rose from necessity, but it was a friendship just the same. Her heart raced as she neared closer to his dugout. She'd stolen kisses from a man who was already taken. Regret began to swim in her soured stomach. No, he couldn't live here. And it wasn't just because of his betrayal. Aubrey couldn't live day in and out watching Cort care for another woman.

A long sigh escaped her. It was beyond her reasoning. She might not ever admit it aloud, but she knew it to be true, no matter how awful. Jealousy overtook her at the thought of that Cassandra Stanton.

She turned around and stomped back toward the path up the embankment, more determined than ever to build her dream, her mama's dream, without depending on anyone. A lot of good came from having Cort's help these past months, but it seemed that Aubrey had become too soft in the process. She should not give another minute of consideration to her confusing feelings toward another woman's man.

Ben met her at the top of the ridge. "Cort has visitors. Didn't even care that my cast is off. Didn't even notice." The typical agitation creased his brow at his mention of Cort.

"Don't let that get to you. It seems Cort's family surprised him with a visit." Aubrey forced herself to stare only at her sod refuge. "Come on, brother. Give me the letter to Pa. I'll post it tomorrow along with a letter of my own."

This peaceful day was sabotaged by a storm of uncertainty. It seemed best for everyone to go their separate ways and leave Aubrey to her original plan. She hooked her arm around her brother's and they carefully made their way to the house. A light flickered to her left, in the old clearing where they'd first set up camp. She could make out the outline of two people.

Cort and his sweetheart, Cassandra, obviously wanted to be alone.

Chapter Fifteen

"Seems your little house is cozy enough for Trevor." Cassandra spread out her skirt on the blanket. Cort walked around the fire and crouched a good distance away. "He fell asleep without any dinner."

"You've traveled a long way to find me, sister." Cort swallowed hard. "Now that the boy isn't in earshot, how'd it happen, Cass? How did Charles die?" He dug his nails in his palms, trying to feel something more than the overwhelming loss. His brother might have heaped trouble on both of them, but Cort had loved him nonetheless.

"Typical Stanton way. A brawl at Ted's saloon. Got sideways with a man from El Paso. Similar to your daddy, huh, Cort?" Her cynical smirk spread amid the dancing light on her pretty face. "As far as I've been told, Charles started it."

He sat back, hooking his arms on his knees. "The man had everything going for him." Cort had made sure of that. He'd been determined to serve a sentence within the four walls of a prison. All for that little boy curled up on a pallet on his fresh-swept floor. "If only he'd seen how good he had it."

Cassandra leaned on her palm, pressing her cheek to her shoulder as she looked at him through her long lashes. "He didn't see it, did he? But you do, and you deserve the life that Charles refused."

Cort snorted. "What makes you think I deserve anything?"

"*We* deserve happiness, Cort. After all I've been through with Charlie's shenanigans, and you...well, look at what happened with you. You went to jail for murder, and the whole prison burned down around you."

Cort grew tense as her words knifed the quiet night air. He'd never allowed them to form on his tongue, and now his sister-in-law released them for any listening ear. He darted his gaze around. The horses were tied in the usual spot. The orange of Aubrey's lantern tinted the blackness from her window. What would Aubrey think if she heard all that Cassandra said?

Cort had expected to be cuffed and taken away before he'd ever have the chance to tell Aubrey. And in a way, that'd be best. If he'd get to the point of explaining everything to Aubrey first, it would be at the risk of someone finding out that Charles was the guilty one. He would never live with that, even for love.

But now? Charles was dead.

Cort rubbed his jaw and dared to ask the question, even if he dreaded the answer. "How did you find me here?"

"A man approached me at Charles's funeral. A Mr. Swanson. He said that he was up in Alva working and noticed your name. Was planning on telling the authorities after seeing the wanted posters, but then he heard about the brawl at Ted's. He couldn't bring himself to devastate the family any more. So, he told me where I could find you."

"You mean, he's not going to turn me in?"

"No. And I told him that I'd make you an honest man." Her smile grew. "My mama's all by herself down in San Antonio. Thought we could start over. You, me and Trevor." She inched closer to the corner of the blanket.

He stood and began to pace. "Now, look, Cassandra." He didn't want to hurt her: she'd been through enough, what with losing her husband. But Cort knew her too well. She was a woman who would do anything to get what she wanted. And there was nothing she could do to persuade him. Even if it meant raising his nephew, whom he loved. He felt nothing but sorrow for Cassandra. "You want a husband who will cherish you and love you. I care for you very deeply. But as my sister. Nothing more. And besides, I have no desire to go south anytime soon. It would be risky, to say the least."

She scrambled up and skirted around the fire till she was right up next to him. "Cort Stanton, are you playing hard to get?" She cocked her head. Her eyelashes fluttered and she gave him a wry grin. "You belong with me, Cort. I'm promising you a whole lot more than this desolate prairie can offer." She fiddled with his collar. As she searched his eyes, her ice-blue eyes rounded, reflecting the orange flames of the fire.

"I haven't been happier in years than I've been here," Cort said, looking over his shoulder at the inky black mass of his house, and the flicker of Aubrey's lantern.

His heart sped up as he thought of those afternoons spent building the walls in the company of Aubrey Huxley. And how close they'd come to being more than business partners. He longed for so much more at his weakest moments—when Aubrey laughed or softened enough to trust him.

"It seems the Oklahoma sun has dried up all your decency." Cassandra crossed her arms and pouted. "Happier in years? Do you know all I went through to get up here? To bring you the news that you escaped a murder sentence because of that kindhearted land surveyor?"

"Now, Cassandra, Alva isn't so bad. Why not stay here for a while? I can find you a nice room in town. I'd love to get to know Trevor again. He was only a little tot last time I was in Amarillo. All is not lost. You are my family, and I'll be here for you." He tilted her chin up. "I just can't marry you."

"Do you know how easy it will be for me to collect that money on your wanted poster?" She shoved her hand in her pocket and pulled out a folded piece of paper. She flattened it out on his chest and crammed it in his hand. The notice announced a reward for his capture. A shiver went up his spine as she spit out, "Cassandra Stanton is not going to be humiliated by a prairie-struck cowboy."

A sudden whinny split the tension. They both looked over to where the horses rested. Nothing seemed out of the ordinary, but he felt as exposed as the newly built frames of the Main Street shops. The night air knew his secrets. He grew paranoid that it'd carry those secrets to the ears of others. Or worse, to Aubrey's. Could she hear everything they'd said?

"What if I told you that I wasn't the one who murdered that man? What if I told you that the only reason I was in jail was because I took the blame? I love your boy so much that I thought if Charles had a second chance, he would change his ways for his son."

"What?"

"That's right. Because I'd betrayed his gunslingers and alerted my boss before their arrival, Charles nearly disowned me. I had no idea that he was a part of the group until it was too late. They were all captured. Well, I hated myself for it, and even though I was happy in Wyoming, I paid Charles's bail and he convinced me to go back to Texas with him. On our last night at camp, Charles killed a prominent cattleman and fled the scene. I was nearby and got caught. Of course, when questioned, Charles turned mute. I knew that you and Trevor needed him more than this world needed me. I was fine by it. After all, I don't have the most noble of pasts. It was about time I paid my dues."

"So it's true?" Cass fiddled with her lip. "You didn't kill that man?" She shook her head, seeming to reflect on more puzzle pieces than Cort had given.

"No," Cort admitted. "I begged Charles to change. To take this as a chance to raise an upstanding family. To redeem our Stanton name down in Amarillo." Cort wagged his head. "He obviously didn't take me seriously."

"No, he didn't." Her voice was small. She covered her mouth with her glove. A small hiccup and then a sob escaped through her fingers. "And I should have listened—"

"There's nothing we can do now, except support each

other." He gathered her up in his arms to give her some sort of comfort. But she just slapped him and stormed off toward his house.

Cort sighed, kicking at an escaped ember in the dirt. Sleeping under the stars again. An old habit, but a welcome one. Although he felt the weight of the stars and moon on his shoulders and didn't know if he'd get a wink of sleep. Poor Cassandra. Poor Charles. He felt his eyes sting with frustrated moisture. If only he'd found God before Wyoming, maybe he could have shared the Good News with Charles before his demise?

Cort dragged his feet to the blanket. He dropped to his knees. All he could do was pray. Before a supplication left his lips, he realized something was amiss. He squinted, hoping the black night was playing tricks on him.

Aubrey's horse was gone.

"Cort?" Aubrey took tender steps toward the dying fire.

"Aubrey, someone stole your horse." His voice shook as he approached from the trees to the west of the property.

Her heart sank. She had a hunch. "I am afraid it might've been Ben." She pulled her shawl around her shoulders and knelt beside the weak flames. "He tried to get me to leave with him. Said it wasn't safe here and we needed to go back to Kansas." Aubrey's pulse seemed to pound in her ears. "He said that the surveyor sent Cassandra here after seeing your wanted posters." She grimaced. "I knew your secret had something to do with the law."

"Aubrey, I can explain—"

She held up a shaking hand in protest. Ben's well-being was all she could consider right now. "He has so much healing to do, I am afraid for him." All the anxiety that had dogged her from the sidewalks of Alva to her sprawling acreage was now strangling her strength, squeezing out a flood of tears.

Cort's muscular arm slid across her shoulders and she leaned into him, allowing his warmth to soothe her—until she remembered Mrs. Stanton. She pushed away. She mustn't draw strength from this man one moment more.

"You have to tell me the truth, Cort." She wiped her eyes with the backs of her hands. "What happened back in Texas? And why didn't you tell me about your family, Cort? Why in the world would you hide a wife and child?"

"Wife?" He blinked. His lips slightly parted. Then he shook his head, gathering her hands in his, searching her face with a desperate tilt of his brow. "I'd never keep that a secret. She's my sister-in-law, not my wife."

Aubrey nearly let out a cynical snort. She tugged her hands from his. "So your sweetheart is your brother's wife?"

"What?"

"Cassandra certainly made it seem that you were smitten."

"What she implies and what is true are two different things." He sucked in a jagged breath. "She came up here to tell me that my brother was killed. And she wants to try and make things work between us."

The distant howl of coyotes carried on the night

wind. All was still except the flickering flame and the dancing grasses.

"I am sorry about your brother," she mumbled, her hand involuntarily reaching out and resting atop his knuckles.

"Thank you." His emerald eyes were washed golden with the fire's light. "And we'll find Ben, I promise." He turned his hand over and twined his fingers between hers. She bit her lip, watching the contour of his sun-tinted fingers caress her own. Her stomach burst with flutters. Crackles of wood eaten up by the flame serenaded them in the quiet night of an Oklahoma winter.

"I hope you know that I am not the kind of man to go and leave behind the woman I love. And it would certainly take more than a land rush to leave a wife and child behind." His voice was low and gruff. He now placed his other hand on top of both of theirs. "I don't love Cassandra."

"You'd said that you missed your chance on love. I just assumed."

"I missed my chance *to* love." He squeezed her hand. "The future is not promising me one ounce of hope right now. And I can't drag another person into that."

Her heart leaped. So his mention of love wasn't about his secret after all. How foolish she was to think that Cort would be devious like that. He had shown his loyalty and nobility all this time. At every turn of this adventure, Cort had been there helping and caring and giving her hope in a future bright enough for her mother's watch in Heaven above. How could Aubrey doubt him for a second?

"You have changed my mind on many things, Cort."

She leaned toward him and gently cupped her hand on his stubbled jaw. His eyes danced with excitement. "You are a good man, no matter your past mistakes. I don't care about any of it."

"You don't know how much your words mean to me, dear Aubrey." His nostrils flared and his jaw grew tense beneath her palm. "But if there's one thing I've learned tonight, it's that no matter how many chances someone gets, the past still threatens." He pulled his hands from hers. "Don't get too attached, Aubrey. You deserve so much better than me."

A sobering truth lay between them, thick like a massive wall that would never be torn down. No matter how much she could trust him, outside forces might steal him away and leave her crippled. She needed to stop depending on him. She'd given away too much of her independence already. How close she'd come to agreeing with him that her dream was sewing, not ranching. He was holding her back from Mama's dream. Even if he wasn't married, it was time to end this uncertain dance with the possibility that Cort Stanton would disappear and leave her alone. The more he was around, the more she wanted him to stay—almost more than the ranch she'd promised to build for so long. She mustn't play this game any longer. He'd forfeited the land, and she'd won it. Ben had healed, and she had earned quite a bit from sewing. It was time for Aubrey to begin to separate her heart from her actions.

"With Ben gone, I'll be able to manage much more on my own." She rose to her feet, gathering up her shawl. Cort stood with her. "If you need to leave and help Cassandra back in Texas, then don't feel obliged to me. I am ready to do what I set out to do long ago. Manage this ranch on my own."

"There you go again, acting as though there was nothing to getting a hundred and sixty acres under your thumb. Aubrey, I am not saying that I won't help."

"Hush. I need to do this for myself, Cort. I can't let my heart get in the way of Mama's dream."

"Your heart?" Cort's voice softened. He stepped closer. His breath was warm on her forehead, and she fanned her fingers against his linen shirt, planning to push him away, but her touch melded into him.

"I meant—" What did she mean? Where was her heart invested? In threads and buttons? Or in this man who'd given her a chance to trust again?

"I meant that you tripped up my heart, Cort. There's no denying that." The last fortress wall fell, and Aubrey's heart was now exposed to the full. She thought it would make her shrivel into weakness, but right now, she felt strong and alive as she owned up to the effect of this handsome cowboy.

"You shouldn't say things like that." His chin jutted out in a challenge. But his eyes smiled bright.

"Well, you shouldn't have asked." She looked away, unable to hold such an intense stare as Cort's.

He rocked back on his heels and ran a hand through his hair. "I don't know how long I'll be here. It seems that everything is catching up with me now." His voice was a contemplative growl. "Tonight, I found out that all I've been hiding from you was in vain. My brother is dead, and the truth won't hurt anyone anymore."

"The truth?"

"The truth about my crime." He gathered her up,

a hope-filled grin on his face. "I was caught for my brother's crime. I didn't want to admit his guilt to anyone for fear that he might be found out and his little family will suffer. But he's gone and gotten himself killed in the end."

"Then you are innocent? Nobody is coming for you?" That unfortified heart of hers began to beat wildly again.

A storm brewed in his eyes, on his brow. His arms tensed against her waist. "I am not sure. Cassandra is primed for revenge since I refused to marry her. She wants to collect the reward money."

Aubrey couldn't stop a smile from growing. That woman was all that stood in his way to true freedom? "Surely your own sister-in-law wouldn't turn you in?"

Cort guffawed. "You don't know her like I do. She's more of a spitfire than even you are." His dimple appeared with a crooked grin.

She narrowed her eyes playfully. "Well, I'd never turn in an innocent man. I doubt that she could, either. Nobody else is coming for you?"

"I—I don't think so."

The stampede of flutters filled her stomach as this rotten day ended and her heart soared to a height greater than the twinkling stars above. "Then you'll be my ranch hand tomorrow? And the next day?"

His lip hooked upward. His arms no longer tensed, but pulled her against his chest. "And the next, God willing."

She leaned in and brushed her lips against his. They were soft, sweet with peppermint. He pulled away, but Aubrey only searched for them again, satisfying her tingling mouth with his gentle touch once more. Her senses were completely consumed by this cowboy's hold. His familiar taste, his earthy smell mixed with leather and the force of his grip, powerful but somehow gentle, like he held something fragile and dear.

At this moment, with the prairie wind slipping in and out of their embrace, Aubrey forced herself to release any doubt. She surrendered to an even bigger dream—sewing, ranching and Cort. Loneliness was no longer something she'd have to own. It was no longer a part of her dream. She had never imagined all she'd find that day of the land race.

Cort's fingers laced into her hairline at the base of her neck, and his lips pressed more determinedly upon her mouth. She wrapped her arms around his neck. Her lashes fluttered, skimming his cheek. He pulled her closer. Cort Stanton was the very reason her dream had come true.

He clasped her elbows. The cold air met her lips as he shoved her out in front of him.

"I'm sorry, Aubrey." His eyes were large and round and desperate. "This isn't fair to you. Just like I said before, I would never do anything as rotten as leave a woman behind. And I can't make any promises to stay here." He snatched his hat from the prairie floor and crammed it on his head. "Even if Cass doesn't turn me in, who knows when word will get around down south? That surveyor knows it's me up here. It's only a matter of time." His nostrils flared and his jaw flinched. "We mustn't continue like this when there might not be a next day."

He walked away into the dark, moonless night, leaving Aubrey heartbroken. She longed for a chance to give Cort the assurance of his future, just the same as he had given her.

She cared enough for this man to want what was best. She might not have convinced Ben of his noble character, but Cort Stanton deserved to know that he was a good man. At least she'd had the chance to tell him that.

Two days passed, with Cassandra and Trevor taking over his soddie. Cort had moved back to his dugout. Cassandra threw a fit whenever he tried to come inside the house, and it was enough to keep him away. Every once in a while, Cort would spy his nephew playing around the trees and he'd have a chance to make acquaintance with the only Stanton young enough to truly change their reputation.

The boy warmed up to him gradually. Trevor was more into chores than Cort had ever been at his age. On the second day, he helped build a fire for the noon meal and then gathered water from the creek.

"Good job, Trev. Good honest work never hurt anyone," he reminded his nephew after each job well done.

By the end of that second day, the boy's wide grin brightened Cort's hope that Cassandra might cool down and muster up some loyalty for her brother-in-law.

On the third morning, the sky was too overcast for Cort to keep his spirit up. Only by the high-pitched reprimands coming from his house did he know that Cassandra was still on the property. Every time he heard her, the hair on his arms stood on end. The less he saw her face, the more he wondered what she might be scheming behind those dirt walls.

He began to stomp toward the eastern part of the land to begin building another fence. It would be good to get the post holes dug before the ground froze, and it was a decent amount of work to forget his grieving heart—for his brother, but also, for the gloomy future that'd keep him from following the greatest desire of his heart: a life with Aubrey.

"Want some breakfast?" Aubrey stood at the corner of her house, holding the handle of a kettle with one hand and cradling a basket in the opposite arm. Her eyes were bright in the pale morning light, and her usual ivory skin was complemented by a rosy pink along her cheekbones. Loose strands of hair danced about her shoulders in the prairie breeze. She was beautiful. "You've been skipping breakfast lately."

"You noticed?" He winked at her, unable to resist coaxing her to smile. And she obliged, filling in for the sunshine that was lost on this day. He put his shovel against the pile of firewood. "I am sorry that I couldn't find Ben." He'd gone into town each day, searching for her brother and her horse. But there was no sign of either, and no witness of a man with a sore leg and a strong brown mare. A foreboding gloom clung to Cort's spirit.

"It is what it is. He is a grown man. His choice to leave makes it easier in a way." She offered the basket to Cort. He took it and she grabbed a mug and poured him some coffee. "I pray that he's safely back in Kansas now."

Rocks rolled in his stomach. After all that was said with Cassandra that night by the fire, he'd wondered how much Ben might have heard. Her horse was stolen during their conversation, wasn't it?

He squatted to his knees and hung his head. "If I recall correctly, he didn't stick around to hear the whole story." The whinnying of the horse had interrupted them before he explained his innocence.

Ben had left here thinking Cort Stanton was a criminal. But did he know that he was wanted for murder?

"Well, if I ever get a chance to see him again, he'll know the truth. Promise you that." Aubrey squeezed his shoulder as she walked past him. "I'm sorry I led him to believe you were—"

Cassandra cleared her throat from his doorway. She looked as though she was ready for an outing more than emerging from a self-imposed two-day house arrest. Her hair was neatly pinned on top of her head, and her dress was a bright cobalt blue.

"Good morning, Cort." Her cool demeanor iced the air as she walked toward them. "And...Miss Huxley."

Cort gave Aubrey a questioning arch of his eyebrow. Aubrey seemingly understood and explained, "We crossed paths at the creek while you were collecting the posts from town."

Did Cassandra spy on him all day to see when he'd leave so she could come out? No doubt. The woman was nearly as stubborn as his brother.

"Would you care for a biscuit?" Aubrey offered her basket.

"I would. I am famished. And I am sure Trevor will be starving when he wakes up. A few cans of beans will only carry one so far." After taking a couple of biscuits, she turned to Cort, her sapphire eyes bubbling with tears.

"I am wondering if you can take Trevor and me into town."

Besides the aggravation from her taking over his home, a sudden rush of compassion filled him. Her sallow cheeks and turned-down mouth were pitiful. The once-rosy lips were pale and chapped. He could almost make out old tear trails. Prairie life did not do this city girl well at all. Even if she came here for the wrong reasons, Cassandra and Trevor were family—the part of the family he'd sacrificed his freedom for. Perhaps he could sway her to ignore that reward money.

"I'd love to spend some time with Trev," he said truthfully. "Cassandra, you are welcome to stay awhile. I have a fine dugout that I can sleep in."

At that moment, the little boy ran out from the soddie, his face red and his eyes wide with fear. "Mama! I didn't know where I was. Thought you'd sold me or somethin'!"

A low rumbly laugh emerged from Cort, and he finally allowed his shoulders to loosen. Nothing like a child to bring some lightness to a situation. He knelt down in front of Trevor, who was hanging on to Cassandra's skirt.

"We've been having some mighty fine conversations, haven't we, Master Stanton?" He reached out to tousle his dark Stanton hair. Cassandra turned him away from Cort's reach.

"Don't you touch him," she seethed. "You aren't treating us like family now. Not after the mess you've gotten us in."

"Mess?"

He skittered a look to Aubrey, whose eyes were as big as chestnuts.

"You think it was easy for me to come all the way up here?" Cassandra dug her fist in her hip. "That man down in Amarillo did us a favor by not turning you in, and instead of being thankful and stepping up to take care of your family, you brush me off like an acquaintance. Well, no more, Cort Stanton. I am through with you no-good Stantons."

His jaw dropped. The realization of what she'd said crept across Trevor's face. He peered up at his mama, his button nose all scrunched up. "But, Mama, we're all Stantons."

She faced her son and bent down level with him. "We'll fix that, dear. Your gran and pop are Wilburs. So am I, and you are half me."

"Now, Cassandra, that's not right." Cort's lip trembled with anger. "Don't talk to the boy like that."

"Just take us to town, Cort." She turned briskly and walked away.

He grabbed his hat and flung it on the ground. That woman! She didn't know him at all. Didn't she see anything noble in his act to protect their young family and take the blame for Charles? Did she even believe him?

Aubrey gathered up the basket and kettle.

"Wait." He gently clasped her hand and pulled her away from her busyness. "I am not the man Cassandra implies. There is a lot in my past, like you know. But she only knows the old me." He gritted his teeth. If he had something to punch right now, he would. How that woman riled him up in the worst way.

Aubrey slipped her fingers from his palm and pressed

her hand against his cheek. "Don't worry, Cort. I know you. Really." The warmth of her smile melted the icy silence Cassandra had left behind. He stepped closer to her, wanting to promise to always be there for her.

But he couldn't promise her that, could he?

Chapter Sixteen

Aubrey kept busy, trying to convince herself that the peace and quiet of a lonesome land was welcome in her future. But her heart ached from memory of the broken look on Cort's countenance as his sister-in-law spewed hateful words.

There was a time when Aubrey had been tempted to give in to the same vulnerable pain Cassandra showed. An outpouring brought on by loss. Aubrey knew it well after they'd buried her mother and she'd caught Pa scouring the room for Mama's savings.

Aubrey had been in the kitchen with the neighbors, receiving meals, trying her best to forget the smell of Mama's fine powder that enveloped her from the high lace collar of her dress. It must have remained there from the last time Mama had worn it. The silk taffeta gown with the neat row of shank buttons down the front, whose collar and cuffs she'd enhanced with leftover glass beads from the shop, was her mother's best dress. The last time Aubrey had seen Mama wear it was the day she'd gone to make her first purchase of full breeds.

"Oh, darling, this old thing will just gather dust once we are true ranch owners. Life will be too busy to get fancied up," Mama had said while Aubrey helped her hang the dress in her wardrobe. "But since you like it so much, I want you to wear it next. You're catching up with me fast with those long legs of yours."

Who'd have known that the first time she'd get the chance to wear it was at Mama's funeral?

Aubrey had said goodbye to the last of the neighbors, then gone upstairs to find out what all the rummaging was about. That was when she'd caught Pa. He'd admitted it forthwith, without a look of remorse, and he'd kept on looking but never found it. How she'd wanted to disown Pa at that moment. But she had nowhere to go. Just like Cassandra probably felt as a widow.

There was one thing different, though. Cassandra had lashed out at a man who was nothing like Aubrey's father. Cort Stanton would never steal from her. Well, the one thing that cowboy had stolen besides her breath on occasion was her heart. And a stolen heart was nothing she cared to admit, or risk chasing after, with her future as unsettled as the darkened skies.

She began to sweep her westward-facing back porch, smelling the fresh scent of moisture in the air. She wondered if rain would come soon. They needed it, that was for sure.

Cort returned from town and tied up his horse. He crossed over the property with his hands shoved in his pockets and a piece of long grass hanging from the corner of his mouth. Once he drew closer, Aubrey could see the creases on his brow. He was deep in thought.

She continued sweeping, even though her heart raced as he neared.

Aubrey Huxley, this is no way to be.

"Hello, Aubrey." His rich voice was soft. "I got Cassandra and Trevor settled in a room at the Alva inn." He rocked back and forth on his heels. "I want to ask you a question."

"Very well." She tried to keep her shoulders square, her chin up. "What is it, Cort?"

"I've been thinking. There's a whole lot of time to think on the way from Alva." He lifted his head and squinted past her to the east. "It seems my family needs me." Now his gaze was set on hers, a desperate, longing stare that flipped her stomach. His words scared her, but his look drew her toward him.

"Of course they do." What turmoil did her own face show?

"What would you say if I gave Cassandra my house, and lived in the dugout for the time being—"

"Oh, no," Aubrey blurted. She could not live with that woman just across the way. "I don't know how that would work… I—I don't think we'd get along at all."

Cort bounced his head in a knowing nod. "She's quite a spitfire. But she's hurting, Aubrey. Maybe my future would depend on it?" He stepped onto her dirt porch and laced his fingers in hers. "Aubrey, if I could give Cassandra a fresh start out here, maybe I wouldn't have to worry about being caught anymore. If I could convince her of my innocence, then if the law does come around, I'd have the testimony of the criminal's wife."

Aubrey searched his eyes, trying to ignore the warmth

of his hands. "Do you mean…you'd marry her?" Her throat began to tighten. She begged her tears to stay away. There was no use in crying. Nothing this man was saying would stop her from Mama's dream.

But what about her own dream?

Cort widened his eyes and chuckled deeply. "No, no, Aubrey." He pulled her in so that her arms rested on his broad chest.

Aubrey watched his mouth as he formed the words. "She's not the woman I was hoping to marry." His peppermint breath tickled her nose.

Her ears couldn't soak his words in fast enough. She wondered if she was hearing him correctly. Did she assume too much? But he squeezed her near. His lips brushed against her forehead. Her eyelashes batted closed, and her whole body melted.

A loud rumble of hooves interrupted her anticipation for more glorious words from Cort's lips. They separated and spun around.

In the distance, two men galloped toward them. As they slowed, Aubrey felt a droplet on her hand. She peered up at the sky. Would it rain? She'd prayed for it often during the treacherous drought. Her thoughts halted. The man nearest to her slid off his horse gingerly.

It was Ben.

"What on earth?" she mumbled, unsure if she should embrace him. He stood stoic, with no kindness about him. The other man wore a uniform of some sort. Almost like the scouts on the day of the race.

Cort put his hand on Aubrey's shoulder. "Perhaps

you should go inside, Aubrey? I assume this is about me." He kept his eyes on Ben, who glared back at him.

"No, she can stay. Seems she needs to know what's going on sooner than later," Ben growled. "Want to tell her what this is about, Cort Stanton?"

"Why don't you tell me, Ben." Cort shifted, squeezing Aubrey's shoulder and then releasing his hand.

Doom coated her stomach like the gray clouds stuck in the sky. Another droplet. And another. As much as she'd wanted rain, a different storm was coming. She could feel it.

"This is Sheriff Thompson. From Amarillo, Texas."

Aubrey heard Cort release a long breath. "Amarillo is a long way to go with your sister's horse."

Ben's nostrils flared. He took an abrupt step with his good leg. "I needed to make things right."

"What are you talking about, Ben?" Aubrey's voice broke. Ben looked more like her father than ever before. His sneer. His beady eyes squinting to hold in all the conniving a Huxley was capable of.

The sheriff raised a hand. "Cort Stanton, you are under arrest." He pulled out handcuffs.

"Officer, you've got it wrong." Aubrey stepped closer. "He's not the man you are looking for. His brother—"

Ben bellowed, "I said you can't trust this man, Aubrey." He spit at the ground just as the rain began to pour. "Not only did he cripple me, he's wanted all over the state of Texas."

Aubrey flashed a look at Cort. His face wore the same broken expression as when Cassandra had hurled hurtful words at him. Why didn't he speak up for himself?

"He's wanted for murder, sis. You've been harboring a murderer."

Aubrey stumbled backward, the rain sliding down her face. "Murder?" She didn't know the crime was that serious.

"That's right, Aubrey. Shocking, but true," Ben said.

Did she just foil her plea of his innocence? "No, I just didn't know what the crime was, but it's true that Cort is not the convict." She ran up to the sheriff, who only shook her away. "Please, sir, he's not the Stanton you want."

"His face is all over the state, ma'am. Perhaps he's convinced you, but that don't mean he's innocent." The sheriff yanked him along toward his horse. Cort craned his neck around to speak, but Ben interrupted.

"I didn't know how dangerous he really was until I saw a poster down south." Ben reached out to her. "I tried to protect you, Aubrey. You're my only sister. But you refused to listen to me."

"You hush, Ben. Even if you were trying to protect me, there's more to it than that, isn't there? You did this because you wanted revenge and, perhaps, money. If you were concerned about me, you would have stayed."

As the sheriff walked away with Cort, Aubrey could only sob into her hand.

She dared not believe that Cort had lied to her. And she was certain that the man she'd almost given her heart to was not a killer. The Stanton name might carry much shame, but Cort had proved there was at least one Stanton who was honorable and just. The Stanton name meant something different on the Oklahoma Strip than it did in Texas.

Aubrey had wanted it for herself.

"Wait!" Cort tried to wrestle his arm away from the man's grip. "Aubrey, please. I've told you the truth." He tried to turn to her again, but the sheriff kicked him in the back of the knee. He yelped with pain.

"There's no explaining necessary." The sheriff tightened his grip. "I've been around Amarillo long enough to know all about you. Bought yourself some time escaping that jail fire." He yanked Cort's arm closer and spoke through gritted teeth. "You best be quiet, Mr. Stanton. Or else this could get ugly real fast."

The rain was loud and booming. When Cort had a chance to look back at Aubrey, she was gone.

His ride to town with Sheriff Thompson was a miserable one as they cut through sheets of rain and a nipping wind. He didn't have much time to think, but he found the chance to pray. He begged God for a second chance, actually a third or fourth. But mostly, he prayed that this would all end quickly, because he couldn't bear the thought of life trapped in a prison cell knowing that Aubrey was somewhere without him.

Regret overwhelmed him, and his shoulders sagged with the weight of his coat from the pelting rain. If only he'd told her the truth about his brother from the very beginning, then she'd have known all along. Did she still believe him now?

As they came up to Alva's Main Street, the sheriff steered his horse to the inn where Cort had bought a room for Cassandra and Trevor that morning. The rain subsided to a drizzle and he was lugged off the horse by the sheriff.

"We are heading to Texas first thing in the morning. For now, I am going to catch a wink. It's been a long three days." They entered the bottom level of the new building. There was a small saloon with a hotel desk to one side. The sheriff situated Cort between himself and the stairwell while he arranged for a room with the desk clerk. Cort looked about the area, trying to ignore the stares. He caught the attention of one particularly blonde gal and her son.

Trevor's eyes grew big as he ran across the room. "Uncle Cort!"

"Hi there, son." A wave of emotion filled him. He was staring into the freckled face of his own brother as a child. Back then, their biggest iniquities had been damming up their own creek and laughing at the fleeing fish. Nothing like the trouble that found them as they grew. With an absent mother, the only guides they had were their own boyish desires and the footsteps of a lawbreaking pa. How he wished that Trevor would at least have the chance to find an honorable man he could model his behavior after, a noble male influence. It seemed everything was spiraling into the sinkhole of a pitiful heritage.

"Cort Stanton." Cassandra approached, decked out in that blue dress that enlivened her long-lashed eyes. "I guess I'll not benefit from your reward money after all." She gave an exaggerated pout as she eyed his handcuffs. "How in the world did you find him, Sheriff Thompson?"

The sheriff leaned on his elbow, admiring Cassandra with a lopsided grin. "Oh, Mrs. Stanton, seems your brother-in-law was quick to make enemies up here. Found their way down south and turned him in."

"Cassandra, please." Desperation soaked Cort's words more than the rain saturated his jacket. "You know the truth about me." He held out his sore wrists. "About this."

She turned her nose up.

"Cass! You aren't getting the money. Besides, I know you. Your heart's bigger than that. Come on." He relied on Aubrey's reasoning that his own sister-in-law couldn't go through with such vengeance.

She tucked her bottom lip back in and searched his eyes. Her nostrils flared. She leaned into him, yanking him by his collar and pressing her cheek against his. Her lips grazed his ear as she whispered, "This would all go away if you'll come to San Antonio with me. You promise to marry me, and I'll set you free."

Cort jerked his head back. "Blackmail, sister?"

"All these years, I've learned a thing or two from you Stanton boys." She snickered, her teeth resting on her lip as her devious eyes devoured him.

"Would you want to marry a man that didn't love you?"

"It's only a matter of time, Cort. Those old flames can't be too hard to kindle." She stepped back and planted her hands on her hips. "So, what do you say?"

"Even if I agreed to this, the sheriff will need more than your word. It's useless."

Cassandra took her fan and tapped it on her chin. "Well, there's the rub. But what if I do have more?"

"I'd need a witness," the sheriff interjected.

Cort shook his head. "There are none."

Cassandra studied him with a glint in her eye as if she knew something more. She opened her mouth to speak, but was interrupted. Aubrey stormed through the door, soaking from head to toe, with a wild look that reminded him of the day she'd nearly lost all one hundred and sixty acres.

"Cort Stanton, I need to talk to you."

Aubrey was flustered after galloping across the prairie. She had tried to talk herself into forgetting Cort and moving on with her plan. But there was one thing that stopped her. When Ben argued that he'd done the right thing as they dried themselves off in her soddie, she heard Cort yelling to her through the rain. Ben nearly tackled her as she tried to get to him.

"He's not the man you thought, Aubrey." He stared down at her.

"He told me he was innocent. Don't you think he's proved to be trustworthy, Ben?"

"But I heard it that night they were by the fire. He didn't argue about it not being true."

She looked hard at Ben, examining each feature—his long cheeks, dimpled chin and that glint of conceit in his eyes. She loved her brother, but trusting him was a whole different story.

"You didn't stick around long enough to find out. Cort's integrity has never failed. Why would it now? I've got to go to him."

Now she stood in a puddle on the newly waxed floors, wordless, in front of a small Texan audience.

"Aubrey, I'm so glad to see you." Cort tried to step

forward but the sheriff barricaded him with an out-stretched arm. "You believe I'm innocent, don't you?"

Aubrey stepped forward, her heart beating double-time. She cared too much for this man whose trouble was far greater than she'd imagined.

Cort's nostrils flared. He narrowed his eyes in Cassandra's direction. "You're holding something back. Aren't you?"

Cassandra just cocked her head, nibbling her lip.

The sheriff interjected. "As far as the state of Texas is concerned, Mr. Stanton, you are guilty and awaiting your sentence. Like I said, you need a witness, and I am sure these women don't know anyone who'd be affiliated with such a dire circumstance."

Cort curled his lips. "All of that is true, except the guilty part. I did not kill that man. It was my brother." He shot a pleading look to his sister-in-law then back at Aubrey. It was the same look she'd seen at the chuck wagon dinner when that land surveyor appeared. "Aubrey, remember what my old boss used to tell me? To always step up and admit when I'm wrong? It's a safeguard for future mistakes."

She could only nod. She remembered. It was when he had apologized to her, before their first kiss.

"I admit it. I was wrong to keep this from you all this time. You know that I have done some rotten things in the past, but my life changed the moment I found God back in Wyoming. So much manipulation had gone on during the caravan back to Texas that I allowed my guilt to trick me into taking the heat off my brother. He had a family and a chance to change. I had nothing but time. So I gave my time away with a plea that wasn't mine."

Her eyes flooded with tears as she hung on to his every word. "I believe you, Cort." The blubbering declaration escaped her lips as tears streamed down her face. "You've not given me one reason to not believe you." These past months had built up this man to be strong and noble and trustworthy.

"I'd never lie to you, Aubrey." His green pools flashed with determination. "I tried to save my brother that day, not take the life of a stranger."

A smile forced its way to her lips. "That sounds just like the man who'd give up a whole chunk of land to a desperate gal." He narrowed his eyes at her, the corner of his mouth twitching upward.

A hero through and through.

The only trigger he'd pulled was in her heart, and she'd never be the same.

The man behind the counter called over to the sheriff.

"Cort, time is running out," Cassandra said, eyeing the back of the sheriff as she spoke. "My offer still stands. And I promise, I can follow through with my end and offer up exactly what Thompson wants."

Cort's brows knit together as he cast a confused look at Cassandra. "What do you mean?"

She cackled. "You first. I need you to hold up to your end first."

The sheriff spun around with keys jingling in his hand. "If you'll excuse us, ladies." He stepped in between them and took Cort by the arm. "I need to sleep before we head south."

Cassandra plucked Cort's chin, sending a shiver down Aubrey's spine. "Well, darling, what do you say?"

Cort, with his soaked hat and cuffed hands, turned his face toward Aubrey. All the hopelessness he'd conveyed over the past months weighed down his countenance. She ground her heels into the wood floor for fear she'd try to push away Cassandra and the sheriff and spend the rest of her life loving him into hope again.

"You are a good man, Cort Stanton," Aubrey said. "No matter your past or what the law says, I believe you are one of the best men I know." Could her words speak away his hopelessness?

For a brief moment, light filled his eyes and he squared his shoulders. But a dark shadow fell on him when he muttered, "Remember me that way." Then he turned to Cassandra and said, "I don't know what you are up to, but my life is at your mercy if what you say is true." He turned up the stairs and the sheriff stepped behind him, pushing him out of sight.

Was that the last she'd see of Cort Stanton?

The tall blonde woman twirled her skirt around and clicked her tongue. "What a shame." Her nose was red as if she had cried, but her eyes were dry as the prairie dust.

"What did you say to him, Cassandra?" Aubrey put her hands on her hips, trying to appear strong. Her fingers trembled and she felt like she would retch.

Cassandra narrowed her eyes to thin cobalt slits. "Why should I tell you anything? It's because of you that he won't come back to Texas with me."

"Because of me? That's not true and you know it."

"He just declined to marry me in exchange for his freedom. I daresay it's because of your little speech. You talked him out of living."

"What?" Aubrey reached for a chair and crumpled into it.

"That man's in love with you. I offered him a chance to be free." She lifted her nose. A tiny crinkle revealed possible remorse. "With the chance to marry me."

"You gave him an ultimatum?" Aubrey had told Cort that his sister-in-law wouldn't follow through with her threat. What decent person would do such a thing? But now she was confessing that she had the ability to free him and wouldn't do it? "What could you possibly do to set him free?"

Cassandra began to fan herself, rolling her eyes.

"You're bluffing, aren't you?" Aubrey would get it out of her. "Cort said he told you that he's innocent. But our word is nothing against the Texas law." The magnitude of an empty life without Cort suddenly crept in on all sides of her. Was he really leaving? Now, when she'd realized how much good he'd brought in her life? "I just don't see how you can be so hateful to him."

"I've got a long history with Cort and Charles," Cassandra said, pulling a chair out and sitting across from Aubrey. Her face was chiseled like a statue. No emotion, no regret. Cool as stone. "I never wanted Charles. Practically threw myself at Cort during our growing up. He never seemed to care. And the thing is, he didn't have another woman. What's wrong with me?" Her stoicism cracked as her eyes swam with tears. She shook her head. "So, because of his stubborn pride, I chose Charles. And look at the mess he's caused. Going and getting killed when he has a wife and child to care for."

"I am very sorry." She was ready to let a man die because of old heartache? Aubrey pushed away judgment, though. Hadn't she said good riddance to Pa because of old hurt? She didn't want him dead, but she allowed herself to stew in her own heartache. She folded her lips together and prayed for forgiveness for both of them.

"Charles had one chance to change his ways, and he didn't take it. When I found out he was spared for that murder along the trail home, I could hardly see past my anger to mourn properly."

Mourn properly? Did she find out before Cort told her? "When did you find out that Charles was guilty?"

Cassandra just flicked her curls and swiveled around. "You are nosy, aren't you? I suggest you find yourself another cowboy to build your ranch. Cort Stanton doesn't deserve as much as a goodbye."

Aubrey shoved her chair back. "You knew before you came up here, didn't you? You knew he was innocent."

Cassandra's shoulders flinched upward, her gold curls cascading between them. "So, what if I did? I had my guesses, anyway. He's always been a softy. Could hardly believe it when they brought him home in cuffs while Charles only got a reprimand for gunslinging."

Aubrey warmed at the thought of Cort's unwavering goodness, but anxiousness soon swept over her. "What information are you holding back?"

Cassandra just traced the wood of the parlor table.

"You are bluffing." Aubrey's throat tightened and the same hopelessness that overwhelmed Cort promised to drown her in a flood of mourning. She spun around and rushed toward the door.

"Thing is—" Cassandra spoke loudly, stopping Aubrey midstep "—the man who told me Cort was innocent is leaving for a cattle drive to Wyoming, any day now."

"You mean there's a witness?" Aubrey turned toward her.

"Mmm-hmm." Cassandra stood. "Cort doesn't know, and I daresay Charles didn't, either. Buck Lewis ran when he saw Charles kill the man. He knew how persuasive Charlie was. Thought he'd get wrangled into the mess. Probably would have, just like Cort. Buck showed up back in Amarillo just before Charles died. That's when he saw Cort's wanted posters and came to the house, causing a ruckus and blaming Charles for the murder." She adjusted her hat. "I heard them talking in the parlor while I fed Trevor his supper."

Aubrey rushed outside and Cassandra followed.

"Where are you going?"

"To find Buck Lewis."

"They've probably left Amarillo already. Do you know how much land is between here and Wyoming?" Cassandra laughed. "By the time you do, Cort will be long gone."

Aubrey turned the horse around toward the south. She'd gallop toward Amarillo and hopefully catch them. "I'm going to try."

"A young woman alone? That's ridiculous. Why do you care so much about a ranch hand, anyway?"

"Because I love him," Aubrey said.

If Ben could ride all the way down south to avenge his ridiculous notion that Cort was the enemy, then Aubrey would double his miles to prove to all of Texas that one Stanton was worthy of living.

Aubrey mounted her horse and galloped through

Alva, puddles splashing and soaking her hem. Her pulse raced as she tried to beat out the sun on the horizon.

Lord, show me the way.

She wasn't running for a land claim now. She was running for her heart.

Chapter Seventeen

"This is farewell, Mr. Stanton, Mr. Thompson." Cassandra straightened her hat with crimson feathers. The pale morning light filled the quiet parlor of the inn.

A ripple of resentment shook Cort's spirit. "You could at least admit that I'm innocent," he seethed. "It's not going to change anything. But for your own conscience, Cass."

She bounced her stare from Sheriff Thompson to Cort. Her eyes were pretty jewels, disguising her haughtiness with their sweetness.

Trevor clomped down the stairs, his lip trembling. "Mama! I thought you'd left me again."

"Oh, child, not again." She slumped her shoulders and blew a stray curl from her ruby lips.

"Uncle Cort, are you coming on the train?" Trevor tugged on his elbow and the cuffs slipped down in clear view. The little boy's expectant brow dropped. "Oh."

Cort crouched down. "We're taking the sheriff's horse, Trevor. You take care of your mother."

"We've got a long ride ahead of us," the sheriff said, pulling Cort up by the elbow.

After the sheriff settled up with the innkeeper, they stepped into the bustling Alva square. Cort had once worried he'd be seen for fear of being caught, but now? Now he was ashamed to be seen with cuffs around his wrists.

"Where's my sister?" Ben climbed off Cort's horse and stormed over to him.

Cort ground his teeth then continued walking toward the hitch with Sheriff Thompson close behind him.

"Did you hear me? Where's Aubrey? She never came home last night."

"What?" Cort exclaimed in panic.

"She's got it in her head that she'll find a witness," Cassandra called out from the door of the inn.

He swiveled toward her. "How could she even know where to start?"

With a drawn-out sigh, Cassandra pushed her shoulder off the frame of the door and strutted toward them. "Somewhere between Amarillo and Wyoming, I suspect. My offer still stands, Cort."

"Why would she look for a witness, Cassandra?" He wanted to grab her by the ribbons tied to her hat. "You know how dangerous it is for a woman to travel alone on the prairie." Cort wouldn't put it past Cassandra to send Aubrey on a wild-goose chase just out of sheer resentment of Cort's affection for his landlady.

"She's in danger?" Ben bulldozed his way between Cort and Cassandra. He stared hard at Cort, their noses almost touching. "This is all your fault. If she's hurt, well, I'll—"

"No need to worry, son," Sheriff Thompson said, pushing Ben back by the arm. "Justice will be served for his deeds, regardless."

"Sheriff, let's go. We've got to find Miss Huxley," Cort demanded. A fear crawled up Cort's spine, just like the anxiety that gripped him when they'd lost little Adelaide. He tried to push back the pictures of venomous snakes and robbers and wild men out on the prairie surrounding Aubrey. He turned to Ben. "I don't care what you've done to get me here, but I won't let these cuffs stop me from making sure Aubrey's safe and sound."

Cort grew impatient as everyone stood still. He felt like his feet were filled with jumping beans. They needed to go, quickly. "Let's go. Now!"

Sheriff Thompson obeyed him with wide eyes. Perhaps he thought Cort was crazy, but Cort didn't care. He couldn't stand knowing Aubrey was out there somewhere, looking for a fictional witness on his behalf.

Cassandra whistled and then said, "Cort Stanton, you really do love that woman, same as she loves you?"

His chest constricted as the sheriff helped him up on the horse. "It doesn't matter now, does it, Cassandra? I am off to die, but I need to do what I can to help Aubrey."

His sister-in-law came up and firmly gripped the rein before the sheriff urged the horse forward. Her lashes were moist and her lips drawn in a frown. "While you're looking for her then, find Buck Lewis. He saw Charlie kill that man."

Cort's mouth dropped, and he searched his memory. Buck had been nearby, but Cort had thought he was sleeping. That was the last time he saw Buck, come to think of it.

"Ma'am, you better be telling the truth," Sheriff Thompson warned. "This man's life is at stake."

"Oh, I am, Sheriff." She folded her arms and near pouted. "But I know when a man's heart is taken. Can't persuade him like I hoped."

Cort sucked in a jagged breath, trying to untangle his anger at Cassandra's mind games and the relief that she'd confessed to an eyewitness. But one thought weighed him down—Aubrey was out in the wild prairie all by her lonesome.

Could he live if any harm came to her, no matter what eyewitness came forward to give him freedom?

Aubrey had brought him hope again. His life would only be worthwhile with her by his side.

They traveled in the barren prairie for hours, seeing no semblance of life except for dormant grasses and the flutter of birds in the gray sky. His eyes hurt with the constant strain of searching the horizon. Nothing but vast land and open sky.

After a cold night beneath a starless sky, they continued. Cort's insides began to implode with despair. What if she was hurt? What if they'd passed her just like they had passed Adelaide at first? But Sheriff Thompson, although willing to question about an eyewitness, was not considerate in searching for Aubrey. He wanted to get home, and get home fast. The only searching they did was from the trail. There was no veering off.

By the time they reached Amarillo, he could hardly contain the emotion filling his chest. He'd die not knowing the demise of the one person he cared about most, and the one person who'd given him a reason to want to live.

"I am sorry, Mr. Stanton. Just because we didn't find her doesn't mean she's in danger." The sheriff led Cort up the steps of the newly built prison. The front facade was the same, but where the fire had devoured most of the cells, there were fresh timbers, much like the buildings in Alva. "I'll put an ad in the newspaper requesting Buck Lewis to step forward. If he doesn't show up, we'll ready for execution."

Cort hung his head and dragged his feet across the wooden stoop. The sheriff led him to a cell and he slumped in the corner.

Lord, keep her safe, wherever she is. I don't care if Buck Lewis ever shows up. I just want Aubrey safe.

Aubrey had ridden through the night, unable to even think about sleeping. It had been the ride of her life— the ride to truly redeem everything Cort had holding him back from freedom. In the deepest wilderness, fear had nipped at her heart, just as it had done the night before the race. But prayer carried her through.

Her stomach growled fiercely the second day. She slept off the hunger near a creek in the daylight. Her heart leaped each time she thought of her mission, and she shooed away the dread of being too late.

A cattle drive spread out before her as she crossed the Red River. The men were resting, and the cattle were grazing. She was thankful when the head cowboy offered her food, but mostly when he took her straight to Buck Lewis.

"Do you know how much pay I'd lose if I came with

you?" Buck whispered between gritted teeth as they ate at a small distance away from the other men.

"But his life depends on you," Aubrey pleaded. "How could you leave him to die?"

"He's a Stanton. Not so difficult," Buck said.

"Please. He's not who you think. He's a good man."

Buck sighed, shaking his head.

She fiddled with the purse strings tied to her waist. She'd carried Mama's savings with her, not wanting to leave it with Ben when she left her house.

Perhaps it was her only hope to help Cort?

If Mama were here right now, would she expect Aubrey to give up the chance of love for the chance to raise horses? Deep down, Aubrey knew the reason Mama dreamed so big. It was because her life had become so small in the eyes of her husband. Mama needed a dream to get away from the reality of marriage to a broken, selfish man.

But now?

These past months had shown her that she was living a dream. And it had nothing to do with a ranch or sewing or independence. It had everything to do with the man who'd stayed by her side and proved his worth, and hers, with every action, every kindness and a faith that shone brighter than any she'd ever known.

Cort Stanton was her dream.

"How much pay will you give up if you come with me?" she asked, wincing in anticipation.

He spoke it quietly, looking around his shoulders, probably concerned that his boss might hear their negotiation.

Aubrey gasped. The number was nearly the same

amount as Mama's money. And with the last payment for her dressmaking, she had enough. She knew it now. Her savings would best be spent on ensuring that Cort would have just as bright a future as he had bestowed upon her present time.

Buck agreed to take the money once he saw that she was good for it. And together, they galloped hard at sunset. By the time they reached Amarillo, the town was sleeping and only hoots and hollers from the saloons filled the air. Buck convinced her to get a good night's rest, declaring there was nothing they could do until morning.

"Hangings are at noon. We'll head over to the prison first thing. That's if we aren't too late." He wouldn't look her in the eye. Just bade her good-night and headed to his room.

The only other night Aubrey had felt such anticipation for the next noon hour was that night before the land run. At least then it was with joyful expectation. Tonight, she curled up on the bed in the tiny inn room, with a sickening dread, wondering if they were too late.

A bright orange washed her room when she woke up. The sun was much too present for the early morning hour she'd hoped for. Surely it wasn't past noon? In a frenzy, Aubrey dressed quickly and ran downstairs, praying that Buck was still around and that Cort was alive.

She nearly tripped on the last step. Sobs caught in her throat, and her stomach ached with anxiety.

The same dark figure that she saw on the morning of the land run, framed by the bright sunshine pouring from the parlor window, stood at the bottom of the stairs.

"Good morning, Boss." Cort's deep voice carried on the crisp air, embracing every ounce of her worry. "Glad you met my old friend Buck."

From the corner of her eye, Buck stood up at a table. Aubrey rushed past him and threw her arms around Cort's neck. "Is it true, Cort? Are you free?"

He laughed deeply, his arms wrapping around her waist and his breath warm on her ear. "Yes, Aubrey. Buck came by the prison first thing. I'm free."

Aubrey held his broad shoulders tightly, her sure rock on the prairie.

His dimple appeared with his mischievous green pools. "Mind giving me a ride to Alva, Miss Stanton?" He turned and offered her an elbow.

"Of course not, as long as you'll make supper." She slipped her hand in the crook of his arm.

They said their farewells to Buck and rushed into a glorious sunny Texas morning.

Their journey was a sweet one. Conversations by the fire at night, and an invigorating sun-soaked run through the plains during the daytime. When they finally galloped past the growing town of Alva, the setting sun welcomed them home with a soft pink wash.

Cort barreled straight toward home. "Almost there."

Aubrey rested her cheek on his shoulder blade. She felt lighter than ever before. Besides surrendering to the frenzy of butterflies as they galloped, she let go of something else. All the resentment for Pa and the puny life he'd shown her dissolved into the cool prairie wind. Everything that had happened had brought her to this moment. This second race toward her land was more satisfying than the first because she'd found more than Pa had ever offered. She was living the dream her mama had always wanted, and then some.

The journey was nothing like Aubrey had expected, and she'd given up all that money for the ranch. She found herself to be penniless again. If she wanted to replenish her purse, buttons, threads and silks were in her future indefinitely. That made her giddy. Cort was right all along—Aubrey Huxley's dream was sewing. Or at least part of it. She was holding on tight to the rest of the dream she had just realized. And he provided more joy than she knew existed.

She looked back over her shoulder toward Alva. The sun shone brighter than it should this time of day. Her heart skipped, and she praised God.

Thank You, Lord. The greatest of these is Love. Just as Mama had said.

It had been easy to cling to Mama's dream of the ranch, but not until Aubrey had found love could she understand the deep wound of Mama's heart and the dream of a ranch filling in the gaps of a troubled husband.

The hooves raced across the muddy land, nearly at the same speed of her heart and Cort's, which pounded in her ear. When they approached the line of mesquite trees, she remembered Ben. He didn't know she'd taken the money with her that day. Good thing. This whole day might've turned out differently.

As they slowed, she prayed for a softening of Ben's heart, too.

Cort didn't head over to the hitching place for her

horse, but trotted a little farther north, to a spot Aubrey often reflected upon, but rarely visited.

They came to a stop.

Cort turned and held her by the waist. He drank in her gaze, never looking away as he gently lowered her down.

She stretched her arms and faced the west, admiring the fiery sphere on the horizon.

Cort encircled her waist from behind and rested his chin on her shoulder.

"A perfect end to this day," he cooed. "Isn't it?"

"Yes, perfect." She leaned her cheek against his. The rushing sound of wind drowned out the pulse in her ears. For that moment, they were the only two on the prairie. Cort's lips grazed her neck with sweet kisses trailing up to her lips. She turned and placed her hands on his warm skin, receiving a kiss she'd longed for.

He leaned his forehead on hers. "Aubrey, I love you."

"I love you, too." She did. More than the land, more than the buttons and bows. More than she ever thought a man deserved.

He guided her a little farther through the grasses. "It's here, right?"

"I think so."

He swiveled around on his boot heel, taking his hat and placing it on his heart. "I didn't know what I was in for when I staked my land in this spot."

"You certainly weren't my favorite person that day." She giggled.

"Am I now?"

She curved her lips in a sassy grin. "What do you think?"

"I'm about to find out." He wagged his eyebrows.

She crinkled her forehead in confusion, but when Cort lowered to one knee on the very spot where he'd staked his claim, she understood perfectly. Her cheeks filled with a warm blush as she peered down at her cowboy, overcome with this perfect moment.

"Aubrey Huxley, I wrestled with my feelings for you these past months. God had offered me grace long ago, but I didn't know how to receive it." Cort's hand trembled as he took her own shaky fingers. "All this time, I didn't think I deserved much of anything. But then you came along and made me want more for myself than I ever thought possible. You've given me a dream, Aubrey. And I want to live the rest of my life making your dreams come true." A stubborn chocolate curl rested on his tanned forehead. His eyes were bright green, sparkling and pooled with tears. She pressed her lips together, trying to contain the blubbering mess that she was sure to spill out. He wiped his eyes with the back of his hand and squinted up at her. "Who says cowboys don't cry?"

They both laughed into the creeping dusk.

Cort grew serious once more and squared his shoulders. His hand squeezed hers tighter. She studied his mouth, anticipation fluttering around in her heart.

"Miss Huxley, would you do me the honor of becoming my wife?"

A smile blossomed on her lips before she squealed, "Yes!"

He sprang up from his knee and twirled her around.

God had so much more planned than a staked claim on that day of the land race long ago. This whole adventure was not just about one hundred and sixty acres. After all, two hearts were at stake. And only God knew how to make their dreams come true.

Epilogue

Alva, Oklahoma
Spring 1894

"I told you I don't need a wedding present." Aubrey adjusted the handkerchief covering her eyes. Fresh sawdust filled the air as they hustled down the nearly built-up Main Street of Alva.

"You said you didn't need help all those weeks last fall, either. Did you, Boss?" Cort squeezed her to him, his cheek pressed against her temple. "Would you just let me pamper you a little? I'm your husband now."

"All I want is you. Don't need one other thing." She couldn't help but reach her hand out, worried that she'd bump into something. "Cort, this is ridiculous. We've been married for nearly four months."

"You gave me a present. Why can't you accept mine?" His warm minty breath tickled her forehead.

"I have no idea what you are talking about." She tilted her head up at him, looking into the block of white from the handkerchief. "I didn't get you a present. We agreed it wasn't necessary back in November."

"You bought my freedom, Mrs. Stanton." She could hear his grin as he spoke. "And the chance to work and build your mama's ranch."

"That's hardly a gift. But I sure do appreciate your work while I sew. So really, that's a gift from you, Cort." She threaded her fingers through his hand on her waist. If he only knew all that he'd given her. When the perfect moment came, she'd share even more with him.

"I'll build ten ranches for the chance to see you wear a dress like you did on our wedding day." He softly chuckled.

She leaned her head back on his shoulder and sighed. "That is a lovely dress. Just like my mother's. Wish she'd have seen it."

"I am sure she was smiling down that day."

Aubrey had replayed the most amazing fall afternoon in her mind at least a dozen times over this past winter. While Cort had built benches for their prairie wedding, Aubrey had sewn her dress diligently. She had plenty of help getting ready, too. Cassandra had agreed to stay for the wedding and moved into Aubrey's home with Trevor. The widow had only one condition in gracing the prairie with her presence for the long term—that she could pamper Aubrey just like every bride-to-be deserved. Cassandra busied about the place, preparing for the guests with elegant bows fashioned from dried prairie grasses, and practiced beautiful combinations of braids and curls with Aubrey's hair each night as she sewed. Cass had quickly become the best wedding attendant, and the only sister she'd ever known.

On her wedding day, Aubrey had approached the small affair without any blood relatives present, but her heart was full just the same. Only the Jessups, the Hickses, Cassandra and Trevor witnessed their union. Everyone had sat comfortably at sunset, and she and Cort exchanged their vows where they had staked their claim on the land. Aubrey had found the land she'd always hoped for, but she was overwhelmed by the new family she'd discovered, too.

"Okay, Boss, you can stand right here." He took her hand now and twirled her around, kissing her nose before facing her away. His strong arms snaked around her from behind. "Mrs. Stanton, your neck is covered in goose bumps. You sure you're not excited about this present?"

She playfully elbowed him. "Maybe a little." Those wild butterflies that he'd riled up so often now began to stir along with a faint nagging that tugged more often these days.

"Well, you're standing right in front of it."

"Am I?"

He nudged her forward and whispered, "Go ahead."

She pulled down the handkerchief from her eyes.

The spring sunshine stole her sight for a moment. She rubbed her eyes. They stood facing the street. Townsmen and horses with carts passed by.

"Where's the surprise?" Perhaps he'd bought her a horse? Maybe one to break in the new corral he'd finished last week. The ranch was slow-going, but Cort was a strong worker and had even hired a hand of his own. She looked up and down the street, wondering which hitched steed might be hers.

"Over there, Aubrey."

She followed his pointing finger. The wooden walk on the other side of the busy street was new, as were the many buildings that seemed to spring up at the last frost of winter. There was a blacksmith now and a new hotel. A mercantile and a—

"Tailor's? Did Mr. Caldwell change locations?" Directly across from them was a large window with an empty wire mannequin displayed.

"Look up, wife."

She raised her hand above her eyes and squinted upward. A sign hung above the door said Dresses by Aubrey Stanton.

He heart flipped and she gasped. "What in the world?" She faced her husband and took him by the shoulders. "Cort, what did you do?"

"I am making your dreams come true. All of them." His green eyes sparkled with so much love and excitement she threw her arms around his neck. He spun her around just like he'd done after their first kiss as husband and wife.

"Come on—let's go inside." He grabbed her hand and they rushed across the street. "There's more."

"More?" She swallowed hard, trying to ignore the dizziness from spinning and the topsy-turvy roll of her stomach.

They entered a small space lined with empty shelves. A fresh wood scent filled her nostrils. Their footsteps echoed as she circled the room with Cort close behind. She began to envision the swatches of fabrics and spools of threads.

"Cort Stanton, this is too much." She reached a trembling hand for his, unable to focus on any one thing.

He took it and squeezed. "It's just enough. I think there's plenty of room to grow a business. Don't you?"

"Plenty." She reached up and gave him a soft kiss. "Thank you."

"Thank you. I finally don't have to hide my name anymore. Did you see it on the storefront?"

She smiled wide. "I did. But that's my name, too. I'll never hide it." She winked and continued to explore the space.

Her fingers shakily brushed a gorgeous Singer machine in the corner. On the desk next to it was an envelope with her name on it. The handwriting wasn't Cort's, but it was familiar.

She opened it and read:

Dear sis,
I'm sorry I didn't stick around for the wedding. I know you and Cort both forgave me for the mess I caused. Just took some time to shake off all the ill feelings, and also, to forgive myself. Pa's same as ever, but he's slowing down a bit. I seem to catch him with your letter nearly every day. He's even started going to church when he's sober.

Thought I'd send you a wedding gift. I've been working for the doctor in town and have started saving. This machine is supposed to be every seamstress's dream, according to Maureen.
Love you, sis. Keep in touch.
Ben.

Aubrey's eyes flooded with tears. "This is from my brother?" She nearly hugged the sewing machine, thinking of all the redemption it represented. The stolen horse, the broken dreams of her mother, fetching the sheriff from Texas and all the old ways of Pa seemed to fade into old memories, replaced by this beautiful gift. "Can't believe he sent this."

"Yes, it's the perfect addition, don't you think?"

"It is." Her stomach flipped and she thought it was the perfect time to give Cort his own surprise. "Speaking of additions."

He lifted his hat and scratched his head. "I was going to tell you that we've started the plot for that barn at the back—"

"Not that." She rushed up to him and gathered up his hands. "Cort, I think this is a perfect little dress shop to make little dresses, too, don't you think?" She placed his palms on her belly.

"Little dresses?" His mouth fell. "What, are you—"

"Yes," she warbled through tears. "We're going to have a baby, Cort."

Those emerald pools filled up, and she caught his first tear on the tip of her finger.

"I never dreamed in a million acres that I'd be a pa," he whispered.

"There's no other man that I'd trust with that task," Aubrey said. "And no other name I'd want for my child than Stanton."

"I thought this day would be all about you, but you've gone and made me the happiest man alive, Aubrey." He wrapped her in his arms and she breathed in the familiar scent of leather with peppermint.

"No happier than I am," she said, perfectly content in his embrace. She sighed and held on awhile, because there was no place she'd rather be than in the arms of her cowboy.

* * * * *

If you enjoyed
THE OUTLAW'S SECOND CHANCE,
look for
THE MARSHAL'S MISSION by Anna Zogg
or
FAMILY OF CONVENIENCE by Victoria W. Austin.

Dear Reader,

Thank you so much for taking this journey with Cort and Aubrey. The Oklahoma Land Run is one of those special events in American history that has fascinated me since my teen years. I was thrilled to dream up a land-run story where romance grew as quickly as the land was settled.

During my research, I discovered that outlaws and women were noted among the more than 100,000 settlers who arrived to stake their claim in 1893. This venture was not for the faint of heart. The race took place during a nationwide depression, and the Oklahoma territory had yet to recover from a severe drought. I was amazed at how quickly towns were built after the run, and how resourceful those settlers had to be when they claimed a quarter section. Some soddies even became generational homes for families. Imagine living in a home that was built by the hands of your family members, from the very land found in such adversity on that hot day in September. To endure such hardships, I would say you'd have to have Aubrey's determination and Cort's work ethic. Wouldn't you?

Please visit my website, angiedicken.com, for updates on upcoming novels. I would also love to connect with you on social media.

God bless,
Angie Dicken

Get 2 Free Books,

Plus 2 Free Gifts—

Love Inspired HISTORICAL

just for trying the Reader Service!

"Mr. Arness—I'm sorry, Preacher Arness—I'm here to apply for this position."

"How old are you, Miss Marshall?"

"I'm nineteen, but I've been looking after my brothers, my father, my grandfather and, until recently, my niece since I was fourteen. I think I can manage to look after one four-year-old boy."

That might be so, and he would have agreed in any other case but this four-year-old was his son, Evan, and Annie Marshall simply did not suit. She was too young. Too idealistic. Too fond of fun.

She flipped the paper back and forth, her eyes narrowed as if she meant to call him to task.

"Are you going back on your word?" she insisted, edging closer.

"I've not given my word to anything."

"'Widower with four-year-old son seeking a marriage of convenience. Prefer someone older with no expectations of romance. I'm kind and trustworthy. My son needs lots of patience and affection. Interested parties please see Preacher Arness at the church.' I'm applying," Annie said with conviction and challenge.

"You're too young and…" He couldn't think how to voice his objections without sounding unkind, and having just stated the opposite in his little ad, he chose to say nothing.

"Are you saying I'm unsuitable?" She spoke with all the authority one might expect from a Marshall…but not from a woman trying to convince him to let her take care of his son.

He met her challenging look with calm indifference. Unless she meant to call on her three brothers and her father and grandfather to support her cause, he had nothing to fear from her. He needed someone less likely to chase after excitement and adventure. She'd certainly find none here as the preacher's wife.

"I would never say such a thing, but like the ad says, Evan needs a mature woman." And he'd settle for a plain one, and especially a docile one.

"From what I hear, he needs someone who understands his fears." She leaned back as if that settled it.

Don't miss
MONTANA BRIDE BY CHRISTMAS by Linda Ford,
available October 2017 wherever
Love Inspired® Historical books and ebooks are sold.

LIHEXP0917

Inspirational Romance to Warm Your Heart and Soul

Join our social communities to connect with other readers who share your love!

Sign up for the Love Inspired newsletter at **www.LoveInspired.com** to be the first to find out about upcoming titles, special promotions and exclusive content.

CONNECT WITH US AT:

Harlequin.com/Community

 Facebook.com/LoveInspiredBooks

 Twitter.com/LoveInspiredBks

LISOCIAL2017

Looking for inspiration in tales
of hope, faith and heartfelt romance?

Check out **Love Inspired**®,
Love Inspired® **Suspense** and
Love Inspired® **Historical** books!

New books available every month!